D0445492

SOUTH of the CLOUDS

JOHN D. KUHNS

Post Hill
PRESS

ALSO BY
JOHN D. KUHNS

China Fortunes
Ballad of a Tin Man

A POST HILL PRESS BOOK
ISBN: 978-1-68261-372-6
ISBN (eBook): 978-1-68261-373-3

South of the Clouds
© 2018 by John D. Kuhns
All Rights Reserved

Cover art by Cody Corcoran

This book is a work of fiction. People, places, events, and situations are the product of the author's imagination. Any resemblance to actual persons, living or dead, or historical events, is purely coincidental.

No part of this book may be reproduced, stored in a retrieval system, or transmitted by any means without the written permission of the author and publisher.

Post Hill Press
New York • Nashville
posthillpress.com

Published in the United States of America
Printed in Canada

"Jade, a shade of pain, and then you die."
—*Seal, Deep Water*

With apologies, and many thanks, to Richard Hughes

———————

For Mary, and J. W. and Carol Woermer

CHAPTER 1

The man on a bicycle drove down the road, heading toward the edge of the hill. His right pedal swiped the chain guard during every rotation. A morning shower had just ended. Raindrops trickled down through layers of jungle undergrowth, whispering amongst themselves. A few dripped onto the man's straw hat. Mist rose from the edges of the pavement as the tropical heat made short work of the precipitation; the sunny center of the road was already dry. Butterflies fluttered out of hiding and returned to their mating rituals in the high grass.

Only a few steps removed from the smelter office, Jack Davis stood still in the musky quiet of the Yunnan rainforest, his face sunburned, wearing jeans and a black cotton tee shirt. He held his breath as he watched the Chinese soldiers. Gathered behind a stand of bamboo across the road, they were wearing camouflage uniforms and their faces were painted. Jack had first spotted them only seconds before he saw the bicyclist. He couldn't make out all of the soldiers, but he knew there was a group. The two standing out front weren't talking but a murmur of voices came from behind them, careless voices that continued as the man on his bicycle rolled by.

Jack heard the truck before he saw it. Crawling up the steep incline from the river, its driver wasn't taking it through the gears, but staying in second as it approached the peak of the hill. It must be empty, Jack thought, not detecting any strain on the engine. The driver seemed complacent; he should have already shifted to third.

Jack was about to resume reading the texts on his mobile phone when the truck came over the crest of the hill. It was a big blue Forland transport truck, its rear cargo deck covered with a canvas roof. The dead boy was wired to the truck's front grill, his arms out to the sides, legs arranged under him swami-like, as if he were sitting down. His head was wrapped in a white funeral headband, eyes covered with white patches. The boy's clothes were caked with blood. Jack turned off his phone's flash and snapped a photograph.

As the road flattened out and the truck left the hill behind, it still didn't pick up speed. Jack could see two people inside the cab. When the truck was twenty yards away, the pair of Chinese soldiers walked out of the jungle, unshouldered their weapons, and held up their palms, motioning for the driver to halt.

The driver eased off the gas, but the truck didn't stop right away. It kept rolling, coming closer to the soldiers, closer and closer until it stopped only yards away from them. The soldiers were very young. Their uniforms looked brand-new. The shorter one on the right glanced at his counterpart, who continued staring at the passengers behind the windshield.

The truck's engine remained running, the cab's two inhabitants staying inside. The driver had on sunglasses. Both men wore headbands. To Jack, they didn't look Chinese, but he couldn't get a good look at them from where he stood.

The soldiers waited for the men to get out of the cab. When they didn't, the short soldier spoke to his partner, who snapped back at him, still staring up at the faces behind the windshield. After a pause, the taller soldier barked an order, and waited. When nothing happened, he raised his voice and yelled again.

The door on the driver's side creaked open. The driver dropped down to the road in a crouch, not making a sound as he landed, his feet and hands hitting the road at the same time like an animal. He straightened up, started brushing the dirt off his hands, and kept rubbing his hands on his trousers as he walked around the front of the truck to where the soldiers stood.

The soldiers hadn't changed position since giving their orders. The short one looked over the barrel of his assault rifle at the driver, while the taller one continued to stand erect, his gun down at his side. As the driver came abreast of them, the short soldier said something to him. The driver took off his sunglasses, stuck them in the breast pocket of his shirt, and smiled. He was good-looking, his features delicate, almost effeminate. Jack figured he was a little over twenty.

The driver went as if to dust off his hands on his backside once more, reached behind his back and pulled a pistol out of his waistband. He shot the short soldier in the forehead, his skull exploding as if the bullet had punctured a melon, blood and bits of flesh splattering over the three of them. The lifeless soldier flew backward, his boots dragging along the pavement several yards. As the taller soldier turned to run, the driver shot him twice, winging him the first time and then shooting him again in the back of the head as he spun and fell to the road.

The passenger inside the truck's cab stuck the perforated barrel of an old-fashioned twelve millimeter machine gun out his window and began spraying the bamboo alongside the road, the deep staccato of the gun crashing through the quiet of the jungle. Return fire rocketed wildly out of the foliage, raking the truck, bullets smashing into its fender. As the driver leaned over the soldiers in the road and shot the tall one again in the back of the head, the rear gate of the truck banged down and a half-dozen guerillas with AK-type automatic weapons jumped to the road and ran into the rainforest after the retreating Chinese.

Jack held up his phone and snapped more photographs.

The passenger in the cab of the truck stopped firing the big gun and jumped out carrying an assault rifle. He ran down the road forty paces and disappeared into the bamboo.

Jack heard crashing undergrowth as shots and yells trailed off in the forest, then nothing.

A minute later, making no sound, two Chinese soldiers crept out of a thicket of bamboo twenty yards down the road and ran toward the crest of the hill. They had ditched their weapons. Running fast, they didn't look behind them. None of the guerillas had re-emerged from the jungle. The two soldiers were running downhill now, almost out of sight as they sprinted past the man who had gotten off his bicycle and stopped to watch. As they ran by the man, the passenger stepped out of the forest, aimed his rifle, and shot the two Chinese men dead, hitting each one in the back of the head.

The man leaned against his bicycle and finished his cigarette.

Minutes later, the group of guerillas emerged from the bamboo where the truck's passenger stood standing over the two dead Chinese in the road. The guerillas were of varying ages. Most were shirtless, wearing headbands and camouflage bottoms. Laughing and joking, they frisked the two bodies lying in the road and then flung them into the bushes. They walked back up the road and repeated the procedure with the two dead soldiers lying in front of the truck. Then they threw their weapons into the truck, its engine still running, and climbed aboard. The driver hit the gas, dropped the truck into gear, and continued up the road.

The man with the bicycle tossed the butt of his cigarette and headed the other way, coasting slowly down the hill.

Jack watched him until he was out of sight. Then he turned to follow the path of the truck as it continued up the road, for the first time seeing the temple where its spires poked out of the trees on the mountaintop. He listened to the truck driver take the rig through all four gears.

CHAPTER 2

"You heard that, right?" Jack said to his junior partner Victor Romanov as he burst inside the front door of the silicon smelter's office building.

The two-story structure's cinderblock walls were stained with vertical stripes of greenish mold and pocked at intervals with rusty metal-frame windows. The first floor smelled vaguely of urine. It contained a product sample laboratory and washroom for silicon customers alongside two small offices, each jammed with cheap fiberboard furniture. An outside stairway led upstairs to another set of rooms and a bathroom. When Jack and Victor had arrived from the states a day earlier, they had taken one of the offices for themselves, leaving the other for the smelter staff, and commandeered the upstairs rooms for their living quarters. Jack hadn't any sense yet as to whether he could leave the factory unsupervised, and didn't want to spend the money on a hotel in any event, even one of the cheap ones up the road in Mangshi, the main town in the Dehong prefecture.

Across the road, the silicon smelting machinery fired up, the roar rattling the windowpanes. A moment later, the de-dusting tower kicked in with a whine, sucking toxic dust out of the crushed quartz and charcoal being fed into the furnaces to be melted to make silicon.

"There you are," Victor said, ignoring Jack's question. He stopped punching the keyboard on his computer. Like many workout specialists, Victor exuded an appearance of calm, but to do so required him to smoke incessantly. Using Jack's interruption as an opportunity, he stubbed out the remainder of his cigarette and extracted a fresh one from the box in his shirt pocket. "New York's called three times," he said, his eastern European accent barely discernable over the racket from the factory.

"To hell with New York," Jack barked over the din. His six-foot, two-hundred-pound frame filled the doorway like the linebacker he had once been, blocking the light and leaving the room's interior shrouded in gloom. "Did you hear those guys?"

"What guys?" Victor asked, exhaling a cloud of cigarette smoke.

Peering into the unlighted room from where he stood, Jack discovered the Chinese girl in the far corner, trying her best to disappear.

She wasn't going to be able to hide. Tall and dressed in a man's clothes—a white cotton shirt two sizes too big with the sleeves rolled up and khaki trousers tucked into brown leather boots—the girl's long black hair was piled atop her head, highlighting her cheekbones and translucent skin, and exposing silver earrings. Her face was not round, China-doll cutesy, but sleeker and elegant like an empress. The girl's dark eyes, soft as a foal's, stared uneasily at Jack.

"Who's the movie star?" Jack said to Victor.

"Mei, this is Jack Davis," Victor said. "He's the boss. Jack, meet Mei, the translator the agency sent down from Kunming."

Jack looked the girl over, and then turned back to Victor. "Can you step outside for a minute?"

The two men ducked through the doorway.

"What in God's name are you thinking?" Jack said to Victor over the roar of the smelter.

"Don't look at me," Victor said, unfazed. "You're the one who called the agency and requisitioned a translator. While you were out back exploring, one of our guys drove in from the airport saying he was delivering someone from Kunming. She gets out, and he drives away. End of story."

"But she's just a girl. What are we going to do with her?"

Victor shrugged. "Your call. Trade her in if you want. But it'll take three days to get someone else, and we've got work to do," he said, ducking back inside and reclaiming his seat in front of his computer.

Jack looked inside at the girl. He had to send her back. "I need to talk to you," he said to her from the doorway.

Trying to hold his gaze, she didn't move. Her full lips opened to speak, trembled, and finally stammered, "Isn't New York important?"

"What's that supposed to mean?" The last thing Jack needed was a conversation.

"I know New York's important for people like you."

"What do you know about me?"

"When you contacted the agency, we looked you up on the internet."

Victor exhaled a plume of smoke across the room, and then punched more numbers into his computer.

In spite of thinking she should leave, Jack found himself trying to get a read on the girl. He stepped back inside the office. "Well, you must have been disappointed."

She didn't reply.

Jack said, "Where'd you learn to speak English like that?"

"I lived there for two years." The girl remained glued to her seat in the corner, as if moving would be tantamount to giving up. "New York City, I mean. That's why I know it's important."

"Everyone there just thinks it is," Jack said as he remained standing in the doorway. "Well, I've got to admit: listening to you, I doubt we could find anyone more fluent. May—like the month? Is that how you spell it?"

"M-e-i." She tried to smile, but was too nervous.

Jack said, "Most professional Chinese translators take English names."

"But it sounds English, don't you think?"

"You know what I mean," Jack said.

"They gave me an English name in New York." She pressed her lips together, as if regretting her words. "But I didn't like it."

At least she had some spunk. "You know what I'm going to ask you now, right?" Jack said.

She just sat there looking at him.

"What was it?" he asked.

She didn't answer at first. "Bunny." She spit out the word.

Jack couldn't help it—he laughed. "Bunny? What'd they name you that for?"

"It's what I was supposed to do," she said, her eyes defiant.

"Next subject," Jack muttered to himself.

"My father said foreigners would respect a Chinese person who kept their real name," Mei continued.

"What does your father do?" Jack asked, happy to change topics.

"He was in submarines. In Dalian. He died young," she said.

"Submarines?" Jack looked over at Victor. "And your mother?"

"She was in the air force; she's not alive either."

Jack said, "Well, at least you must have been raised with some discipline."

"I really need this job, Mr. Davis."

Jack tried to get a look at Mei's hands. A good-looking girl like her, she'd probably never done any real work in her life. And she couldn't be more than twenty-five. But Victor was right: they didn't have time to wait for a replacement. "Where are we on those property transfer papers?" he asked Victor.

"The English versions are all done," Victor said, grabbing a sheaf of papers and holding them up in the air while continuing to stare at the screen in front of him.

Jack took the papers and held them out in front of Mei. "I should warn you," he said. "This task isn't simple translation. These are legal documents, and they must be correct. Have you ever done anything like this before?"

"Of course," she said, taking the documents from him. Spreading them out on the conference table in front of her, she began to review the paperwork, as if Jack was no longer there.

"We need them in Chinese as soon as possible," Jack said, glad to wash his hands of the subject of her employment. He looked back out the door. "You really didn't hear anything a minute ago?" he asked Victor once more.

"Nope." Victor rejoined Jack at the doorway. He followed Jack's gaze in the direction of the rainforest. Then he fished another cigarette out of his shirt pocket and lit it, the flame of the match illuminating his loyal Cossack face, the handsome features beginning to wear from the stress of his trade. "I was too busy taking phone calls," he said after exhaling his first drag, waiting for Jack to calm down, the two of them used to each other. "What was it I was supposed to hear?"

The smelter shut down as abruptly as it had started up.

Irritated with the foibles of the machinery, Jack glanced sideways at Victor. "Are we still convinced this contraption can lead the way to China's solar revolution?"

Victor shrugged. "It's been doing that all morning," he said. "No rhyme or reason to it; just starts and stops whenever it wants. I can't believe the operators know what they're doing."

"Assume we've got to replace everyone."

"For now, I'm just as glad the thing's screwed up," Victor said. "You can't think when it's running. The guys inside are probably brain-dead."

Visualizing a cartoon-like scene of demented Chinese operators bouncing off the smelter's walls, Jack wanted to laugh but couldn't. He had felt like he was jumping off a cliff the last few months, ever since he had decided to roll the dice and go back to China to take over a silicon smelter in the middle of the jungle. And seeing some guys killed right behind his office hadn't improved things.

With the smelter down, the factory compound grew silent except for the drone of cicadas. As the sun rose, the heat and humidity escalated, wrapping around Jack and Victor like an electric blanket.

A door slammed as Mr. Liu, the smelter's general manager, walked out of the staff office next door. He saw his new bosses and approached them, smiling and bowing. He couldn't speak English, but took the opportunity to shake their hands for the third time that morning. After an awkward interlude, he crossed the driveway and got into a late model, five-door Toyota Land Cruiser.

Victor took a drag of his cigarette. "Nice car."

"Too nice," Jack said. "Dead giveaway."

"If the car wasn't, his fancy clothes sure are. The guy's probably been busy lining his pockets since the day he took this job."

"That's what they all do here. Let's just close this deal before we waste any time on him," Jack said. He stepped outside the door past the birds-of-paradise growing at the corner of the building and peered into the rainforest, trying to see any movement along the road. But he couldn't fool himself. He was stalling, trying to defer the consternation waiting for him in New York at the other end of the telephone line.

The jungle was still, as if holding its breath. Not even the drip of a raindrop disturbed the solitude. Jack looked up the hill the truck had ascended, through the clouds of mist clinging to the temple's spires and the mountaintop beyond. Nothing.

The sky spit rain again, the drops heavier this time, rat-a-tat-tatting on the corrugated metal roof of the office building and splashing on Jack's face, coldly reminding him of his predicament. He glanced across the way at the massive silicon smelter. Originally built by Metalclad Industries, an international mining and natural resources conglomerate, and containing two electric arc furnaces, the brand-new but temperamental factory produced silicon for sale to hi-tech solar and semi-conductor customers. The biggest buyers were Asian and located nearby, in Korea, Japan, Taiwan, and increasingly, China itself. One of the largest silicon smelters in China, the business had been a disappointment for Metalclad, which had defaulted on the factory's bank loan from Continental Bank. A big shareholder of Metalclad, Jack was betting the restoration of his stateside reputation, as well as his financial future, on restructuring his ownership of Metalclad and the defaulted bank loan, and taking over the factory.

"So what's the bank's verdict?" Jack asked Victor matter-of-factly, stepping back inside the office and slouching in one of the plastic garden chairs arrayed around the conference table.

"The verdict?"

"Come on, Victor. First, I'm seeing things when I say I watched some guys get gunned down behind the office, and now you're saying the bank didn't give you our purchase price."

"Who got gunned down?"

"I'll tell you later. What'd New York say?"

Victor shook his head. "You think they're going to tell me? You're the managing partner; I just work here."

"For Chrissakes."

"I don't talk to those guys," Victor said. "That's your job."

The office landline jangled. Victor acted like he didn't hear it. Jack picked up the receiver. "Hello?"

"Jaaacck—we were beginning to worry about you," said Alan Kester, Jack's former business partner. The line clicked and sputtered, the overseas connection scratchy.

"Hello, Alan," Jack said, his eyes hardening.

"How's China?" Alan asked. "You're down in the southwestern corner somewhere, right? Someplace in Yunnan called Dehong?"

"Oh, things are wonderful here," Jack said. He heard Alan laugh.

"We've been trying to reach you for an hour," Alan said.

"Try texting next time. Mobile phones don't accept calls in the middle of the jungle."

"We both agreed this was for the best," Alan reminded him.

"I must have been out of my mind," Jack said. "But don't keep me in suspense: what's the bank's purchase price?" Jack asked, and then was forced to listen, the connection cutting in and out, while Alan droned on describing the process Continental Bank was using to value Metalclad's Chinese smelter asset.

Victor lit a cigarette but didn't move from his seat. Mei had stopped studying her documents, her eyes glued on Jack.

Alan exhaled as he reached the conclusion. "The bottom line is, they're asking eighty million."

"To hell with that," Jack exclaimed, standing up at the table and kicking his chair into the corner. "Eighty million? Forget the whole thing. You can tell the bank to go fuck themselves," he said. "This smelter is barely functional. No way we're paying those idiots eighty million dollars. Send them over to take a look for themselves."

Victor gave Jack a thumb's-up sign, egging him on.

"The bank's got an appraisal from Enterprise," Alan whined. "What am I supposed to tell them?"

"No wonder," Jack said. "Enterprise is an American firm; they don't have a clue about China. Look, the bank can either sell us this hunk of iron for the twenty million I offered or we're walking, and they'll never get a nickel out of the place."

"That'll blow our whole transaction," Alan moaned.

"Easy for you to say, sitting stateside with your half done," Jack said.

"That was the deal," Alan said. "You've done business in China before; you're the only one who knows the place. That's why your upside's much better than mine."

"If things work out," Jack said. "Digging out of a hole back in the states sounds a lot better right now."

"Let's stop arguing and try to figure out how to deal with the bank," Alan said, toning it down. "I could…"

Jack cut Alan off. "Sorry, but we're capped at twenty million. That's it."

Holding the receiver away from his ear, Jack glanced over at Mei watching him, her exquisite features irritatingly out of place in both the room and the conversation. He forced himself to concentrate on Alan blabbing away on the phone.

"If the bank says no, we're both fucked," Alan warned.

"Twenty million is more than fair."

The line got scratchier. "Let me see if I can work something out overnight," Alan offered.

"I don't think so," Jack said. "I'm not camping out here another day, especially after what I saw a couple minutes ago."

"What happened?"

"I'll tell you some other time." He allowed Alan a few more words. "Look, I mean it. I need to know today. The bank doesn't want to accept our proposed price, we're out of here. I'll mail them the keys on my way through Hong Kong."

"I'll try to talk some sense into them," Alan mumbled.

"You know where to find me," Jack said, and slammed down the receiver. "Goddamned two-bit bank." He saw the alarmed expression on Mei's face, and quickly switched demeanors, forcing himself to grin to buck her up. "You're not getting off that easy; I was just bluffing. We're not leaving. The bank'll agree to our terms. They've got no choice."

While Mei tried to recover, Jack stood up and paced back and forth in the cramped space. "Let's get the purchase contract ready," he said to Victor.

Victor stubbed out his cigarette. "It's almost done," he grunted, staring at his computer screen and punching entries into the keyboard.

The silicon smelter roared back to life, the de-duster beginning to whine. Then the machinery belched, and staggered to a halt.

Jack exhaled as he stared out the door at the big smelter, already rusting in the Chinese jungle although it was only completed the year before. He had done a lot of business in China, first going there in the eighties to buy hydroelectric power equipment, then raising money as an investment banker in the US for Chinese companies in the nineties, and ten years later living in Beijing and building a huge Chinese hydroelectric company—the best enterprise he had ever created. And then the Chinese had stolen it from him and broken his heart—and his bank account. When he had left China the last time, he swore he would never return. But here he was once more.

He watched a roach as big as a small animal crawl across the concrete floor of the office, and squashed it with his boot, the noise causing Mei to jump halfway out of her chair. Jack needed to be strong. He fought the urge to second-guess himself. There was no way he was paying a nickel more than twenty million for the factory, and he was starting to wonder if even that amount was too much. He glanced at Mei sitting at the other end of the table, head bowed as she returned to analyzing the property transfer documents. Undoubtedly, she had figured this was going to be just another humdrum assignment with some naive white guys from New York City. She probably wouldn't last a day.

"He'll call back in a minute," Jack said to Mei as he stood up and walked toward the door. "The guy from New York. When he does, if I'm not back, come and find me." He walked outside to look into the rainforest one more time.

The intermittent showers ended. Minutes later, the sun's rays burned a hole through the clouds. From far down the hill, Jack could hear the dull roar of the Mangshi River spilling over a waterfall. His eyes followed the silvery course of the river across the valley floor, winding through rice paddies on its way south to the blue-green hills of Burma in the distance.

———————

Mei came outside five minutes later. "That man from New York is on the phone again."

"See? I told you," Jack said.

Probably thinking she should show some enthusiasm, Mei smiled for the first time.

Jack followed her back inside the office.

Victor blocked the doorway. "You've got him on the run," he said to Jack. "Remember, Alan's not our friend here. He just wants to get off the hook with the bank."

"Right you are," Jack said, walking into the office and picking up the phone. "So what's it going to be?" Jack asked Alan, while Victor watched Jack intently.

Alan sounded like he was out of breath. "They'll do it, but your note's got to have a short fuse," he said.

"How short?"

"One year," Alan muttered.

"Jesus Christ," Jack said, raising his eyes to the ceiling. "One year to pay them twenty million? That'll never work," he said, glancing over at Victor.

Victor held up a forefinger, sat back down and checked his computer screen. And grimaced. "That's way too tight," he said in a low voice.

"We need more time than that," Jack said to Alan, feeling like the best thing would be to bolt and run if he had anywhere to go.

While Alan rambled on, Jack watched Victor pound some more numbers into his computer. After a moment, Victor held up three fingers.

"At least four years," Jack said to Alan.

"Impossible," Alan said, sounding like he meant it.

"They're that dug in?" Jack said.

Victor made some new calculations. He leaned toward the screen to double-check. "Anything less than three years and we'll need to refinance," he called over to Jack.

"Fat chance," Jack said, and decided. "Three years, and we'll buy it," he said to Alan. "Otherwise, forget it."

"Come on," Alan moaned. "Twenty million's a great deal for you guys."

"Not if we've got to pay it back in one year," Jack said. "Three years or we're out of here," part of him happy to pack his bags.

Alan exhaled. "I'll have to go back to them."

"You can do it," Jack said, switching to his encouraging tone.

"But there can't be any more loose ends," Alan said, tired but insistent. "Tell me what I'm missing. You're buying the smelter in exchange for your Metalclad shares plus twenty million. And the bank's lending you the twenty million for three years, at which point their loan is due. Right? Have I got it right?"

"That's the deal," Jack said. "We'll finish the draft purchase contract by the end of today, and it'll be in your e-mail when you wake up. And Alan? I'm saying draft, but it's just an expression—don't let the lawyers screw this thing up. We want to close in twenty-four hours."

"You owe me for this," Alan said.

"Give me a break," Jack said. "If anyone's thanking someone, it should be you thanking me."

"We both did our part," Alan said, sounding worn out. "Take care of yourself," he added, and not waiting for a response, hung up.

Jack slumped in his chair. "I guess we're in the smelter business," he said to Victor.

"No," Victor said, laughing darkly through a cloud of cigarette smoke, "we're in the smelter business in China."

———

Jack and Victor spent the rest of the day drafting the purchase documents. At six, one of the female factory workers, wearing overalls and a hard hat, appeared with dinner. Despite being covered with dust, the woman was striking, her brown face accented with high cheekbones and bright eyes, features which Jack knew meant she was not Han, the majority strain of Chinese. She and Mei spoke in Mandarin Chinese, Mei smiling, seeming much more comfortable with one of her own kind.

The woman finished talking with Mei, laid out bowls of steaming vegetables, tofu, and rice, and left.

"What a beautiful creature," Victor said to Mei as both men dove into the food.

"She is Dai," Mei said.

"Dai?" Victor asked between mouthfuls.

The food, although simple, was delicious, and tasted more Thai than Chinese. Jack figured Mei had to be starving, but she refused to eat with them.

"Yes," Mei said. "The local minority here in Dehong. Their women are very good workers."

"I can see that," Victor said, pushing more rice into his bowl with his chopsticks. "She's wearing a hard hat."

"Well, we know she can cook," Jack said to Mei. "What did she say she does in the factory?"

"She's a rock crusher," Mei said, and turned her head quickly at the two men, who were choking with laughter.

After dinner, they returned to their work until midnight, when Jack stood up from his computer and stretched. "That's it for the words. How're you doing on the numbers?" he asked Victor.

"I've got another hour or so. Go ahead and turn in; I'll be all right. As soon as I'm done, I'll send everything to Alan and get a confirmation that we're closing on schedule. Anything special you want to say to him?" Victor laughed.

"Let's make sure the deal is closed before that. If all goes well, we'll have the final papers in the morning and be done by noon our time." Jack glanced over at Mei. "Not to get ahead of ourselves, but what potential is there around here to celebrate?" he asked her.

"Celebrate?" Mei hesitated.

"You know, have a party. There's a good chance we'll own this place by tomorrow evening," Jack said. "A few drinks, some good food; that type of thing."

Mei's expression was baleful. Like most Chinese Jack had worked with in-country, she didn't appear comfortable making a recommendation to superiors. "I don't know, Mr. Davis. Don't you like the food from the workers' kitchen?"

"Workers' kitchen?" Victor scoffed. "This man can't be expected to mark the acquisition of this pile of iron with mere victuals," he said, grinning at the befuddled girl. "The events of the day call for a fitting celebration."

"She doesn't know you're kidding," Jack said to Victor. "Mei, he's just joking."

"I know he's joking," she said, not smiling. "I understand Western humor."

Victor tried to help her out. "The truth is, food is secondary. Where can we drink our troubles away?"

"Mangshi's an hour up the road," she replied. "There are restaurants there."

"How about down past Ruili? Mai Ja Yang, to be specific," Jack asked.

Mei appeared alarmed. "But that's on the border with Burma," she said.

"So?" Jack said.

Mei looked down at the floor. "I don't recommend going there."

"What goes on in Mai Ja Yang?" Victor asked.

"What doesn't go on in Mai Ja Yang," Jack replied. "How far is it from here?" he asked Mei.

Her brow furrowed. "Maybe an hour further than Mangshi. But it's right across the river from Burma. They're fighting a war down there."

"No, no," Jack said. "You mean between the generals and the rebels? They've had a truce for a decade."

"I don't know about any truce," Mei said, insistent. "Things happen down there. In Burma."

"You mean Myanmar, according to the generals," Victor said.

Jack scoffed. "I'm not calling it Myanmar. To be fair," he explained to Victor, "I should warn you. Mai Ja Yang isn't in Burma, but it's right on the border. It's—how do I put it—a place of ill repute. Ever since the American GIs holed up there during the war. Gambling, prostitution, drugs—it's all there."

"Including good restaurants?" Victor asked.

"Well, don't get too excited. But they're probably better than Mangshi," Jack said. "And they have other things too, if you're interested."

Victor clapped his hands together. "Why didn't you say so?" he said. "You deserve a massage. Mei, let's make sure he gets the hot stones."

Mei observed Victor with no reaction, awaiting Jack's decision.

"Mai Ja Yang, here we come," Jack said to Victor as he clapped him on the shoulder and headed upstairs to bed, "but I don't recommend taking a chance on hot stones in this part of the world."

CHAPTER 3

When he awoke in China the next morning, Jack lay on his cot listening to the angry noise of the bugs fighting to infiltrate his mosquito netting. It sounded just like the place he had left on the other side of the world.

———

Eighteen months earlier, in 2008 on a cold March night, a taxi dropped Jack off in front of his home on the Upper West Side of New York City. The townhouse was dark. He punched the security code in the panel and unlocked the door. Jack came into the foyer and hung up his coat, depressed.

His blind date had been, once again, a disaster. She had been beautiful and intelligent, and worked on the trading desk of a prominent investment bank. But in the get-to-know-you part of the evening, his honesty—and perhaps one too many glasses of wine—had ruined things. Without being asked, he had volunteered that he didn't think he would ever truly get over his wife. Although their conversation remained pleasant for the balance of the evening, that was that.

The truth was, he had been married once, and had no interest in doing it again. He realized that complicated things for almost any potential partner. He had been through several of them. Which was why he now felt obligated to bring up the subject sooner rather than later. Not that he didn't second-guess himself. Hadley had died from cancer a long time ago. What else was he supposed to do at this stage of his life?

Heading for the stairs, he changed course and stepped into the study. His favorite place in the house, the room was like a second skin to him. One wall held a picture window looking out onto the street, the opposite, floor-to-ceiling bookcases, and the two others were covered with his favorite artworks and maps, every item significant. He leaned over the piano and stared at the score of photographs arrayed across the Steinway's black enameled surface. There were his parents when they were younger, liberal arts professors who had remained somewhat in a state of shock that their son had become a Wall Street financier. The older he got, the more he looked like them. Looking at a family photograph, he examined his face as a younger man, trying to confirm evidence of his business excesses—extreme optimism, together with a dangerous misjudgment of challenges—knowing that despite years of acquired experience, traces of his afflictions remained.

His eye travelled down the rows of photos, past the ones of him with his Georgetown football team and Harvard Business School rugby mates. He stopped to examine some group shots of people involved in businesses he had built from the ground up, mostly renewable energy companies, including his biggest and best, the hydroelectric power company in China. It was the creation he was most proud of, but the same one where his two trusted Chinese friends—Tie Liu and Lin Boxu—had betrayed him, forcing him to sell out at a bargain basement price to a group of Princelings, the de facto rulers of their country. Scanning the faces in the photographs, he realized he hadn't seen anyone portrayed in a long time.

A photograph of his wife, Hadley, in her twenties smiled back at him, reminding Jack of the only time he had truly been in love. He had always assumed that it would happen again, but as the years passed, he knew his chances were dwindling.

An orange glow streamed in the window from the phosphorescent street light out front. He gazed at pictures of his children, all grown now and out of the house, moving on with their own lives, just like he had done. He glanced back at his mother's photo, reminding himself guiltily that when he had left the house for the last time right after high school, he had been so focused on matters at hand that he hadn't even said goodbye. Even though his own family was his sole emotional anchor, like Jack and his siblings had been for his parents, the last ten years had taught him that he had become a category for his children too. Someone to remember on birthdays and holidays. He used to anticipate family gatherings, the long car trips when they talked about history and politics, and books and movies, followed by get-togethers where participants shared their dreams, destinations, and interests. Even though he knew his children loved him, they rarely did those things now. And when the family did get together, it seemed that no one wanted to hear what he had to say anymore.

In a way, he knew he deserved his fate. In one photo, a group of them posed at his beach house when Hadley had still been alive, her auburn hair blowing in the wind and Jack—what? Distracted. Probably the best way to put it. Wavy brown hair tousled, his blue eyes glancing off to one side, as if not sure how long he would stay. Part of the crowd for the moment, he would soon resume the trajectory of a detached life after the other bodies in his galaxy ceased their gravitational pull.

The heating system knocked quietly along the baseboard, performing a percussion arrangement with the grandfather clock ticking in the corner. He had paid a fortune for that clock. But it had grown on him. It wasn't just the clock's familiar, soothing beat, but more its embodiment of an idealized, family-centric life. Money had never been important to him, even though some of the symbols of that life, like the clock, could be conveniently acquired. But emotional substance, his real goal, could not. No matter how hard he tried, he seemed destined to derive solace from photographs and clocks, as opposed to something better. Whoever that might be.

Jack awoke later than usual the next morning, his head still abuzz from too much wine. Wandering into the dressing room, out of habit he glanced over at Hadley's side to double-check that she was truly gone. He dropped to the carpet to do his exercises, like he had done every day since he turned twenty-one, his parents telling him habits made the man until his character took over. Glancing out the window at sheets of rain washing the street, he opted for sweats on his jog around Central Park. Showered and shaved two hours later, he stopped in the Starbucks on the corner of 103rd Street and Broadway to have a cappuccino and read the sports page, and rolled into his office around ten.

His Chinese assistant, Vivian, the sole remnant of Jack's hydro-electric business, paid close attention to her desk as Jack shuffled by on the way to his wood-paneled corner office. Two minutes later, she brought him the business papers and his coffee and disappeared.

Alone in his office, he glanced around: money-green carpets, a roll top partner's desk, and Abstract Expressionists' works on the walls. Arrayed along the windowsills, mementoes commemorating deal closings marked Jack Davis as a Wall Street player, and his firm Davis Partners as a respected, if somewhat obscure, investment organization.

He started to read the newspaper, and then returned his gaze to his deal souvenirs. Some would say there should have been more of them. He had had his moments of fame, but nothing compared to others he knew. He smiled to himself as he recalled the question from another failed blind date a few years back: "Why aren't you richer?" He had had no answer then, and didn't have one now. For some reason, all of the businesses he had started—struggling mightily to raise himself and his latest, impossible-to-pull-off concept up to the firmament of the New York Stock Exchange, together with all the co-founders, employees, investors, and other hangers-on—had always ended in disappointment. Not abject failure. But not glorious, spectacular success. The demise of the Chinese hydro company had been the toughest to take. Of all his efforts, it was the one that should have enabled him to ring the bell. To make millions, yes, but more importantly, to garner the accolades of his contemporaries. The one deal that would have allowed him to say: "This was enough. You're done." It's probably what kept him going.

He put down the paper, drank some coffee, lit a Cohiba Robusto, and sat there in his five-thousand-dollar bespoke suit and his two-thousand-dollar handmade crocodile shoes. Feeling ridiculous. The day before, he had reviewed the audited numbers for the firm's prior year financial statements. After splendid performances in 2005 and 2006, his fund's 2007 returns were negative. By double digits.

Something was going on in the market, but he couldn't put his finger on it. A big part of his problem was that he wasn't a passive investment type. He had always been best at creating things, from when they were kids deciding whether they were going to make tree houses or Roman catapults, to his college days when he had declined a pre-law major to study sculpture and drawing. From then, he had moved on to his first career as an investment banker. After raising huge sums of money for others, he had secured his reputation building successful companies from nothing, something few could do. One after another, he had taken a half-dozen enterprises from concepts to corporations listed on major stock exchanges. But it was exhausting, and he wasn't in his twenties anymore. With his last such business, the Chinese hydroelectric company, he remembered his optimism at the outset, and how foolish he felt later as the agony of the process became apparent. The pain he felt when he was forced to sell to the hated Princelings was even worse. Trying to do it again had seemed out of the question.

When Jack sold his Chinese hydro business, his friends advised him to come home and slow down. If he still chose to work, he could manage an investment fund, they said. He had been tired, and happy to do so. But even now, when he was supposed to be merely an investor, his instinct was always first to try to make a better company rather than to maximize his fees.

He had formed Davis Partners, brought in Victor as a junior partner, hired a small staff, and raised a billion dollars to invest. Small as investment funds go, the firm was the right size for Jack and the oddball transactions he pursued. He knew his investors well. In his fund's initial two years, he made money for them from crazy deals in crazier places, investments like the companies he used to build. They loved him for it, and were happy to see him become wealthy—as long as their returns were even more substantial. But when the 2007 numbers were published, some of them were sure to begin redeeming their limited partnership interests and taking their money back. If the deal he was working on now—a blockbuster acquisition of Metalclad Industries—wasn't a home run, his firm was in serious trouble.

His interoffice line buzzed. "Alan Kester is on the phone," Vivian said. "You've had some calls from limited partners as well."

"Listen, I'm a little under the weather," Jack said. "Tell Alan I'll call him back."

"What about the meeting?" Vivian asked.

"What meeting?"

"You were scheduled to have an all-hands conference call with Alan and the Metalclad deal team an hour ago," she said.

"Oh, Jesus Christ." Jack looked at his watch. "All right, give me a minute."

"I'll tell him you'll be right back to him. Go ahead and collect yourself, and while you're at it, you need to read the front page of the *Journal*—there's an article on Metalclad."

"Two minutes max—and please ask Victor to come down here."

"Read the article."

"I will." Jack picked up the paper. According to the article, Metalclad Industries, the poorly performing mining and natural resources conglomerate, had announced its sale to Whitestone, a private equity fund. The management of Metalclad also declared the unsolicited acquisition proposal from Davis Partners and Uranus Capital, Alan Kester's firm, unwanted and inadequate.

Jack heard a knock at the door. Vivian stuck her head in, her eyes assessing Jack's level of alertness, and then opened the door to admit Victor.

"This should be fun," Victor said as he sought his favorite chair across from Jack's desk.

"What's the inside scoop?" Jack asked, still scanning the remainder of the article. Feeling lousy but needing to focus, he put down the paper and waited for his lieutenant to answer.

Victor got up, closed Jack's office door, cracked a window, and lit a cigarette. "How's your cigar?" Victor smirked.

Jack knew what was coming. "I think Vivian just doesn't like cigarette smoke."

"At least not mine," Victor said. "Late night?"

"Very."

"A repeat customer?"

"You know me better than that."

"Sometimes I think I don't know you at all," Victor said with a slight smile. "But I digress," he said, blowing a plume of smoke toward the open window. "I spoke with a few of the guys last night. Alan is going to say he's surprised the Whitestone bid isn't higher, that it gives us a lot of running room. And that we should counter aggressively and put everyone out of their misery."

"And what do you think?"

Victor said, "It all depends on Continental Bank. If they're willing to accept the appraisal we deliver, the money's there for us to top Whitestone."

"What's the bottom line?"

"China's the bottom line, and that makes me nervous."

"You're supposed to be nervous; that's what I pay you for. What's bothering you about China?"

"All the upside in the deal depends on China," Victor said. "Take a look at the numbers—ours, not Alan's. Metalclad's mines around the world comprise the majority of their asset base, but they're low-margin and stagnant. No amount of layoffs and cost-cutting is going to change that. Any material growth in the company's profitability depends on their big new silicon smelter in China. But it's unproven, and so far, the results have been mixed. Investing Chinaside requires real work—you know that more than most. We acquire Metalclad but can't significantly improve production at their Yunnan smelter, maybe the banks get repaid, but we're working a long time for nothing. And it's Davis Partners that would have to do the heavy lifting over there. Alan knows nothing about China—I doubt he's even been there."

"I'll grant you the silicon smelter's twitchy now," Jack said, "but it could be a gold mine."

Before Jack could finish, Vivian knocked, and walked in. "Alan has called twice since Victor came. Can I set up the call now?"

Jack shrugged, and nodded.

Vivian dialed Alan on the speaker phone. Harried by the morning's false start, she blew wisps of hair out of her eyes. "Ready?" she asked. Without waiting for a reply, she pressed the speaker key, and then left the room to Jack and Victor.

Alan was already talking, "…a lot of money at stake and I don't appreciate your lackadaisical attitude."

Jack and Victor looked at each other.

"Hello?" Alan said.

Jack sighed. "We're here."

"Did you hear what I just said?"

"Every word," Jack said.

"Well?"

Jack said, "Look, I'm terribly sorry about the delay. So where are we?"

"Where we're supposed to be," Alan bellowed. "Whitestone made our job easy yesterday. Our proposal last week put Metalclad in play, and now the company has used Whitestone to set the bar on an acceptable price. And it's a low one. My guess is all we've got to do is top Whitestone's bid by twenty percent, and the company's ours."

"Twenty percent? Hold on. We've already offered a very full price," Jack said, leaning over, his face close to the speakerphone.

"Jaaacck," Alan said, "come on, now. Remember what we agreed? Leave this one to us. We've got the mining experience, and besides, we know the appraisers. If we need to leverage this thing a little more, I'm sure we can get them to raise their estimates," he said conspiratorially.

Victor's expression indicated he wouldn't be convinced by anything Alan had to say.

Vivian knocked on the door again, and then glided into the office to give Jack a new cup of coffee and his telephone messages. Jack flipped through the messages, spying a couple of his smartest investors' names. They could smell the advent of poor returns a mile away.

Alan was still pontificating.

"Alan…Alan!" Jack shouted over the din of the speakerphone to stop him from talking. "So let's say we forge ahead. Same arrangements we discussed earlier?"

"Of course," Alan said. "Same deal. We split the fees, fifty-fifty."

Jack said, "Look, I don't think we're ready to agree to that yet, but let's come back to the subject after we're done with the fundamentals. You still think Continental Bank is prepared to lend us all the debt and equity we need to acquire Metalclad, even to pay our fees, right?"

"Absolutely," Alan said. "Had dinner with them last night."

Victor nodded confirmation at Jack.

Jack said, "Even though we're about to bid the valuation of this thing through the roof?"

"Jaaacck," Alan said, his bedside manner back on display. "You're too conservative. How'd you ever to get to be a private equity guy anyway?" he laughed.

"I was stupid enough to think it was a real business," Jack said. "Anything else?"

"I believe we're done," Alan said, his tone indicating he expected the call to end.

"Victor?" Jack asked, fighting his inclination to run to return the calls from his investors. He sensed that Victor, who usually remained silent, wanted the last word this time.

Victor took a slip of paper out of his shirt pocket and glanced at it. "If memory serves, metal prices are at all-time high, and yet the worst-case numbers in your scenario only reduce revenues twenty percent. You guys may be the mining experts, but doesn't common sense dictate a larger reduction?"

"Wake up and join the real world," Alan lectured. "There's a middle class now in China if you haven't noticed, and they're pushing worldwide commodity prices through the roof."

"Jack's very familiar with China, although I haven't noticed your firm closing any deals over there," Victor said. "You're convinced the country's growth will continue unabated—right? No new outbreak of SARS. No hiccups from other world events?"

"It's all just beginning over there. Everyone knows that," Alan responded, making it clear he wasn't in a mood to listen. As if on cue, Alan's subordinates began vomiting data to support the idea that the deal was a home run.

As Jack listened to the facts flying back and forth, Alan weighing in sporadically, he waited for Victor's gambit. He didn't know what it would be, only that in the rare times when Victor spoke during one of these sessions, it was for a reason.

"This deal depends a lot on China. Knowing the country as we do, I remain dubious," Victor said in what sounded like a concluding tone.

"Right…" Alan said, waiting for the punch line.

"And it looks to me like the company's upside depends on commodity prices around the world remaining high, and the Chinese assets performing well."

"Yeah…"

"So," Victor said, pausing to light a cigarette, "due to the importance of China for this deal, I'm advising Jack that we should get a majority of the fees on this transaction. And if the deal craters and we all get sentenced to the rock pile, we divide up the assets in the workout. You guys work on the balance of Metalclad's assets around the rest of the world, and we'll do you a favor and take China."

A muffled silence emanated from Alan's end of the line. Jack could hear voices whispering in the background on Alan's speakerphone. "Wait a minute," Alan yelled into the phone. "A majority of the fees? That's not our understanding."

"I've got to listen to my troops," Jack said.

More mumbling ensued on Alan's end of the line. "Jack, I'll call you back in a minute," Alan said. "On your private line."

The phone went dead.

Jack looked at Victor. "Want to tell me what's going on?"

Victor exhaled. "I know you need this deal, and you'll get it. It's just free money from the bank. The real issues are where the upside is coming from, and what business is going to suck more in a downturn. Alan and those guys have this thing so debt-strapped it's barely viable, and if it goes under, the bank's going to chase us to hell and back to recover our fees. But the future of Metalclad is its Chinese smelter business. Alan and the lenders don't know China, so we should anticipate that they're assuming China is a relatively worthless piece of the puzzle, and structure our deal accordingly."

"You're saying carve out China for next to nothing," Jack said. "I get that, and completely agree. I like the Chinese silicon smelter. But you sound really pessimistic on this one."

"I am pessimistic. Alan's numbers are a pipe dream."

"So why are we doing it again?"

Victor took his time lighting his third cigarette. "This is what you do—swing for the fences." He stood up to go. "By the way, I've been here for three years now. When is Vivian going to bring me my coffee in the morning?"

Alan called Jack back five minutes later and made a big deal about Victor being out of line. When Jack said Davis Partners was probably out if they stuck to the original deal, Alan roared like a wounded animal and then harangued Jack for a half-hour on the fee split, never mentioning divvying up the assets as a concern. Jack then feigned capitulation, and said he would overrule Victor and accept an equal fee split. All was forgiven. The point about China was immaterial, at least as far as Alan was concerned: Jack could take the Chinese assets in a workout if he wanted them. Metalclad would never fail anyway.

The Davis/Uranus group lobbed in their new offer to Metalclad a day later, the stock price soared, Metalclad's shareholders were thrilled, and the Metalclad management started to sound much friendlier. Jack and Alan continued to buy the company's shares in the market, pushing the stock price higher and keeping the shareholder pressure on management to come to the table and make a deal. After three weeks during which the newspapers dutifully documented every scrap of Metalclad deal rhetoric, Whitestone dropped out of the bidding. The reason, according to unofficial Whitestone sources quoted in *The Wall Street Journal*: "The future of Metalclad Industries depends on China, and we just couldn't get comfortable with the place."

Subsequently, Metalclad accepted Jack and Alan's proposal, and they began moving toward a closing. Whitestone's decision about Metalclad didn't seem to give Continental Bank pause. But Jack had heartburn. In the past, every time he had told himself 'one more deal,' it was always the one he shouldn't have done. Now, here was a warning from Whitestone, a well-respected financial industry player.

He didn't know what would be worse, to miss out on the Metalclad deal, or to land it.

On August 1 they closed, purchasing Metalclad Industries for four hundred million and taking it private. Jack and Alan's teams were ecstatic. In addition to all the capital necessary to purchase Metalclad Industries' shares, Continental Bank's loan included proceeds enough for the Davis/Uranus group to pay themselves twenty million in fees.

"Not a bad return on zero equity," Alan chortled to Jack. Then he lobbied hard to celebrate their windfall by renting an ocean-going yacht to take their teams to Bermuda. It wasn't Jack's style, but he was tired of arguing with Alan. Their ship sailed back into New York harbor a week afterward, just in time for the groggy revelers to witness the greatest financial crisis since the Crash of '87. First Bear Stearns and then Lehman Brothers collapsed, and the Street dropped off a cliff. At Metalclad, as economies around the world stalled and commodity prices plummeted, the company's revenues dropped by fifty percent.

In retrospect, as Jack looked back on it, he doubted the Metalclad balance sheet ever had a positive net worth, but if it did, it was erased by the losses piling up through December. That's when Continental Bank began calling every day, insisting that Jack and Alan return their fees.

The Metalclad deal had hardly been the elixir to keep Jack's fund afloat. Instead, it and the recession accelerated Davis Partners' decline. As the news regarding Metalclad and the worldwide recession got worse, Jack's limited partners deluged him with redemption notices, demanding a majority of the fund's capital be returned to them. Never having had a down year, Jack had little experience with redemptions, and was slower to sell assets than he should have been. By the end of the first quarter of 2009, Metalclad was on life support, and Davis Partners was hemorrhaging cash. Worse, whatever remained of his reputation was in tatters. The articles in the business journals were cruel, while the gossip rags had all but declared him suicidal.

The carnage solved one problem: no one called anymore to set him up on blind dates. It was the same with other aspects of his life. At Christmas, Jack counted: he sent out over two hundred cards, but received only fifty.

On a dreary morning at the end of March 2009, Jack sat at the conference table in his office studying his Willem de Kooning painting, trying to find what the curators said was a woman hidden in the gobs of paint. He had never been able to make her out. Vivian fussed with papers at his desk behind him. "Did you know that before de Kooning became a famous artist, he was a sign painter?" Jack asked her as he continued to scrutinize the painting that had cost him a fortune. It wouldn't be his much longer.

Hearing no response, Jack turned around to look at Vivian. "Do you think if his fine arts career had blown up, de Kooning would have been happy going back to painting signs?"

Vivian looked up from where she was storing documents in his filing cabinet. "You'll figure something out," she said. "You're a survivor."

"We've got to mail our audited statements tomorrow," Jack said. "It's a death warrant. I may have to close the firm." The words were painful, but he was more worried about her and the other employees.

"I'm not going to let you," Vivian said, her face uncharacteristically firm. And then she smiled. "Just kidding. I'll be fine," a tone of false gaiety in her voice. "I'm worried about you."

"I doubt anyone's ever going to give me another chance," Jack said, running his hand through his thinning hair.

"I will." She smiled again. "Why don't you just retire? You've got money put aside. Your houses are paid for."

"You know me better than that. It's never been about the money," Jack said, taking a cigar out of his humidor. "I just don't want to end things this way. Besides, I've got the bank breathing down my neck."

"But they're only posturing, right?" Vivian asked, her positive mien dissolving. She pulled out a chair at the conference table and perched uneasily across from him.

"Every time one of these deals collapses, the lenders always say the sponsors milked the company," Jack explained, queasy enough to seek relief in his own words. He cracked open a window and lit his cigar. Outside, a drizzly wind ruffled the feathers of a lone pigeon perched on the stone ledge.

Vivian frowned. "Look, I really need to know. I signed papers as the corporate secretary of the Metalclad acquisition vehicle."

"You weren't a decision maker, so you're not on the hook," Jack said, trying to say something to comfort her. "We've got a lot of high-priced lawyers working on this," he added.

"What's fraudulent conveyance?" Vivian asked, her eyes fearful, skin tight around her cheekbones. "That's all the bank wants to talk about when they call for you."

"Wishful thinking on the bank's part, at least so far," Jack said. "Metalclad's got to get a lot closer to bankruptcy before they can come after the firm on a fraudulent conveyance claim."

"But say they did," she said.

Jack exhaled. "Fraudulent conveyance means we paid ourselves fees from company funds when we knew the business would crater."

"They can't prove that," Vivian exclaimed, indignant. "Besides, Metalclad could still come out of this fine."

Jack shook his head. "Right now, it doesn't look that way. And the bank could really do a number on us in court," Jack said. "Think about it. Continental Bank? All the lawyers they could put on a case?" His voice trailed off.

"We didn't take anything," Vivian protested.

Jack shrugged. "We borrowed way too much."

"That's not a crime," she said.

"The fact pattern is lousy. After not investing a penny of our own money, we stripped out twenty million of fees," Jack said.

"The bank was pushing to do the deal as much as we were," Vivian said. "I heard them. Everything would have been fine if the recession hadn't come along."

"I was too anxious for a big score." Absentmindedly, Jack played with his wedding band. "That stupid cruise."

"What if they win?" Vivian asked.

Jack considered his words. "Davis Partners would have to fork over ten million it doesn't have."

Vivian slumped in her chair. "What did you do with the fees?" she whispered.

"Paid them out to the limited partners, of course."

Her face brightened. "Thank God! So the bank will go after them for the money instead," she said.

"I'd never raise another dollar from investors if that happened," Jack said, shifting in his seat. He had been turning over the issues in his mind for weeks, and the last thing he wanted to do was talk about the subject. But Vivian deserved to know. "I can hold the bank off for a while. They'll try to foreclose on the equity we own in Metalclad first," Jack said.

"Which should be worth way more than ten million," Vivian said, her face showing signs of optimism.

"Who knows? This recession could drag on, and Metalclad could be wiped out. Unless the China assets save the company. I don't know what would be worse," Jack mused, "going bankrupt or my investors crossing me off their list forever." He scanned the ledge for the pigeon. The bird had flown off.

"So what are you going to do?"

"Go out for a walk." Jack stubbed out his cigar, got up from his chair, and put on his suit jacket and overcoat.

"I meant about the bank."

He was halfway out the door. "What you always do when you owe money to a big bank. Settle with something other than cash."

Continental Bank took their time. Their legal complaint alleging fraudulent conveyance by the Davis/Uranus group didn't arrive until the end of June. The bank demanded that all of the Metalclad deal fees—twenty million dollars, plus interest—be returned to the company.

Jack knew the bank's feigned dispute over the fees was a sideshow. Everyone had heard the news about Continental Bank's lending mistakes. They had made a worldwide bet that commodity prices would rise at exactly the wrong time, and not just with Metalclad Industries. The bank stood to lose not only their entire investment in Metalclad but billions in similar loans to a slew of industry players.

A week later, someone from the bank's legal department left a message after hours at Davis Partners. They wanted a face-to-face meeting at the bank's headquarters the following afternoon with Jack. Alone.

He had expected the invitation. That night, he poured himself a stiff drink and sat in his study, pondering whether to fold up his tent, or step up to the plate one last time. For about two minutes. He had never quit anything in his life, and wasn't about to start now, even if his solution required a return to China. He picked up a pad and began outlining notes for a plan, then spent another hour refining the words into a written presentation.

The following morning, Jack called Vivian and told her he would work from home to avoid distractions. The meeting with Continental was a session he could only have once. The day was a scorcher. Still, Jack dressed in a suit. In midafternoon, he let himself out of his townhouse and began walking, what he always did on his way to important meetings. So he could think, get ready. From the Upper West Side, he headed southeast across Central Park. People huddled in the shade under the trees, the lawns toasted by the hot July sun.

At Park Avenue and 47th Street, Jack entered Continental Bank's headquarters and presented his driver's license to the guard at the security desk. He wiped the perspiration from his forehead. "Don Smith, please," Jack said, referring to the senior corporate loan officer in charge of the bank's loan to Metalclad Industries.

The guard got one of those looks on his face. He punched some numbers into his telephone. "I've got a guy here wants to see Don Smith," he said to someone on the other end of the line. "That's what I thought," the man said a moment later, and looked up at Jack. "Don Smith is no longer with the bank," he said, as if that ended things.

"Let me talk to them," Jack said, reaching for the phone.

The guard hesitated, and then handed Jack the receiver. A woman was on the line.

Jack said, "Look, I'm one of the owners of Metalclad Industries. You guys made the company a loan and someone here in the bank's legal department called to request a meeting with me. I thought Don would be involved, but I guess he's gone. Whoever it is, someone up there asked me to here be at three o'clock. Perhaps you can direct me?"

"I see. Just a minute, Mr....?"

"Davis. Jack Davis, of Davis Partners."

"Hold on."

Jack waited several minutes, leaning against the reception counter. The guard went back to reading his copy of the *Daily News*.

A new voice finally spoke on the other end of the line. "Mr. Davis? We're sorry to have kept you waiting. Do you have counsel present?" the man asked.

Jack said, "No one told me it would be that kind of meeting."

"Of course. Come right up—forty-first floor."

"I thought you guys were on forty."

"That's the loan department. We're in workouts."

Jack stepped into the elevator, encouraged by what he had just heard. The workout department. Maybe he had caught a break.

At the forty-first floor vestibule, a man with short red hair and a jacket two sizes too small stood waiting. "Mr. Davis?"

Jack shook the guy's outstretched hand. It was clammy.

"Follow me, please," the man said and proceeded down a hallway lined with small meeting rooms and bullpen offices, a majority of the occupants overweight men sitting in front of computers wearing short-sleeved shirts and fake Florsheims. Jack looked closer at their computer screens as he walked down the hall; most of them were playing internet games.

"Right in here," the red-haired man said, opening the door to a spartan conference room with scuffed walls that hadn't been painted in a decade. The room contained a small Steelcase table surrounded by four metal chairs, a bookshelf full of plastic binders in one corner, and a window with a view of the back side of the office building next door. "Something to drink?"

"That's all right, thanks."

The man shut the door.

Jack sat looking out the window. He knew that bank meetings stemming from a borrower's problem were predictable, like in the rare cases when Jack had gotten behind on a money-good loan. Then, the bankers forgot about lunch in their wood-paneled rooms, threatened foreclosure, and scolded him for his personal failures.

But when things turned bad for the bank—enough so that it shifted the loan into the workout department—deals could be made. Usually by that point, the loan had been written down on the bank's books, often to zero. Now, instead of fighting with loan officers trying to preserve the loan and their jobs, a borrower dealt with non-bankers, green-eyeshade types who had no vested interest in the value of the loan, only in their paperwork and procedures.

The door opened and a beefy man who hadn't seen his belt buckle in years walked in. "Mr. Davis?" the fat man asked as if he didn't care. He took a seat and tossed a binder of papers on the table. "Don Smith's no longer with the bank. Your Metalclad loan has been transferred to us here in the workout department."

"I gathered that. It's your meeting."

The fat man flipped through the papers on the table. He finally raised his head and through watery eyes took his shot. "When are you guys sending us the twenty million in fees?"

Jack made a show of looking at his watch. "Listen, Continental's loan at Metalclad is current. The company isn't in bankruptcy. Meanwhile, your bank has suffered some big hits, but it's not fair to take it out on us."

The guy pulled a spreadsheet out of his folder and put it in front of Jack. "Metalclad's out of cash. Says so right here. By my calculation, the company's loan will be in default in another month, maybe two," the man said, lifting his eyes up to the level of Jack's chin before they fluttered down to the spreadsheet again. "At that point, we will definitely force the company into bankruptcy. And come after your ass."

Jack felt the tops of his ears burn and the back of his scalp begin to itch. "You'll never recover a dime if you take that approach."

The fat man's face was pale enough to make his bone-colored eyes actually look blue. He folded up his spreadsheet. "We need cash, Mr. Davis. I don't care where it comes from. That's the bottom line."

"The last place to get it is from me. But," Jack said, pausing, "I could probably solve your problem."

The man stopped stuffing the spreadsheet into his folder. "Do you have a proposal?"

Jack straightened up in his chair. "It just so happens I do," he said, taking a two-page stapled outline out of the breast pocket of his suit jacket and sliding it across the table. "What's your name, anyway?" Jack asked the man.

The man scanned the proposal without looking up. "Larry," he said a minute later. Larry breathed in and out, loudly, and then wheezed. He finished with the first page, and then flipped to the second. He hadn't seemed tired when he walked into the room before, but now he did. "I don't see any cash."

"You will when I pay off the purchase-money note you're taking back from me," Jack explained.

Larry turned back to the proposal's first page and read it again. Slowly. "Let me get this straight," he said when he had finished. "You're proposing to swap all of Davis Partners' equity ownership in Metalclad Industries with us. We give you Metalclad's Chinese silicon smelter, free and clear except for a purchase-money note in favor of Continental Bank equal to no more than thirty percent of the appraised value of the smelter. And then, after a period of time, you get us cash by paying off the note."

"Correct," Jack said, "subject to the valuation of the smelter being set by a third-party appraisal, and the bank's release of any claims against me, Alan Kester, Davis Partners or Uranus Capital."

"What do you think the smelter's worth?" Larry asked, his watery eyes finally meeting Jack's.

"I've got to get over there and see for myself," Jack said, "but a good guess would be about twenty million."

Larry sighed, and reread the proposal's second page. "I assume Mr. Kester would agree to the same arrangement," he said.

"There's no role for him to play in China," Jack said. "But I imagine he'd be thrilled with any deal that takes him off the hook regarding the bank's complaint."

Larry dropped the proposal on the table. "Why should I do this?" he asked Jack.

"Because the smelter in China is Metalclad's most valuable asset, but you're not going to realize a dime out of it any other way," Jack said. "Someone as crazy as me has got to go over to that god-forsaken country and make it happen."

Larry glanced at the proposal one last time and then started to put it in his folder. He hesitated. "You realize you'll have to personally guarantee the loan."

Jack had been expecting as much, but the words still caused the warm feeling in his ears to engulf his neck as well. "In that case, you'd better take the deal before I change my mind," he said.

Larry looked out the window. "This might just work.... I've got to go back to the credit committee," he said as he got up, the meeting over.

Jack remained in his seat at the table, trying to get comfortable with what he had just done. "I can wait," he said.

CHAPTER 4

Dehong's heavy August rain drummed on the roof, and drove Jack out of bed. Outside, birds in the rainforest canopy chirped and squawked. Jack lay down on the concrete floor to do his exercises, and then showered. When he was finished, Victor crawled out from under his mosquito netting and shuffled into the bathroom, grumbling. "Hey, look at the good side of things," Jack said through the bathroom door. "Monsoon season will be over in a month."

Bareheaded, they made their way through the downpour to the workers' cafeteria. Jack carried a jar of instant coffee he had picked up coming through the airport in Kunming the day before. They could barely see their way through the rain.

"Where's this rain come from?" Victor yelled as they slogged through puddles a foot deep.

"India."

In the kitchen alongside the cafeteria, clouds of steam wafted toward the ceiling. Jack lifted the lids of the iron pots bubbling on the wood-fired stove, inspecting their soupy contents. Vegetables. One after the other, he inspected the row of pots: more vegetables. Not an ounce of protein, not even hard-boiled eggs. He found some congee. He filled two clay bowls, one for himself and one for Victor, adding some bread crumbs and a dash of chopped chives on top of the porridge. As one of the rock crushers poured hot water into two mugs, Victor stirred in instant coffee. Each man picked up a bowl and a mug and sat down on one of the long wooden benches in the refectory. They ate in silence alongside scraggly Chinese workers, disturbed only by the men's slurps and burps.

When Jack and Victor returned after breakfast to the soggy office, Mei was already working. Sitting in the spot she had occupied the day before, she was wearing the same clothes. Jack got the sense she had been there all night, but decided not to ask.

Jack and Victor examined the lawyers' comments waiting for them in their emails. The bank had approved the final terms of the deal; they were good to go. They spent the remainder of the morning making last-minute adjustments to the papers. An hour before noon, final versions of the purchase contract, property transfer, and related loan documents were agreed to by all parties, and signature pages were emailed back and forth and executed.

In exchange for Davis Partners' fifty percent ownership share of Metalclad Industries, Continental Bank and Metalclad's other creditors sold them the Chinese smelter business, subject to a twenty million purchase-money note in favor of the bank, payable in a lump sum in three years. The bank provisionally released its claim against Jack and Davis Partners for fraudulent conveyance. However, if Continental Bank's loan was not paid on time, all bets were off. Jack would be on the hook personally both for the unpaid loan and Davis Partners' portion of the deal fees, an amount that could total over thirty million.

"Here's some money for us tonight," Jack said to Mei, handing her a wad of Chinese RMB as soon as the transaction was consummated. "It's better that you manage the checkbook." He looked at his watch. "We'll need to leave shortly. How are we getting down there?"

"Chin can take us," she replied. "Mr. Liu's driver." Mei didn't look away as she took the money from Jack. She appeared more comfortable than she had during her first day, which made her look even more beautiful despite her lack of sleep. She wore no makeup—she didn't need to. Her lips were full, her skin pink and lustrous over her cheekbones. Under her left eye, a tiny vein crinkled beneath the surface of her skin whenever she smiled. She had let down her long hair, her silver earrings peeking out. "I think you've met the guy," she said. "When he picked me up from the Dehong airport, he told me he had done the same for you a day earlier."

"I remember him. The guy who looked like Hop Sing," Jack said, realizing as he spoke that she was way too young to have watched *Bonanza* on television.

Mei ignored his comment, Jack beginning to understand that was how she reacted when he said something she didn't fully comprehend or agree with. "He's probably over at the dormitory," she said, stepping toward the door. "I'll go fetch him."

Jack said, "Wait up," as she walked out. "Time to inspect my new domain."

Outside, it had stopped raining. A thick mist hung in the air, making it difficult to see across the road.

The huge smelter was the size of a football field. Cutting through the rear garages, Jack and Mei covered their faces as they were enveloped in a cloud of blue exhaust. Two flatbed trucks sat idling at ground level while men loaded them with bags of crushed silicon ready for market. In windowless concrete rooms alongside the loading dock, flocks of sledgehammer-wielding Dai women, their heads wrapped in scarves to prevent inhalation of deadly needles of silicon dust, pounded at slabs of cooled silicon the size of tree-trunks, crushing them into gravel-sized pellets.

"Those hammers must weigh half as much as some of these women," Jack said to make conversation as they walked by, Mei smiling politely but not saying anything as she led the way. The women continued to bang away, the ones in Jack's sight line concentrating on their tasks while those on the periphery whispered through their scarves as their bright eyes followed the *laowai* who— little did they know—was the new master of the realm.

The entire building shook as one of the electric arc furnaces above them on the main floor started up with a deafening roar. Mei cried out and grabbed Jack's arm, and then, embarrassed, kept walking. Dirt and grit rose off the ground and floated back down in a dusty cloud. Jack and Mei shielded their eyes and made their way up a rickety iron staircase. Alongside the furnace, they passed a group of men with metal poles stoking quartz as it melted under the hearth's blue, three thousand-degree flame.

They exited the building toward the dormitory at the other end of the feedstock yard. Spread across a field of several acres, piles of whitish-yellow quartz and ebony charcoal sat waiting to be dumped into the smelter. Alongside the feedstock yard, dozens of big blue Forland trucks, including both transport and dump truck models, sat lined up in rows, ready to be dispatched to gather their next loads. "You know how much a truck like that costs new? A hundred grand," Jack said to Mei, speaking loudly over the machinery noise, but she hadn't heard him, had spotted Chin, and was moving quickly ahead.

Mr. Liu's Land Cruiser was parked at the edge of one of the charcoal piles. Two men, one with a misshapen, boyish face and the other wearing a bamboo hat, stood ankle-deep, digging atop a six-foot-high charcoal pile. Intent on their work, they burrowed with their bare hands, soot covering them from head to toe.

The smelter continued its roar. Jack and Mei arrived at the pile and watched the two men dig, waiting for them to look up.

"Chin," Mei called out in a loud voice, trying to be heard over the din of the furnace. Neither of the men on the pile heard her. "Hey, Chin!" she finally yelled.

The men looked up, realized they had an audience, picked up the canvass bags lying at their feet, and scrambled down the pile.

Jack and Mei walked over. Chin appeared sheepish, his face split by a gum-filled grin. He sported one of those silly haircuts where the hair around the sides of his head was shaved to the bone, but the hair on top was longish and mullet-like. Jack paid no attention to him, but focused on the other guy in the bamboo hat. He couldn't be sure, but it looked like the man on the bicycle.

"We just play around," Chin jabbered, uneasy as he brushed his hands free of soot.

"Mr. Davis needs you to drive us somewhere," Mei said to him, her eyebrows furrowed.

"What are you doing in that charcoal pile?" Jack asked. Chin's soot-covered face highlighted the expanded whites of his eyes: it was as if Jack were talking to a frightened horse. The guy exhibited the same sniveling behavior as Tie Liu, the lesser of the two Chinese crooks who had swindled Jack out of his hydroelectric company.

"I am Chin," he said, not answering Jack's question as he bowed up and down, gums and teeth competing for space in his lopsided grin.

"I know who you are," Jack said. "Where's this charcoal from?"

"Burma, boss," Chin said. "Trucks have special permit."

Jack tried to speak over the rumbling of the smelter, but his words dissolved in the racket.

"Too loud here. We get in car," Chin said, the man in the hat following him as they picked up their bags, scurried over to the Land Cruiser, opened the door of the rear compartment of the vehicle, and threw the bags inside. Chin took a solvent-soaked rag out of the car and wiped his hands. Jack started to climb into the back seat, but Chin held him off.

"Wait, boss. Very dirty," Chin said. He held open the car's back seat door and spat Chinese at the man in the hat, who walked around to the other side. They emerged from the back seat with more bags, and hurried to deposit them in the rear compartment of the car. Chin slammed the rear door shut, returned to the back seat and wiped it clean, and motioned for them to get in. When everyone was seated, Chin drove away.

As they pulled up to the office, the man in the hat opened his door and jumped from the vehicle while it was still moving, disappearing around the corner of the building.

Chin asked, "You want to go somewhere, boss? Mr. Liu's car yours now."

"Wait a second," Jack said. "Who was that guy with you?"

"Mr. Tao? He number two guy here, boss. Deputy general manager. Where you want to go?" Chin repeated.

"Mai Ja Yang," Jack said. "Clean up the car, and we'll head down there."

Chin's eyes widened. His grin disappeared.

Mei spoke in clipped Chinese to Chin.

"OK, but must be careful," Chin warned. "Mai Ja Yang can cost you."

———

An hour later, with Victor riding shotgun and Jack and Mei in the back seat, Chin drove the Land Cruiser out of the factory compound onto a cobblestoned byway only slightly wider than a goat trail. Dropping down the mountain toward the Mangshi River valley on hairpin turns, he sounded the horn every ten seconds. Initially wet and shaded as it passed under stands of bamboo and intermittent banyans, the road dried quickly as the open fields provided no defense against the sun. Bouncing through puddles of rainwater, Chin put the car through its higher gears as they reached the valley floor, green swatches of mountain jungle giving way to earthy plots of tilled farmland. Haphazardly constructed farm vehicles, all fan belts and handlebars, buzzed to and fro. A lone, erect woman in a conical hat and sarong walked along the opposite side of the road, oblivious to the traffic, carrying a pole across her shoulders, water buckets on either end. A few lengths behind her, a young boy, one hand trailing a lead rope and the other waving a bamboo switch, guided three water buffalo, tied nose-to-tail to one another, their brown eyes wide as the car rolled by.

Ten minutes later, they approached a busy junction with a major highway. Chin downshifted, hesitating only long enough to glance in both directions, and darted across the oncoming line of traffic, skidding to a halt in the median. Victor raised his eyes heavenward and crossed himself. Waiting as a long caravan of trucks rumbled by, Chin spotted an opening, and pulled into the line of vehicles, gunning the car southwest toward the hazy orange sun hanging over the Burmese horizon.

They passed by a sign saying *320 Guo Dao*, with 'National Highway' written in English underneath. Now in the flow of traffic, Chin turned loquacious, aiming to please his new boss. "Burma Road, boss," he said to Jack in a loud voice over the traffic noise. "American road," he said. "Your road."

"No," Jack corrected him, "this part is actually the Stillwell Road. And please, don't give me any credit for it. You know what they call this road stateside? The man-a-mile road. That's how many men died building it. I've never had to think about being in a situation like that."

"You weren't in the war?" Mei asked him.

"What do I look like to you, Father Time?"

Mei hung her head.

Christ, she was sensitive. But Jack had to admit, he had been wrong about her. She had worked very hard, staying up all night to finish the property transfer documents, which were surprisingly flawless, as if she had done similar work often. When she had questions, he only needed to explain things once. And sometimes, her queries weren't about simple things, but more fundamental issues, as if she was actually trying to learn. He felt he might be able to rely on her, a rare thing anywhere, but in the backwaters of China, close to a miracle. "Hey, I was just kidding; all right?"

She stared out her window toward the rice paddies rushing by.

"Okay?" he persisted, gazing at her in profile. Jack figured after what she had been through in New York, she probably thought all men were assholes. But not only was she a hard worker—she was gorgeous. She had ditched her work clothes and freshened up for the evening's festivities. Wearing espadrilles, slacks and a loose, multicolored peasant blouse, she looked as if she had stepped out of a page in a fashion magazine. Her figure, previously hidden in her men's clothes, was full, and abundantly apparent. Around her neck on a thin chain hung a miniature silver charm in the shape of an artist's palette. Her ebony hair was piled on top of her head and held in a bun with a lacquered pin, her neck softened by wisps of peach fuzz until it disappeared under her shirt collar. Sitting next to her, Jack could smell the scent in her hair. She had put a touch of something on her lips that glistened.

"Sure, Mr. Davis," she finally said, speaking toward the window.

He could have just watched the country roll by, but it was a long way to travel in silence. And he had become intrigued by the beautiful woman sitting next to him. Jack spoke toward the back of Victor's head. "Victor, I don't think you and I have ever talked about it," he said. "The armed forces, I mean. Did you serve?"

Victor lit a cigarette. "Where I'm from, it was compulsory," he said, taking a drag, rolling down his window, exhaling and tossing the spent match.

Quiet returned to the car's interior as the vehicle sped down the road. Chin eyed Jack in the rearview mirror, and when he caught Jack returning his gaze, reverted to looking straight ahead. Victor seemed to be studying the collection of bugs splattered on the windshield.

Jack shifted to face Mei. "It's not fair of me to assume you know about the war, I suppose," he said. "They keep a different set of history books in China, right? We called it the Second World War, but you guys called it the War of Japanese Aggression." He was transfixed by her profile, the silhouette of a lovely woman that could have been lifted from an antique Chinese portrait. He followed the smooth, apricot line of her cheek into the sides of her eyes, not rounded outwardly like a foreigner's, but flat across the front.

When it became clear Jack wasn't going to avert his gaze, she turned away from the window, looked him in the eye, and nodded slowly.

The car hummed south through the Dehong prefecture, rolling alongside an ancient irrigation canal, its clear water running down trenches of stone the same way it had for hundreds of years. Women with babies on their backs, their pantaloons rolled to their knees, planted rice in the paddies. Along the road, dingo-like dogs patrolled the periphery, looking for non-existent road-kill.

"What did they call the Vietnam War here?" Jack asked Mei.

"I didn't attend university, Mr. Davis, so I wasn't able to learn when your wars took place, or what they were called," she said.

"Well, it's OK for you to ask me if I was in that one," Jack said, smiling at her, trying to put her at ease.

"Were you?" was all she would say.

"I got a partial college scholarship to be a commissioned officer in the Navy—something called Reserve Officers Training Corps—but the war stopped the year I graduated. It's too bad. Maybe I would have developed more gumption."

"Gumption," she said aloud, examining the term with interest.

"It's a good word, right? One of my mother's favorites."

"Yes, I've seen it in translation. Resourcefulness, I think it means," Mei said.

"I've always thought of gumption as character, but that makes a person who has it sound too admirable," Jack said. He paused. "It's whatever it is that made me stubborn enough—some would say stupid enough—to buy this business."

"Yes, stubborn sounds like you," Mei said, smiling carefully back at him. Then she frowned. "But there was good reason to buy this business. The workers say it is the newest smelter in China."

"Maybe so, but it's anyone's guess whether we can get it to operate properly. Besides, it's liened to the hilt."

"Is 'liened' something bad?"

"It means we owe a lot of money," Jack said.

No longer turning away, she looked him over. "Perhaps you studied engineering at university," she said matter-of-factly.

"Well, you are correct, in a sense," Jack said, impressed with her statement. "That's what I should have studied to understand this smelter. But I majored in fine arts. Sculpture and drawing. Painting too," he added, looking at her necklace.

Mei eyes widened as she stared into his. She grasped her charm in one hand, but didn't say anything.

"Have you ever heard of Friedrich Nietzsche?" Jack continued.

"No," she answered, not uninterested.

Jack said, "He's a German philosopher who said the best thing humans can do is create. He also said the best type of creation is to dream. But I guess making sculptures—or paintings—is better than nothing." He shrugged.

Mei looked at him differently. "Why would someone like you choose a life here?"

The rice paddies rolled by. Bougainvillea climbed the fence posts, reaching for what was left of the ebbing sun. A flock of birds flew off perpendicular to the highway, the first songbirds Jack had seen in Dehong. "I could tell you what I told everyone in America, that I had no choice. Would you believe that?"

"I'm not sure. You seem to enjoy this. A part of you, anyway. What does your wife say?"

"My wife?" Jack said, surprised.

"Yes," Mei said. "You're wearing a wedding band."

"Oh," Jack said. "I wear it in her memory. She died a long time ago."

"How stupid of me," Mei managed to stammer.

He told her not to worry about it, but it was no use. She stopped talking. It was just as well; he couldn't get Hadley out of his head.

Chin pressed them south. Along the highway, the bougainvillea gave way to hibiscus. The roadway ran up a long straightaway through a gap notched between two mountains. As they cleared the tops of the trees, Jack caught sight of a river winding through the valley below. The early beams of the evening's moonlight reflected off its rippled surface.

"What's that river?" Jack asked Chin. "Still the Mangshi?"

"No, boss. Ruili River. We in Ruili city; close to border now," Chin said.

"This can't still be the American road, is it?"

"No boss. Old road over that way," Chin said, pointing off to the northwest, toward a ridge of jagged mountains. "But still there. Maybe one day you see."

"Yeah, if I'm looking for snakes."

"Snakes everywhere in China," Chin said, croaking a laugh. The right lane of the road began to jam up as civilization approached. Without any warning, Chin pulled the car off the highway into a turn-out, picking his way through piles of refuse that looked like they had been dumped there decades earlier, and stopped. "Please, Mr. Lomanov," he said, mangling Victor's last name, "you take back seat now." He said something in Chinese to Mei. She opened her door, got out of the vehicle, and switched places with Victor.

Victor climbed in next to Jack. "We playing musical chairs?" he said aloud.

"You see," Chin said, hitting the controls to roll up the tinted rear windows as he pulled back out onto the highway. After cresting the hill, the road turned south and began a long, downhill grade. The right lane ground to a standstill as scores of trucks bound for the border negotiated the incline in lower gear. The prehistoric machines, ramshackle and overloaded, inched down the hill, head-to-tail like the water buffaloes on the road earlier.

"Why are all these trucks backed up?" Jack asked.

"You see," Chin said again, his teeth showing white in the dark. At the foot of the hill, they took a sharp right, Chin threading the car between two lumbering trucks as the highway entered a rickety two-lane bridge suspended over the turgid Ruili River fifty feet below.

Jack examined the scene unfolding ahead of them. Darkening the roadway, a grove of banyans provided a sepulchral backdrop to a large customs and immigration station. A group of uniformed Chinese officers stood in front of barriers operated by men in adjacent guard booths. The men were all smoking. They casually surveyed the lines of vehicles heading south to Burma, their disdainful faces blotched intermittently by blue and red blinking lights atop long metal poles extended across the roadway.

"Your passports please," Mei said to the men as Chin slowed the car.

Jack and Victor pulled out their passports and handed them up to Mei. The roadway widened as it approached the guard booths. Traffic sorted itself into two lines. The line on the right moved along briskly, multiple vehicles escaping under the barrier each time it went up. The line on the left—the one subject to more scrutiny—moved slowly. Chin stayed in the left lane, creeping forward.

"Were those guys over there just nice to the cops?" Victor asked Chin about the line to the right.

"That line for trucks with special permits from Chinese government. Like smelter trucks," Chin said. "For charcoal. No wood in China anymore," he said, grinning.

The barrier in their lane went up and down several more times, red and blue flashes violating the night sky. Jack could see the uniformed men clearly now. They wore powder blue short-sleeved shirts with epaulets, faded navy pants, and silly hats with checkered rims that, except for the badges, made them look like they should have been selling hot dogs at Yankee Stadium. None of the guards was wearing a gun.

The car eased up to the guard booth and Chin rolled down his window. The nearest guard recognized him, walked over, and started speaking in Chinese. Chin replied, his voice animated, an unctuous smile affixed to his face, the guard saying something and Chin laughing. The guard kept talking to Chin, speaking casually. He glanced over toward Mei, but did not develop any apparent interest. He couldn't see through the tinted windows into the rear seat of the car.

Backing away, the guard was about to wave Chin through, and then asked one more question. Chin hesitated, answered him, and Jack sensed Mei flinch. The guard stopped backing away, came closer to the car, and said something in a sharp tone to Chin. Chin rolled down the rear windows. The guard looked inside at Victor and Jack, barked something at Chin, and walked away toward a separate station house under the trees ten yards off the edge of the road.

"Well?" Jack said, watching the man walk away.

Chin just sat there studying the guard house.

"He didn't seem very happy with you," Jack said.

"Big boss come now."

Victor took a long pull on his cigarette, the tip glowing bright orange. From over in the other lane, the dull roar of several trucks rolling under the gate reached a crescendo, and then ebbed as the guards dropped the barrier to apprehend an offending vehicle.

The guard re-emerged from the station house, followed by a man buttoning his officer's jacket over a stout girth. The man's head was covered in a chrome helmet, and although it was dark, he wore sunglasses. As he approached the car, Chin began speaking to him in Chinese when he was still twenty feet away.

"So, Chin. With *laowai* friends," said the officer. He stepped toward the car's rear window to get a good look at Jack and Victor, and then leaned the other way to glimpse Mei as well. He lit a cigarette and took a long drag. "They get out of car," he said in English to Chin, blowing a plume of smoke in Chin's face and flicking his matchstick against the car.

"Boss, Mr. Lomanov; please."

Jack and Victor opened their doors and got out, as did Chin and Mei.

The man took off his sunglasses and examined the four people standing in front of him, taking another long drag on his cigarette. "Passports," he said, and accepted the stack of passports Mei offered him without examining them. His squat frame appeared reasonably muscular, and his face was much browner than an average Chinese man's. But as Jack surveyed him in the light provided by the guard house lamp, he was surprised by the man's eyes. They were reptilian, a light brownish color, almost clear, and unfortunately, intelligent.

"American *laowai*. Yes?"

Jack and Victor didn't respond; Chin said something in Chinese.

The officer shuffled the passports without opening them. "One American and another one," he said, nodding to himself. "*Laowai* buy drugs this place," the man said, smacking his lips as he surveyed his prey.

Mei said something in Chinese to the officer. He looked at her, and then stared at Jack and Victor again as if for the first time. He glanced down at their shoes, and then back at their faces. He said something to Mei.

"He said you look like drug dealers, not businessmen," she said.

Victor said, "Tell him investors switched to casual dress ten years ago."

Mei's eyes widened, but her face remained stern as the officer continued speaking to her in Chinese. Then he pulled a flashlight out of his pocket, turned it on, and examined their passports more carefully, first shining the light on the men's faces, and then back on their paperwork. He spoke again in Chinese to Mei, and they talked to each other for a minute more.

Mei said to Jack, "I told him you own the smelter in Mangshi. He said no, his friend Liu owns the smelter. He said Liu sends trucks through here on their way to Burma for charcoal."

Jack shook his head carefully. "Mr. Liu does not own the smelter," he said slowly. "He works for us."

Mei began to translate Jack's words to the officer.

"*Pian zi!*" The squat Chinese man spit the words at Mei.

Mei leaned forward until her head was close to the officer's and hissed angrily in the man's face, clenched fists down at her sides. Jack was as surprised as the officer. When Mei finished, she took a deep breath. "He called you a liar," Mei said, trying to stay calm. "I told him he was wrong, that you own the smelter. I said you have an important business appointment south of here, we are late, and I will be forced to call the American consulate if he detains us."

The officer began to back off, trying to preserve face by flipping mindlessly through the pages of their passports. Then he sighed, spoke briefly in a clipped tone to Mei, and handed her the passports. He pulled a package of cigarettes out of his pocket, shook it open, and offered it to his foreign guests.

Victor took one. Jack was about to put up his hand in refusal, mentally kicked himself, and selected a cigarette as well.

"Mr. Davis, he asks that I introduce you," Mei said. "This man is the captain of China's customs and immigration service here at the Ruili border. As the top official in charge, he welcomes you."

"What should I do?" Jack asked.

"Say hello as you would in America."

"*Ni hao*," Jack said, sticking his hand out to the officer.

"*Ni hao, ni hao, ni hao*," the man said, shaking Jack's hand, and then shaking Victor's too. He spoke again to Mei.

"The captain asks if you will be sending charcoal trucks through here to Burma."

Jack said, "We've got to get the stuff somewhere."

Mei plastered a smile on her face and answered the man, who then rambled on in what Jack guessed was a local business pitch. "The captain recommends you come through here often," Mei said to Jack.

Then the officer took a final drag of his cigarette and flicked the butt onto the ground, the embers skittering in the dirt. Waving his right forefinger back and forth as he spouted some last words at Mei, the man turned his back and walked toward the station house.

Chin hissed at Jack and Victor, "Get in car," and, grabbing Mei, scurried after the officer. Jack and Victor watched the three of them standing on the porch of the station house in the shadows. After

Chin spoke, Mei reached into her pocketbook and gave some cash to the officer. Chin raised his voice at Mei, she spoke loudly as well, Chin yelled some more, and Mei extracted another fistful of money out of her pocketbook and thrust it at the man. He grabbed the cash and scuttled inside the station house, and Chin and Mei quickly walked over to the car and got in. A moment later, the little guard who had fetched the officer raised the barrier, and Chin gunned the car down the open road.

No one said anything as the car zipped past a line of plodding trucks. After a quarter mile, Jack saw signs in Chinese and English pointing the way to Mai Ja Yang, and Chin turned west on a minor road.

"When do we call the consulate?" Jack said to Mei. He could hear her breathing hard as she stared straight ahead into the night, the lights from Ruili fading to the south.

"I've never lied like that before," Mei said.

"It wasn't a big lie. What was the guy so upset about?" Jack asked.

"He's losing a paying customer in Mr. Liu, and he doesn't know if we're going to play the game," Victor offered. "Right, Chin?"

"Yes. He make good money on charcoal trucks with Mr. Liu," Chin said. "We say you foreign businessmen, he think maybe you don't pay him like Mr. Liu. Captain don't know you."

"He didn't look very Chinese," Jack said.

"Muslim Chinese," Chin said.

"From out west in Xinjiang?" Jack asked.

"No, boss. Muslims live this place long time," said Chin. "Many mafia here Muslim."

The road grew thinner, and their surroundings more remote, as the tires thrummed along the unimproved pavement.

"How much did you have to give him?" Jack asked.

"It is better you don't ask about such things," Mei said.

CHAPTER 5

An hour later, the road reached the top of a high plateau and flattened out. "Burma, boss," Chin said, pointing out ahead in the tropical darkness to where a single light flickered.

Shacks appeared along the road. Groups of people floated to and fro. They did not look Chinese. Some of the men wore long sarong-like robes, and almost everyone was barefoot.

"Are these people Burmese?" Jack asked. Buildings lined both sides of the road now, and motorbikes and motorcycles clogged the highway.

"Not all Burman, boss," Chin answered. "Most Kachin. Like Dai in China."

"What's that guy wearing?" Jack asked.

Chin looked at the people along the roadside as they drove past. "That *longyi*," Chin said, and leaned over and spoke to Mei in Chinese.

"He said a *longyi* is traditional Burmese dress for men," she said to Jack.

Jack asked, "Where are the Kachin from?"

"Kachin from Kachin," Chin said. "The far north of Burma; the mountains below Tibet. We go to Kachin now."

"What language do they speak?" Jack asked.

"*Jingpho*," Chin said. "Very difficult."

"Can you speak it?"

"Yes. Me and Mr. Tao both speak," Chin said.

"How did you learn?" Jack asked. "You're Chinese, right?"

"I am Dai," Chin said to Jack. "Mr. Tao is Tibetan. Live along border, must speak many languages."

Another guard house appeared, this time plunked in the middle of the road like a toll booth, its red and blue lights signaling as cars were stopped, and then permitted to pass. Chin eased the car into the gate and paid the guard ten *quoi*.

"What was that for?" Jack asked as they passed through, the blue lights flashing.

"Mai Ja Yang is a border port," Mei explained. "Things are duty-free here, so travelers must pay a tax."

Victor piped up. "A small charge to maintain 'sin city' for the public."

They floated off the plateau down a long hill. Ahead, more lights winked in the night. At the bottom of the incline, the road curved and then straightened out as it entered Mai Ja Yang. The small town looked like an outpost in an Italian western. Two- and three-story buildings lined both sides of the street. In the moonlight, Jack could see a small river running through the grassy plain to the southwest. Men strolled in the streets, ogling clusters of women leaning against the buildings or lounging on steps. As the car rolled slowly down the street, the women turned to check it out.

Victor said, "Reminds me of Amsterdam," rolling down his window to light a cigarette.

"No, no," Chin said as some of the women immediately began to collect themselves. "Sorry; they bother you now."

Several women began slinking toward the car, like so many crocodiles rushing live food that had strayed into their swamp. Coming alongside, the women coaxed and pleaded in Chinese. Victor rolled up his window, Chin hit the gas, and the car spurted down the street.

A triangular plaza formed the center of town. Beyond it, the river ran under a bridge. A red banner stretched across the road, and a large billboard exhibited a black-and-white photograph of uniformed Chinese and foreign soldiers standing next to one another in formal poses. Halfway across the bridge stood a border patrol guard booth.

From each side of the structure, metal barriers extended across the road, blocking nonexistent traffic.

"Lwegel Bridge, boss," Chin said. "Big battle here against Japanese."

"Right," Jack said, "the one they fought over sixty years ago that Mei thinks I was in."

"I didn't say that," Mei exclaimed, laughing.

Chin headed west toward the opposite end of town. In the moonlight, Jack could see people wading across the river.

"That Mai Ja Yang River, boss," Chin said. "Burma on other side."

"What are those people doing wading in the river in the middle of the night?" Victor asked.

Chin said, "Women come over from Burma, meet men friends, have party, men pay for food, women go home."

"A cultural exchange program," Victor said.

The river narrowed into a channel walled on both banks with boulders, circling around a big, man-made bend. In the middle of the bend—on the Burmese side—was a building complex highlighted with neon signs flashing Day-Glo colors in the dark. From parking lots on the Chinese side, wooden footbridges hung across the river, allowing patrons walking access to Burma.

Chin pulled into the entrance gate of the parking lot, paid the attendant, and found a space. He turned around and grinned at Jack. "Casino in Burma."

"We're going over there—to Burma?" Jack asked.

"As long as they take credit cards," Victor said.

Jack said, "What about immigration?"

"No problem, boss," Chin said.

"We needn't go to the casino," Mei said, surveying the decrepit buildings behind them in Mai Ja Yang. "There may be restaurants elsewhere."

"We can't celebrate at a mere restaurant," Victor said. He got out of the car and started walking toward the bridges across the river.

Single file, the rest of them walked between the cars in the unlit parking lot. When they came to the river, Chin led them onto a footbridge outfitted with rope rails swaying over the shallow stream. The group bumped into dark human shapes coming the opposite way, out of the Burmese netherworld back into China.

"We in Burma now," Chin announced when they reached the far bank. "No Chinese police." The casino loomed up in front of them, its multistory facade a bastardized rococo design. The walls were moldy cast-concrete highlighted with neon tubes at the corners, the roof topped with spotlights. Chin led them up to the entrance, dodging a group of drunken Chinese tumbling down the stairs. They went through double doors into a marble-floored lobby where a reception committee of armed guerillas barred the way. Chin ignored the group in rag-tag camouflage and made his way to the man at the front desk who appeared to be some type of army officer wearing a hat and a forest green uniform with red epaulets.

As Chin schmoozed with the officer, Jack and the others stood under a decrepit chandelier hanging from the ceiling. Following the plastic beads dangling from its frayed nylon strings, Jack's eyes ran down the electrical cords stapled in a half-assed fashion along the base of the wall to the chamber's broken windows, and rested on the collection of lizards hunkered in one corner of the room.

Victor was looking at the lizards too. "I guess that's what happens to guys who can't pay their tab," he said.

"What's taking so long?" Jack asked Mei as crowds of Asian people passed to and fro, Chin still talking with the officer.

Mei whispered to him. "Remember, Burma doesn't allow Americans."

Chin finished talking. "Passports," he said to Mei. She reached into her pocketbook and handed Jack's and Victor's passports to the officer. When the man held her gaze, she passed him two hundred RMB notes. He pocketed the cash, shuffled through the passport pages, studied Jack's for a moment, compared his face to his passport, handed back the documents, and waved them through.

"That guy a friend of yours?" Victor asked Chin as they walked down the hallway.

"KIA," Chin said. They followed him across the marble foyer to a hostess stand where an older woman stood surrounded by a bevy of young Asian girls.

"*Ni hao, ni hao*," Chin said to the hostess, while Mei ignored her and examined the color-coded floorplan set forth on the counter. The girls looked too young to be so heavily made up, their eyes ringed with black liner, cheeks spangled with silver glitter. They stared at the visitors with blank expressions under hair piled high on their heads, their dresses slit far up their thighs.

"You got *laowai* friends," the lady in charge said to Chin, displaying an array of gold teeth. "They want bang-bang? Or gang-bang? Ha, ha, ha," she laughed, her mouth wide open like a hippo, metal flashing, as the girls stood doe-eyed, staring at the strangers.

"Oh, please," Mei said, rolling her eyes. She turned to Jack and Victor, her lips pressed. "They have a casino, restaurant, bar, karaoke…. What would you like to do?"

Chin interrupted Mei in Chinese.

Her face flushed, she added, "They also provide massages—and other services."

"With hot stones!" Victor said.

"You're kidding me about that, right?" Mei said to him.

"I could use a drink," Jack said.

"A splendid idea," Victor responded.

Mei spoke to the hostess, who barked orders. Two of the girls opened a door and led them down a long hallway, the walls covered with grubby black felt. Jack could hear karaoke music bumping out of loudspeakers, overpowering singers performing out of tune. A door swung open, noise and smoke spewing out. Two men, propped up by a squad of karaoke girls, staggered out.

At the end of the hall, they entered the casino's crowded saloon. As ratty as the outer entryway had been, the saloon was worse, resembling a smoking lounge in a bingo parlor, every surface shellacked with a gelatinous slime of alcohol-saturated humidity. The smell of cooking grease wafted out of the kitchen. Ceiling fans struggled to circulate the squalid air. A wooden bar ran the length of one side of the room. Behind it, shelves of bottles were stacked to the ceiling, the smudged mirrors on the wall making the room wiggle like a fun house. Beyond the saloon, a pair of swinging windowed doors led to what looked like a restaurant, with gaming rooms beyond.

The room was jammed with Asian men, sweating in sleeveless tee shirts, shorts, and sandals, lounging around tables loaded with partially consumed drinks and overflowing ashtrays, a bluish pall of smoke floating above their heads. A mélange of *laowai* meandered in and out from where they were exiled on an outer terrace. Jack looked through a Palladian doorway at the motley collection of foreigners: a few might be Americans, but the rest appeared to be Europeans, including a lot of Russians. The majority of the *laowai* crowd was overweight men sporting tattoos, with sideburns crawling down their faces.

Skanky madams occupied the barstools at the back corner of the room. When the two new *laowai* walked in, the predators sprang off their seats and swarmed the foreigners, grabbing at Victor, calling him what sounded like 'ruver boy.'

"Jesus, get them away from me," Victor said, laughing as he fended them off.

Chin took Victor by the elbow and led him and the rest of his charges to a table looking out over the terrace.

A sweaty waitress wandered over, her hair hanging in her face. "Some drinks?"

"Ask her if they serve Mai Tais," Jack said to Chin.

"No Mai Tai," the waitress said.

A wan smile passed over Victor's face.

The waitress handed Jack a dog-eared cocktail menu, which he ignored. "How about a Martini, then?"

"No Martini."

"How nice that our waitress speaks English," Victor said.

Jack sighed. "Chin, do me a favor and ask her if they have vodka."

Chin spoke to the woman. "Yes, they have," he said to Jack.

"How about ice?"

Chin spoke again to the waitress. "Yes; ice," he said, nodding.

"OK, then. I'd like some vodka poured over ice. A double, please; ask her to put it in a tall glass."

As Chin spoke to her in Chinese, the waitress nodded and looked over at Victor, who held up two fingers. Mei ordered mango juice, and Chin had water.

When the waitress left, Jack pulled two Cohiba Robustos out of the breast pocket of his shirt and handed one to Victor. "I guess we've earned these," he said, removing the wrapper and biting off the end of the cigar with his teeth. "Jesus, it's hot in here," he said, rolling up his sleeves. The hair on his chest was soaked in sweat. As he unbuttoned the top button of his shirt, and then another, he caught Mei staring at him. For a moment, things stood still as he considered the intoxicating notion that maybe—just maybe—she was attracted to him. He brought himself back to earth. "So Chin, what's the KIA?" Jack asked.

"Kachin Independent Army."

Jack struck a wooden match, watched it flare, and lit his cigar. He took a long drag as he stole another glance at Mei. A thin sheen of perspiration covered her face, making it glow as if she were backlit on a stage. He studied the burning ember of his cigar. He might as well face it—she could become a major distraction if he wasn't careful. "Whose army is the KIA?" he asked Chin.

"KIA belong to KIO—Kachin Independent Organization," Chin said, carefully managing the big words. "KIO boss here."

"I think I know, but tell me: who is the KIA fighting, and why?" Jack asked.

"But surely you know the answer," Mei said, seeming surprised.

Jack said, "You flatter me. But I'd rather learn the answer from people here on the ground than a *New York Times* bureau chief who's been in Asia for six months."

"Kachin people different from rest of Burma," Chin said. "Different religion: most Kachin Christian. Burmans are Buddhist. Different culture too. And Kachin State has jade. KIA want to keep; Burman generals want to take."

"So Kachin doesn't want to be part of Burma," Jack said, taking a drag on his cigar.

"Kachin want to be Kachin," Chin said.

"Incoming at ten o'clock," Victor said.

Jack looked up to see a scrawny white hippy in a pair of stained cargo shorts and a tie-dyed tee shirt heading their way.

"Dude, what's happening?" the man said to Jack when he arrived at their table, his aging face disfigured by a Fu-Manchu mustache. He held a bottle of beer in one hand, his fingers covered with tattoos.

"Not much," Jack said.

"Where you from, man?" the hippy asked Jack, pulling up a chair. He bent over to adjust one of his sandals. Faint traces of marijuana permeated the air as he pulled his long gray hair behind his head, exposing an earring in one ear.

"New York," Jack said.

"Neewww Yoorrrk," the man repeated as he straightened up in his seat. "LA," he said, pointing his thumb at his chest. "You guys in the CIA or something?" he asked. "I heard a rumor the Agency's got something to do with this place."

"Not tonight," Victor said.

The waitress arrived with their drinks. The hippy took a crumpled box of Chinese cigarettes out of his pocket and offered them around, but there were no takers. "Well, what brings you to Mai Ja Yang?" he asked, lighting a cigarette and tossing the match on the muddy carpet.

Jack drank half his glass of vodka in one swallow.

"A celebration," Victor said, lighting one of his own cigarettes.

"Cool. Didn't know there was anything to celebrate around here."

An equally emaciated white woman, a cigarette in one hand and beer bottle in the other, stumbled into the bar from the terrace, saw the hippy with the strangers, and crossed over to their table. "Wha'chou got here?" she said to him.

"New Yorkers. Having a celebration," the hippy said. "This is my better half," he said, introducing the woman to the table. "But don't ask her where she's from—she don't remember," he laughed, exposing a mouthful of crooked teeth. "So," he said to Jack, "what kind of product you guys moving?"

Jack and Victor looked at each other. Feeling like a character in *Easy Rider*, Jack stifled the urge to laugh stupidly. "We just stopped in to get something to eat," he said.

"Hope you like Thai cooking," the better half said, "cause they ain't got no Western food." She pulled over a chair from the next table and sat down next to the hippy.

Mei and Chin remained silent, as if not wanting to involve themselves in a worthless *laowai* conversation.

Victor threw down what remained of his drink. "I think I'm ready to go next door and try some of that Thai food right now."

"Seriously, what the hell are you guys doing here?" the hippy asked.

"We just bought a smelter business up the road in Dehong," Jack answered.

"I get it," the hippy confided to his better half, leaning his head her way. "That way they can use those permitted trucks."

"That's the reason you guys bought the smelter?" she asked. "So you could deal using the trucks?"

"Dealing means smuggling, I take it," Victor said.

"Call it whatever you want," the woman cackled. She turned and gestured at the roomful of people. "Everyone here's doing it."

"She's right," the hippy said. "Jade, rubies. Other stuff."

"How do our hosts, the KIA, feel about contraband changing hands in their dining room?" Jack asked.

"Hell, they're the goddamned ringleaders," the hippy guffawed. "The only law around here that cares is the Chinese. And they won't stop you with stones—just drugs. You definitely don't want anything to do with bringing drugs into China," he said, waving his hand back and forth in a warning gesture.

"Wait a second," Jack said. "Bringing jade over the Burmese border isn't illegal in China?" He looked over to get a read from Chin, who said nothing.

"I have no idea what the law says," the hippy said. "After all, we're in China. All's I'm saying is that they want you to bring it in, man. You know how important jade is to the Chinese? And the good jade comes only from Burma. Stopping you is the last thing they're going to do."

"So the KIA and the Chinese both look the other way," Victor said.

"Dude, they encourage it," the hippy said, emphatic. "With stones, the only thing you gotta worry about is the Burmese generals further south. And like I said, you definitely don't want to take drugs over this-here border."

"I've been called a lot of things, but never a drug dealer," Victor said.

The better half cackled, and blinked several times, as if she had lost her contact lens. "Well, if you're not dealin', wha'chou guys doin' here then?" she asked.

"Just getting ready to have a little party," Jack said, having heard enough. Taking a last drag on his cigar, he stubbed it out and stood up. "Ready?" he asked Victor.

The hippy snorted. "We're all waiting to party," he said. "China: the land of opportunity. I've been here ten years, man."

"What's your day job?" Victor asked as he got up.

"Teaching English," the better half said.

"God help you," Jack said to the two losers. "*Fuyan*," he called, waving over at the waitress and holding up the hippy's empty beer bottle. "Two of these for our friends and the check."

"Hey man," the hippy said. "Thanks. Very white of you."

"Don't mention it," Jack said. "Nice to meet you both."

Mei pulled some RMB out of her purse and paid the waitress, and caught up with the men walking across the room.

"I need another drink," Jack said.

———

In the dining room, amidst a boisterous crowd sitting beneath ceiling fans slapping the smoke-and-alcohol saturated air down on their heads, a waitress seated the four of them and handed out menus. Victor requested a wine list, and she handed him a small card soiled with fingerprints. Victor asked if they had another wine list and she said no. Jack ordered two more vodkas and another mango juice for Mei.

The menus were covered with clear plastic and filled with colored photos of dishes. Jack leafed through his and handed it to Mei. "You'd be better at this."

Mei studied the pages of the menu. "The food here is mainly Thai, with some nice Yunnan items, but they don't serve many dishes with meat," she said.

"We don't need meat. Right, Victor?" Jack asked.

"As long as it tastes like meat."

The waitress returned with their drinks, and Mei ordered for them: a soup, chicken salad with lemon grass and pickled peppers, mint salad with tofu, two kinds of fish, noodles with scallions and spicy sauce, and a Yunnan specialty, fried goat cheese.

"That's well enough," Victor said, "but it will taste much better with a bottle of good wine." He stopped the waitress as she was leaving, holding up the wine list. "Mei, can you ask her if this is all they have?" Victor said.

"I'm sure it is," Mei said to Victor as the waitress stood next to him nodding.

"Perhaps for the occasional stray traveler they keep some good stuff in the cellar," Victor persisted.

"I doubt it, but I'll ask." Mei began to speak to the waitress in Chinese.

"*Meiyou*," the waitress replied with no hesitation.

But Mei didn't give up. Forcing a smile onto her face, she added some words. The waitress exhaled, uttered an exclamation, and fidgeted, wanting to be done with such foolishness. But Mei kept at it, and finally the waitress shrugged, issued an unhappy remark, and stalked away.

Jack said, "She didn't sound pleased."

"She says she'll ask," Mei said grimly.

At the next table, chaos ensued as two waitresses delivered huge platters of shrimp and crabs to a large group of Chinese men who elbowed one another out of the way grabbing for the food, and then tore at the shells, shucking them onto the floor, picking at the pile like a pack of starving animals.

An Asian woman pushed through the swinging doors from the saloon. She was clad in a Burmese sari top and sheath dress with a slit running almost to her hip. As she made her way through the crowd, their waitress spoke to her, and then pointed in their direction. The woman walked across the dining room toward them. As she came nearer, Jack could see she had been beautiful once. Her light brown skin, slightly freckled across a flat nose, was pulled tightly across high cheekbones, her eyes an unusual hazel color.

"Someone said something about wine?" she asked in the direction of Jack and Victor in a voice inflected with a slight British accent. She acknowledged Chin. As she locked eyes with a sober-faced Mei, a flicker of recognition crossed the woman's face.

"We're celebrating," Victor responded. "I was wondering if the house might have a bottle of something better than the table wine on your list."

"And if I did, what would make me offer it to you?" she replied, the makeup on her cheeks streaked with perspiration.

"The goodness of your heart," Victor replied.

"Ha," she spoke without humor, "I ran out of that a long time ago." She scrutinized the two foreigners. "What brings you here?"

"We just bought a smelter up in Mangshi," Jack said.

The woman frowned. "I heard. Metalclad's operation. Why would you do that?"

Jack was surprised; word had gotten around fast. "Just trying to make some money," he said.

"In the business?" she asked.

Victor said, "And what business would that be?"

"The same business that attracts all these lowlifes," she said, gesturing disdainfully toward the crowd in the room. "Moving things over the border. Stones; drugs…women."

"Sorry to disappoint you," Victor said. "We're just investors from the U.S."

"God help you," the woman said. She exchanged a few words with Chin, eyed Mei once more, and started to leave.

Victor gazed up at her with the most polite expression he could muster. "Does your sympathy mean we qualify for a good bottle of wine?"

"How good?" she asked.

"The best you have," Victor responded.

"You know the rules for favors in this part of the world," she said to Victor, her face hardened once more. "The grander your request, the tougher the consequences." She grabbed a busboy, spoke to him for a moment, and then walked back across the dining room and out the swinging doors.

"You didn't seem to like her very much," Jack said to Mei as the waitress arrived with the first course.

"I've been trying to get away from people like that all my life," Mei said as she wheeled the Lazy Susan in the center of the table around so the mint salad was in front of Jack. "Try some," she said.

Victor let his drink sit half-full. "Do you think she's going to come back?"

"Maybe riding on a broom," Jack said, examining the mint salad. He sampled some with his chopsticks. "Not bad." He ate some more.

Victor said, "Prior to hot stones—and good food like this—a glass of decent wine is mandatory."

"No offense, but I'm ordering another vodka," Jack said.

When Jack didn't make any move for more mint salad, Mei reached over with her chop sticks and put some chicken salad with lemon grass on his plate.

Jack leaned down to examine the food. "What is it?"

"It's good," Mei assured him.

He speared some food and chewed. "You're right." He nodded. "You know, serving me isn't part of your job description," he said to her.

"It is my pleasure."

Jack was still thinking how good Mei's answer sounded when the waitress presented the bottle of red wine to Victor.

"What is it?" Jack asked Victor.

Appearing pleased but incredulous, Victor held up the bottle of Nuits-Saint-Georges.

"You sure you want to take it?" Jack said, grinning at Victor.

Victor examined the label. "What kind of a year was 2004?"

"A great year for French pinot noir," Jack said. "If our hostess was right, we must be in for one hell of a ride."

Victor had just passed out after-dinner cigars when the hostess reappeared. "How was your wine?" she asked Victor, standing next to the table with her arms crossed.

Victor said, "I'm afraid to tell you."

"There's someone who would like to speak to you," she said to them. "Chin will know who I'm talking about," she said, and walked away to tend to another table of customers.

"You seem to know everyone here," Jack said to Chin.

"That my job," Chin said proudly, flashing his buck teeth.

Just like Tie Liu at the hydro company used to say, Jack thought to himself. "Who's she talking about?" Jack asked.

"Her boss. Very, very big guy. Want to meet you, you must say yes." Chin spoke in a torrent of Chinese to Mei.

She turned to Jack. "Chin says this man owns the casino with the KIA."

"A Kachin guy?" Jack asked.

"No," Chin said. "He white guy, American. Same as you." Chin spewed more Chinese at Mei.

Mei explained. "Chin says that the Kachin helped the Allies defeat the Japanese here in the War of Japanese Aggression. In return, they were supposed to get their own independent state before the generals in Rangoon made other plans."

"We've heard about that," Jack said. "And they've been fighting ever since. Where does this guy come in?"

"Chin says the rumor is that the CIA helped the Kachin buy guns for several years, but then left, except for this man," Mei said. "Chin says the KIA hope he will bring back the American armed forces."

"Sure he will," Jack said, "just like they did at the Bay of Pigs."

The hostess appeared at the restaurant door, wagging two fingers at their table, indicating they should join her.

"I doubt this will take long," Jack said to Mei as he got up from the table.

"Don't say any more than you need to," Mei warned.

The woman led Jack and Victor through a doorway out of the dining room down an unlit hallway until she came to a cramped, dingy office. She closed the door behind her and sat down behind a desk, picking up a pencil and notepad.

"Colonel Costa would like a word with you," she said. "Your full names?"

Jack traded looks with Victor. "Jack Davis," he said to buy some time, Victor giving her his name as well. The yellow glow of the desk lamp, the only source of light in the room, illuminated the lower half of their faces.

Jack took in the floor-to-ceiling shelves filled with what appeared to be accounting manuals, work papers, and binders overflowing with business forms and records. The only concession to technology was a speaker phone sitting atop a filing cabinet next to the desk. The phone was engaged and on hold, its green light blinking.

The hostess got up and perched on a corner of the desk, her thigh exposed by the long open slit of her sheath dress. She pressed a button on the phone.

"Jack Davis and Victor Romanov are here now," she said, speaking into the phone as it activated, static in the background.

"Finish Googling them?" a voice crackled from the other end of the line.

"Mr. Davis is who you thought he was. I didn't get a chance to do a search for Mr. Romanov." She lifted her eyes. "Gentlemen, this is Colonel Costa on the line."

"You're the Davis in Davis Partners," the guy on the line said, with a raspy voice, like that of a tired old cop.

"That's me," Jack answered.

"You're a long way from New York City."

"Yeah, I'm trying to get adjusted to that myself."

"Seriously," Costa said after a pause, "I need to know what you're doing here." The colonel—Jack had a hard time believing he was really a colonel—was definitely American, his voice a little squeaky. He sniffed loudly every minute or so.

Jack's first instinct was to tell the guy that he was in the middle of dinner and to mind his own business, but there was no reason so far to waste the energy. "Some things stateside didn't go my way, and this is where I've ended up."

"So you're trying to tell me you left your life in the States to buy a smelter in the middle of the Yunnan jungle," the man said.

Jack didn't need this guy to remind him of his plight. "I'm not trying to tell you anything. But the answer's yes—we closed the transaction today."

"And the business strategy behind that?"

"Desperation."

"But it's just a business deal."

"What's that supposed to mean?" Jack said.

"Look, I've got to ask you these questions for security purposes," Costa said.

Jack had heard enough. "No offense, but you're going to have to tell us a lot more about who you are. Colonel."

"The smelter's not a front?"

"A front for what?" Jack snorted.

"Where do you plan to buy your charcoal?"

"I have no idea. The same place we're buying it now, I imagine," Jack said.

"Your general manager Liu buys his charcoal from us here in Burma."

"He's not our general manager—he was Metalclad's."

"He won't be working for you?"

"We haven't made the decision yet, but I doubt it."

"Why?"

"My guess is he's stealing us blind," Jack said. "But that's what happens to all *laowai* in China, right? Look, we're in the middle of dinner. Where's all this going?"

Costa said, "We have a good charcoal business in Kachin, and we'd like to keep you as a customer. And we might want to speak to you about your trucks. Is the entire fleet licensed to enter Burma?"

"I'm really not sure," Jack said.

"How do you feel about your country?" Costa asked.

Jack smelled ripe bullshit. "I don't have much time these days to think about that sort of thing," he answered.

"We're fighting a brutal war here with the *Tatmadaw*," Costa said.

"Who's that?"

"Sorry. The Burmese military."

"Who's we?" Jack asked. "The U.S. hasn't been involved in this part of the world since Vietnam."

"I can't say much more about that now—this line's unsecured," Costa said. "What would you say if I offered you the opportunity to serve your country—on a clandestine basis? I need to know how you feel about the sides down here."

"You mean the Burmese generals—whatever you call them—and the Kachin? No offense, but I could care less."

"Very nice speaking with you," Costa said.

The dial tone sounded, the woman punched a button, and the phone was quiet.

"That guy's not in the CIA," Jack said.

"I didn't say he was," she said with a sigh, standing up.

"And I can't believe he cares that much about charcoal either," Victor said.

"I don't get involved with that part of his business," the woman said.

"I would have thought the casino would be more profitable," Jack said.

"You'd be surprised," the woman said, a perfunctory smile crossing her mouth. "A monopoly on charcoal in Burma helps in unexpected ways. How long will you be staying tonight?"

"We're going to finish our dinner, have a few more drinks, and then we're out of here," Jack said.

"No gambling; no girls?" the woman asked.

"Maybe if Victor is interested, we'll stay a little longer," Jack said.

"Sorry, not tonight," Victor said, "but could I pick up something to go?"

"One of the girls?" She arched her eyebrows. "That would be very expensive."

"I was thinking about a couple bottles of Hennessey," Victor said.

"That we can do," she said, laughing. "No gambling for you, Mr. Davis?"

"I can't afford to lose right now," Jack said.

SOUTH OF THE CLOUDS

"But you've made a big bet on your smelter business."

"And maybe it'll pay off, and we can flip it and get the hell out of here."

The woman packed up her paperwork. "There's probably more upside with your trucks. You should stay in touch with Colonel Costa."

"Hard to imagine why," Jack said.

"I applaud that response," she said with a sad smile. "In this part of the world, you'll find cynicism to be a useful tool."

CHAPTER 6

At midnight, the four of them climbed into the car and headed home. After an hour on the highway, they cleared customs, crossed the bridge over the Ruili River, and surmounted the long hill that took them up through the gap in the mountains to Dehong.

Chin drove steadily north in the night. He was trying hard, Jack thought, admonishing himself not to judge the guy on the basis of his uncanny similarity to Tie Liu, his traitorous partner in the Chinese hydroelectric company.

Up in the shotgun seat, Victor was asleep. Slumping next to Jack in the back seat, Mei dozed, her head leaning back, eyes closed, lips partly open. Her leg rubbed up against Jack's. He was happy to feel her touch. Jack stared at Mei's face bathed in the moonlight, entranced by her beauty. Tempted to lean over and kiss her, he told himself to get a grip. "Who really owns that casino?" Jack asked Chin.

"KIA and American friend," Chin said.

Jack asked, "How much does the American have to do with the business?"

"KIA own building. American own business," Chin said. "Own girls too."

"He owns the girls?" Jack said. "Jesus. Where're they from?"

"All over Asia. Some Chinese. Most from Burma. Casino treat girls good, boss. Sometimes…" Chin shrugged. "Sometimes people need money. Then slave not so bad."

Jack watched the night rush toward the windshield and flinched as a big bug splatted against the glass. "Why does the KIA need an American partner?"

Chin said, "Cash, boss. KIA need cash for guns. American has cash, KIA let him do casino business. KIA do security for casino; get some money. But everything in Kachin belong to Kachin people, boss."

"It sounds like other people want what the Kachin have, though," Jack said.

"Yes, boss. Many people. Burman generals; Chinese people too. Everyone want Kachin jade. Best in the world."

"So what can the Burmese generals do about it? I don't imagine they're going to show up in Kachin and start digging the stuff out of the ground themselves."

"Special tax," Chin said. "Stones go south, must pay big tax to generals."

"So the jade goes north to China," Jack said. "The Chinese get their jade and the Kachin get money to buy more guns."

"Yes, boss."

"So why would the American think I could help with that?"

"You must ask him."

Jack looked out the window into the night, sensing a fog of deception encircling him. Dozing in and out of sleep in the back seat, he opened his eyes when Chin downshifted and slammed on the brakes, the car skidding on the grit of the highway.

Up ahead at an intersection, traffic had ground to a halt underneath a billowing cloud of oily smoke seemingly held aloft by a cacophony of headlights and taillights. Through the confusion, Jack could see a screeching pattern of red and blue flashes emanating from the tops of police and fire vehicles and temporary warning lights placed in the road.

Chin stopped behind a long line of cars and trucks, and then inched forward through emergency vehicles. The commotion woke Victor and Mei. The four of them craned their necks to see what was up ahead.

Chinese soldiers were questioning drivers, inspecting each vehicle. Policemen made circular motions with their flashlights, attempting to route traffic around the source of congestion.

"General Dong coming. Number one drug soldier," Chin said as a dapper man in a military uniform with stars on his hat approached their car. Chin rolled down his window.

The general removed his hat and looked at Victor, and then craned his neck to peer inside the back seat of the car. "Foreigners. I thought so," he said. "You may pass by, but please: no drugs in China. You bring in jade, other things: all OK. These people have drugs; now look what happen. Please: no drugs," he said, flipping his hand as if to shoo them off. Not waiting for a response, he walked down the line of cars.

Chin pushed the car forward a few more yards, and then there it was, in the southbound lane: the remains of the big blue Forland transport truck Jack had seen in the rainforest the day before.

It was the same truck: Jack could see the bullet holes lining one fender. But he would never know if the dead boy was still affixed to the grill, since the entire front end of the vehicle was smashed like an accordion. The truck had veered on an angle into the concrete median wall, evidently in an effort to evade the half-track, a tank-like vehicle topped by a large caliber machine gun blocking the intersection. The half-track was a smashed heap as well.

As they pulled alongside the accident site, what remained of the Forland smoldered where it sat wedged under the front of the crumpled half-track. Flames licked its undercarriage, only half of its original length. The truck's driver had to have been flying, Jack thought. What did the guy think he was going to do, ram a tank and live to tell the tale? Or maybe he had figured they were going to die one way or another.

Alongside the carcass of the Forland, what had been a man lay dead in the road, a bloody stump at the end of his neck. Two soldiers were trying to shovel his remains into a body bag. The policemen yelled at the rubberneckers, flashing their lights and urging traffic to move on. Chin had stopped the car, transfixed by the mess. A policeman slammed the butt of his flashlight against Chin's window, startling everyone.

"Chin, you must drive," Mei urged him in a low voice.

Chin kept staring down at the body in the road. The policeman banged his flashlight against the window again, yelling this time.

"Move us out of here, for Chrissakes," Jack said to Chin.

Chin jammed the car into gear and jerked it up the roadway.

They passed a line of bloodied guerilla captives being prodded by Chinese soldiers into two big white vans with police markings on their sides. Jack couldn't tell whether any of the guerillas were the same ones from the gunfight in the jungle. They didn't look rough anymore, just frightened.

"What are they doing with those guys in those vans?" Victor asked.

"Those are death wagons," Mei whispered.

"What're those?" Victor asked.

"They'll be gassed to death," Jack explained.

"On the spot?" Victor asked.

"That's what happens to you in rural China if you're carrying drugs or guns," Jack said. "Unless you're a foreigner. Then you get a break: only jail for life."

Further up the road, an interrogation was in process. A group of soldiers surrounded a lone guerilla in a headband, his face covered with blood. Acrid smoke, reeking of chemicals and electrical fire, smudged the scene.

Jack looked closer at the guerilla. It was the truck driver from the gun battle on the road behind the smelter. "I've seen that guy before," he said.

"Yes," he heard Chin say.

Multiple soldiers shined flashlights at the guerilla's head. As the guy tried to shield his eyes, an interrogator wearing an officer's hat slapped his hand away, screaming at him. The interrogator slapped the guerilla's face again, and his headband flew off. Standing in a circle around the suspect, a group of helmeted soldiers watched the event as if they were students observing a procedure at medical school. The interrogator screamed at the guerilla again, and this time bashed his head with a truncheon.

General Dong stood a few steps away observing the scene. He was impassive, as if wishing he was somewhere else. As his aide handed him a cigarette, the general turned out of the wind for a light just as the guerilla jumped on the interrogator and bear-hugged him.

The guy had to have a death wish, Jack thought in admiration as he sat in their car and watched the fight. The guerrilla clung to the interrogator's neck, pulling him off balance; the officer's hat fell off and rolled away in the mud. The two of them fell into a pile in the darkness. As the guerrilla clambered onto the interrogator's shoulders, the larger man straightened up, and flicked his lightweight assailant off his back as if he were a bug.

General Dong had seen enough. He tossed his cigarette and snapped some words at the interrogator. At first, the man paid no attention, drawing his leg back and kicking the guerilla's face as he lay on the ground, blood spurting out of his nose. Then the general barked loudly at the interrogator again. As the man straightened up and paused to search for his hat, the guerilla rolled cat-like off to the side. In the dark, he scrambled into the crowd on all fours, through people's legs, and disappeared. The stupid soldiers just stood there, as oblivious as they had been the day before in the rain forest.

"Let's get out of here," Jack said to Chin.

Chin inched the car slowly through the crowd and out onto the highway, gunned it and picked up speed, leaving the scene in the rearview mirror.

"Those men no have drugs," Chin said, his face twisted into a bitter scowl. "General Dong is liar."

"He is not alone," Mei said.

CHAPTER 7

"Staff Sergeant Dennis T. Costa, United States Air Force," Victor read off his computer screen when Jack sat down in the office the next morning.

"Not colonel?"

"Perhaps he gave himself a promotion."

"What unit?" Jack asked.

Victor flipped through more pages, squinting his eyes. "The most current entry just indicates he was discharged."

"Honorably?"

"It doesn't say," Victor said.

"Where he was last stationed?"

Victor clicked his mouse a few times. "Joint Military Advisory Group; Bangkok, Thailand." He scanned the screen. "But he was last posted there in 1998. It's a black hole after that."

Jack sat down at the conference table next to Victor. "Here are the photographs I took during that shootout in the rain forest the other day. Take a look," he said, handing Victor his mobile phone. On the screen was the photograph of the Forland with the dead boy lashed to the grill.

Victor studied the photograph, and then flipped to the next ones. "My guess is these guys are doing what everyone was talking about last night."

"That truck looks familiar, right?" Jack said. "It's the same one we saw smashed in half last night. Look at the next photo. See the guy in the headband? He's the one they were slapping around before he got away."

"The one Chin seemed to know," Victor said.

They finished their coffee in silence.

"I'm starting to get the feeling we're outnumbered," Victor said.

Two weeks later, Jack notified the Chinese managers they would hold the smelter's inaugural management meeting the following day, the first of September. Sitting in the office waiting for everyone to assemble, he listened to the smelter across the road struggle to come to life, hum half-heartedly and then whine, belch, stop dead, and start fitfully again a minute later. The sputter and stutter of the big machinery had become familiar. But it was far from soothing. They needed to gain traction and get out of the ditch.

At nine o'clock, after a round of unctuous handshakes, General Manager Liu stood up to lead off. His teeth were rust-colored, and his hair was dyed coal black and hardened with hair spray. Mr. Liu's face was puffy and his eyes red-rimmed, undoubtedly aftereffects of long nights drinking *baiju,* the white liquor favored by Chinese guys who thought they were big shots. His Tommy Hilfiger sports jacket straining at the buttons around his midsection, he spoke in Chinese from a typewritten report.

A hatless Mr. Tao sat next to him clad in a black pajama get-up, clear eyes set in a lined face under a thatch of gray hair. The other managers, staring mindlessly ahead, were crammed along the back wall like birds on a wire. The humid, cramped office was pungent with the tang of human sweat.

Sitting next to Jack, Mei translated Mr. Liu's remarks. She had resumed wearing her men's clothing, but the outfit was no disguise. Even in the dreary office, she was radiant. Her face was scrubbed and bright, hair parted and hanging down around her shoulders. "Mr. Liu says the employee count is three hundred and forty," she intoned. "Last week, our quartz inventory equaled one hundred fifty-two tons."

"We don't care about all that," Jack said, waving his hand back and forth so Mr. Liu would get the idea. "Please ask him to get to the part about how many tons of metal we sold last week."

Mr. Liu stopped, appearing confused.

"I'll tell him, but please," Mei warned. "If a translator interrupts the general manager, he'll lose face."

Jack shrugged—he wasn't going to quibble when she was taking her job so seriously—and got up to toss the dregs of his coffee. But as Mr. Liu droned on, Mei regurgitating his facts in English, Jack realized the clueless man didn't know the difference between preliminaries and substance.

Mr. Liu paused a few minutes later.

"OK, that's enough face-saving. Tell him we just want to know about sales," Jack said to Mei.

She spoke to Mr. Liu. The man listened, looked over at Jack, checked his notes, and then went right back to his sing-song delivery. He fired off another torrent of Chinese, probably something Jack really needed to know, like the temperature of the molten silicon when it came out of the furnace.

"OK, stop," Jack said, exasperated, fighting a losing battle with his temper. "Let's take a different approach. I'll ask him questions, and he can respond with answers. Short ones."

Mei translated to Mr. Liu.

"*Dui,*" he grunted, turning a wary eye toward Jack.

"How many tons of silicon metal did we sell last week?" Jack asked.

Mei translated, and Mr. Liu waxed eloquent with a long trail of Chinese words.

"Mr. Liu says the smelter is number one in China," she said as Mr. Liu kept jabbering.

"How. Many. Goddamn. Tons!" Jack yelled, as Mr. Liu stopped in midsentence, and the junior Chinese managers cowered. "That's all we want to know, for Chrissakes."

"I don't think he knows, Mr. Davis," Mei said. "As far as I can tell, he's never here."

Out of the blue, Mr. Tao spoke, his speech as clipped as his brush-cut. "Three hundred fifty."

Jack did a double-take at Mr. Tao, while Mr. Liu's eyes narrowed.

"Now we're getting somewhere," Victor said as he picked up a pencil and made a notation on his legal pad.

"You speak English," Jack said to Mr. Tao, surprised.

"A little," Mr. Tao said, grimacing.

"Better than nothing," Jack said. "How come you're the one who knows the answer?"

"I operate smelter," Mr. Tao said.

"Thank God someone knows something about the place," Victor said.

"What's our capacity utilization?" Jack continued.

"Four thousand tons one month," Mr. Tao answered. "Fifty thousand tons capacity."

"Yeah, but that's the theoretical nameplate," Victor said. "You just told us we sold three hundred fifty tons last week; that's only a little over a thousand tons per month."

"Make and sell different," Mr. Tao said, for the first time showing his teeth, which were surprisingly white and straight. Despite his lithe frame, his hands were stubby and gnarled. All of his fingernails on his right hand were blackened, as if they had been crushed in a machine.

"Why is that?" Jack asked.

Mr. Tao's face tightened. "I make silicon. Cannot sell it. Rejection rate very high."

"You're saying we're spending a lot of money to produce stuff that the customers aren't buying," Jack said.

"Yes," Mr. Tao said. "Testing equipment next door," he said. "They need four nines to buy."

"Ninety-nine point nine nine percent pure silicon," Victor said. Mr. Tao nodded.

"Why is the silicon we produce less than four nines?" Victor asked.

Mr. Tao spat out the answer. "Quartz low quality," he said. "Many impurities."

"Why do we do buy such poor quartz?" Jack asked.

"Mr. Liu boss of purchasing," Mr. Tao said.

"What a surprise," Jack said, looking over at Mr. Liu, who was ignoring the conversation going on in English, seemingly fascinated by whatever he was watching outside the window. "Victor, do our records indicate what quality of quartz we purchase?"

"They do indeed," Victor said, flipping through charts on his computer screen. "It says here we've been paying for the best quartz money can buy."

"So Mr. Liu is paying for the top of the line, but we're getting the bottom of the barrel."

"Right," Victor said, eying Mr. Liu. "Now we know where his fancy clothes come from."

"One other thing," Jack said, turning back to Mr. Tao. "Why does the damn thing stop and start all the time?"

"Many men inside no good," Mr. Tao replied. "Some go; then I fix."

"Why not do that now?" Victor asked.

"Mr. Liu's family work there," Mr. Tao said, his lips pressed tightly together.

"Mei," Jack said, "could you let Mr. Liu and the others know we'd like to take a ten-minute break? Except for you, Mr. Tao."

Mei spoke to the men and they filed out. Mr. Tao leaned comfortably back in his chair, waiting for Jack and Victor to continue.

"Where'd you learn to speak English?" Jack asked.

"In Tibet, my home. I was officer in army. Must speak English," Mr. Tao said.

"OK," Jack said. "What do we call you?"

"Tao."

"*Taozong*," Jack said, using the deferential Chinese title, "I'm thinking you could run this business for us."

"Yes," Tao said, as if he had expected such a conclusion all along. He paused. "I need raise," he said with a straight face.

Of course, Jack thought, wanting to laugh out of frustration. "Fair enough," Jack said. "Subject to a six-month trial period."

Tao just nodded, and then spoke a minute to Mei in Chinese.

"Tao wants you to know he is not just a typical peasant," Mei continued. "He is Tibetan, from a Kuomintang military family. You can trust him."

Jack studied Tao's face. "In that case, what can you tell us about the gunfight out back in the rain forest the other day?" he asked.

Tao paused to consider his words, and then, as if to make sure of what he was about to say, spoke in Chinese to Mei.

"Tao says he saw the gun battle, and saw you too," Mei said. "In the trees as he rode his bicycle. He was glad you weren't injured."

"Did he know those people?" Jack asked.

Without waiting for translation, Tao shook his head. "I no know them, but I know why they on road." He spoke to Mei for a minute more.

"It was a type of funeral," she explained, "until the shooting started. The dead boy was Buddhist. He was being taken up the mountain to the temple for his *jhator* the following morning at dawn."

"What's a *jhator*?" Jack and Victor asked at the same time.

"It's a Buddhist ceremony," said Mei. "A sky burial. The monks at the temple manage a charnel ground. It's a high rock where after death, the monks cut up the body and feed it to the vultures so the person can quickly pass on to another life."

"Jesus Christ," Jack muttered. "Who were those men in the truck?" he asked Tao.

"They Thai." Tao spat out the word.

"Why were the Chinese ambushing them?"

"Chinese think drugs," Tao said, looking like he had swallowed something foul.

"Do you have anything to do with them?" Jack asked.

"No," Tao said, shaking his head emphatically. "No drugs."

"Please tell me we can make money at the smelter business," Jack said.

Tao looked puzzled.

"The smelter isn't profitable yet," Jack explained. "I'd hate to tell you how much we paid for this place. When can we make money smelting silicon?"

"In China, no one make money in regular business," Tao said, stone-faced. "Make money other ways."

Jack turned to Victor. "I'm afraid we know what that means," he said in a low voice. "Should we get into it now?"

"Not with that bozo Liu waiting right outside the door," Victor responded.

Jack slumped back in his chair. "All right, let's get this over with first," he said to Mei. "Can you ask Mr. Liu to come back inside? By himself."

She appeared confused.

"Please call him back in here. We've got to fire the guy."

"You're going to fire him?"

"No, we're going to give him a raise and a promotion," Jack said to her. "Of course we're going to fire him. The guy's been stealing us blind."

"I never liked guys in Tommy Hilfiger stuff," Victor said.

Mei went out of the room and returned, Mr. Liu scuttling back in behind her.

Before anyone could speak, Tao stood up. "I talk Liu," he said. "For his face." He spoke in Chinese to a confused Mr. Liu for a minute. Mr. Liu barked some Chinese, and Tao spoke firmly back to him. Mr. Liu surveyed the room with a glower. As Tao led him out the door, he spat on the floor.

Jack watched Mei take a deep breath. The room was silent, the whir of the fan the only noise.

"Mr. Liu's dangerous," she warned. "He's from Henan."

"What's that supposed to mean?"

"People from Henan are very bad."

"That's what people in Henan say about people from Kunming," Jack said, standing up. "Let's get back to work. Mei, please find Chin and tell him to get Mr. Liu's keys."

They filed out of the office. The humid heat of the day smacked them as if they had walked into a door.

"That's one down," Victor said as they stood outside the office entrance flanked by birds-of-paradise, "but we're making a big bet on Tao."

"What choice do we have?" Jack said. "But don't misunderstand me: you can't trust anyone in China. The one you're most friendly with? That's the Judas who's going to fuck you. But I wouldn't sell Tao short," he said. "He sure seemed like a cool customer the other day in the rainforest."

———

A month later, as the morning sun peeked over the ridge to the east and began to dry out the jungle, the smelter cranked up for its first run of the day. From where he sat in the office, Jack stopped reviewing Victor's spreadsheets and listened. The big machines started up, burped once but otherwise hit their stride, the whine of the de-duster kicking in on schedule. A minute later, all of the equipment whirred and hummed in tune.

Under Tao's direction, the business was slowly finding a rhythm. The machinery wasn't belching as much. Payroll costs had dropped by forty percent. Rejection rates of silicon were way down. But the world-wide recession dragged on, choking demand. They remained far from profitable, and they were chewing into their cash. They would require working capital loans to remain operational. Jack knew better than to form quick conclusions, but it was getting difficult to remain optimistic.

The dry season was at hand. In the rising heat, the early morning sky lost its clarity and became hazy. It was nine o'clock, and time for Tao's October meeting. He and his two junior managers, whom Jack and Victor had taken to calling Speak No Evil and See No Evil, filed into the office and took their seats across from the owners. Mei sat at the far end of the table next to Jack.

It was Tao's agenda. The first subject was the production report. Tao unpacked a beat-up computer from an old valise. Turning it on, he pulled up an image on the screen and turned the computer around so Jack and Victor could view it. "Production report," he said.

"What do you know," Victor said as he and Jack, both wearing tight smiles, examined the Excel spreadsheet in Chinese on Tao's screen.

As the men viewed his work, Tao spoke in Chinese to Mei. Speak No Evil and See No Evil, sitting on either side of him, did what junior Chinese managers were supposed to do, and remained silent.

"Well, this is certainly a formative improvement," Jack said, leaning over to examine the report. "But it's in Chinese. What do the numbers say?"

"We sell five hundred tons last week," Tao said, a proud expression on his face.

Jack felt like he had been punched in the gut. At that rate, they were still losing money big time.

"Fifty percent utilization," Victor said, leaning close to the computer screen and squinting.

"Less," Jack sighed. "Christ, we've been at this for two months now."

"Seven weeks," Victor reminded him. He directed his attention to Tao. "You're improving things," he said, nodding to encourage him, "but we're still below break-even."

Tao said, "Customers don't come back yet."

"Who's buying the stuff?" Jack asked Tao, searching for any thread of good news.

"Chinese," Tao said. "No foreign buyers come back yet."

Tao's next agenda item was a brief presentation by two local managers of Farmer's Bank, the big bank that operated across rural China. Tao said they were prepared to recommend making a small working capital loan. All Jack needed to do was show them some respect, say hello for five minutes.

Tao ushered the two managers into the cramped office. To Jack, they appeared to be barely out of college. The manager was a thin-waisted guy wearing a short-sleeved shirt and no jacket or tie. His sidekick, a young girl, who apparently didn't even merit a business card, wore a simple cotton frock.

As Tao was introducing them, Jack leaned over closer to Mei. "Does Tao really think these two have the stroke to commit the bank's capital?" Jack whispered to her.

Mei stayed close to Jack. "Tao said the manager's already been bribed," she said in a hushed voice, strands of her hair brushing up against Jack's temple.

"How?" Jack asked, keeping his gaze focused on the two bank officers as they spoke in casual Chinese back and forth with Tao. The guy did most of the talking. The woman's face was pleasant, her voice light and confident the few times she spoke up.

"In their office," Mei said, sounding matter-of-fact. "When I worked for business clients in Kunming, I learned the businessman takes the banker out to lunch, there's lots of *baiju*, and everyone returns to the banker's office. Then the banker excuses himself to go to the washroom, the businessman stashes a sack of cash in the top drawer and leaves, and he gets the loan the next day."

"They seem awfully young to be taking bribes. That guy's not going to need to shave for the next five years."

"Getting bribes is the only reason anyone works for a bank in China," Mei said, as if Jack should know.

"You said *he's* been bribed. Think she's in on it?" The girl looked as young and fresh as a milkmaid.

"He will give her some."

"I'll bet."

True to Tao's word, the bank officers left a few minutes later.

"Small loan," Tao apologized. "Maybe bigger soon."

"It's better than nothing. Thank you," Jack said to Tao. "Any more bad news?" Jack asked as Mei looked at him, surprised. "He knows what I mean," Jack explained. "Bad news always comes in bunches."

Tao said, "Me and Chin go Burma buy charcoal today."

"How much money do you need?" Victor asked.

Tao turned to Mei and began speaking to her in Chinese. As they were talking, See No Evil's mobile phone started belting out the Rolling Stones' *Jumping Jack Flash* in loud ringtones. He answered his phone—"*Wei?*"—uttered a few words, hung up, and then leaned over and started whispering to Speak No Evil.

When Tao was finished speaking to Mei, she turned to Jack and Victor to explain Tao's words, but her voice was cancelled out by the chatter of the two junior managers.

"What'd you say?" Jack asked Mei over the din.

See No Evil and Speak No Evil became more animated, their voices louder, laughter and snickers mixed in.

"Shut the hell up!" Jack yelled at them.

See No Evil and Speak No Evil stopped talking and looked over at Jack, horrified, as if they expected to be incinerated. Next to them, Tao wore a satisfied expression.

"We need to have some rules around here," Jack said as he eyed Tao, who was nodding. "One person speaks at a time."

"And everyone checks their phones at the door," said Victor.

"Like army," Tao agreed.

Mei continued on the subject at hand. "They're only making a small charcoal run; five trucks. *Taozong* needs permission to pay Costa one million RMB for charcoal, plus your approval to give small money to the customs officer when they cross the border."

Tao said, "Don't worry. No squeeze."

"What does that mean?" Jack asked, turning to Mei.

"Normally here," Mei said, professorial, as if she was describing a standard Chinese business technique, "a manager will quote a foreign owner a price for something like charcoal, then negotiate a lower price with the vendor and keep the rest—the squeeze—for himself."

"But no Chinese guys pay the squeeze, right?" Jack said.

"Oh, no," she said, shaking her head, doing her best to squelch a smile.

"Let's figure out how to bypass those customs turkeys as soon as we can," Jack said. "As far as greasing them now, Tao can do it if he needs to. We're not getting involved in that stuff. But does he need us to help make a deal with Costa for the charcoal?"

Mei started to speak to Tao, but he had understood the question, and laughed as he shook his head. He appeared younger. It was the first time Jack had seen him smile. He spoke in animated Chinese to Mei.

"He says you and Victor can't be involved or we will pay twice as much as we should," Mei said with a straight face.

"Well, I don't want to pay the *laowai* price, but what leverage does Tao have?"

Tao issued a few short words in Chinese to Mei, his face stoic once more.

"*Taozong* will reason with Costa's men," Mei said.

"Sounds like he read *The Godfather*," Jack said, standing up to let everyone know the meeting was over. "Which brings up the question," Jack said to Tao as they all prepared to leave the tiny office, "when you go over the border, are you armed?"

Tao pulled a box cutter out of his pocket and held it up in the air.

"I meant a gun."

"No gun," Tao said emphatically. "Gun in China mean death wagon."

"No gun ever?" Jack asked, gazing carefully at the man's face.

Tao paused, looking Jack in the eye. "Sometimes gun in Burma."

"Tell me what we've got to do to make a profit here," Jack asked, figuring he might as well take advantage of the taciturn man's moment of candor. "We're running out of time."

"We talk soon," Tao answered, his gray eyes clear.

The factory was quiet now. Jack could hear a rhythm of metal on metal as See No Evil and Speak No Evil and their men cleaned charred silicon residue out of the caldrons, backed up by a wacky staccato of smashes and wallops as the women used their hammers to crush the cold slabs of silicon into pellets. The silence of the forest was interrupted by the screech of a parrot. Above the temple's pinnacle on the mountaintop, birds of prey led by a huge raptor circled in the white haze of the Yunnan sky.

Jack stared at the lead bird as it carved lazy patterns in the firmament. "What is that big black bird?" he asked Tao.

"I no know," Tao said. "New here. I not see it before."

"It's new?" Jack asked, looking at the circling bird.

"Yes. Come same day as you."

CHAPTER 8

They worked inside the office for the rest of the day to avoid the burning sun. In the late afternoon, clouds rumbled across the sky. Rain fell half-heartedly. It ended after only an hour, as if knowing its season was over.

At dinner time, Mei left the office. A half-hour later, she returned carrying a tray laden with dishes of food. A rock crusher followed her with a second one. As the men remained oblivious, concentrating on their work, the women put the trays down on the conference table, arranged the food—pond fish, rice, beans, and greens—and left.

Jack lifted his head up from his computer a minute later. The food smelled good. "Where'd Mei go?" he said to Victor as he glanced around, and then walked outside to scan the compound. Moisture dripped off the birds-of-paradise, splatting on the dead leaves clustered on the ground. To the southwest, the setting sun had broken through, its diagonal rays bathing the compound in a mist of golden light.

"Chow's getting cold," Victor said from inside the office.

"She shouldn't serve us and not eat herself."

"Probably one of those Chinese things," Victor said. "I'm starving."

Neither man said another word as they ate. In the late afternoon's balmy air, a jungle bird's whistle echoed across the factory yard. The monks called out evening prayers from the temple on the mountain. A yellow haze of dust, the last vestige of the smelter's workday, remained suspended above the ground. Bugs came out of hiding, carving lazy patterns in the atmosphere.

Victor finished, pushed his tray aside, and got up. He went over to the cabinet at the far end of the room and returned with a bottle of Hennessey and two glasses. "Nightcap?"

"The sun's over the yardarm."

Victor poured a stiff shot for each of them and sat down. "So you're the China expert," he said to Jack. "What do you think's going on here?"

"We're losing our ass," Jack said.

"I meant with our guys," Victor said. "It seems like everyone's doing what Tao said, making money the Chinese way." He gazed through the open door at the mountains marking the border with Burma.

Jack pushed his tray out of the way, swung his feet up on the table, and leaned back in his chair. "Something like that."

"So do we try to stop them?"

Jack smiled ruefully. He picked up his glass of Hennessey and examined the cognac. "Not unless we want to violate a cherished Chinese principle," he said. "If the water's too clear, the fish will die." He downed the rest of his cognac in one swallow. "Do you think she's got anything to do with it?"

"Definitely not," Victor said. He took a drink of cognac. "Speak of the devil."

Jack looked out the door at Mei coming down the smelter road. He watched her walk, tall and supple, her baggy men's clothes billowing in the warm wind like the rippling muscles of a young colt, taking her time, exuding the very grace her outfit was designed to obscure. He waited until she entered the office, smiling her hello. "Who'd you beat up for those clothes, anyway?"

"You don't like my wardrobe, Mr. Davis?" As she started stacking the men's dishes, he caught her smiling to herself.

"Here, we can do that. It's everyone for themselves around here," Jack said, standing up and relieving her of his tray.

She kept on picking up the stray dishes anyway, stacked them and then stood there, out of things to do.

"How about a drink?" Jack said.

She eyed the bottle of cognac on the table tentatively. "A very small one."

"Coming up." Jack went to the cabinet, got another glass, and poured some for her and more in his and Victor's. "Here, take these," he said to Mei, handing her their glasses. "I'll get the chairs. Let's sit outside where it's nice. Victor, care to join us?"

"I've still got work to do. You go ahead."

Jack picked up two chairs, Mei following him, and walked out to a patch of grass along the wall where the view stretched off toward the distant hills.

They sat down, and Mei handed him his glass. Jack leaned back in his chair and watched the last of the sunset smolder over the Burmese hills. He drank some cognac. The bamboo groves, finally drying out at the end of the rainy season, rustled in the breeze. He closed his eyes and tried to imagine he was somewhere with her far away, sitting on an island under a grove of trees whispering in the wind. When he opened his eyes, he gazed toward the temple on the mountain. The big bird was still up there, circling alone on the last of the afternoon thermals. "Think that bird sees us down here?" he asked.

Mei followed the flight of the raptor in the sky. "I hope not, Mr. Davis." She tried the cognac and wrinkled her nose.

Jack said, "You can call me Jack, you know. How did you get the job with the agency anyway?" he asked to make conversation.

Mei's face flushed. "Don't you like my work?"

Taken aback by her reaction, Jack smiled to reassure her. "Don't be silly. You've been doing a very professional job."

She seemed relieved. "That's important to me," she said. "To be good at this job, I mean." Drawing a deep breath, she surprised him by continuing. "The man who owns the agency is Jimmi Zeng," she said. "His knew my parents in Dalian. I've worked for him since I was a girl."

Jack watched as Mei removed the pin from the bun on top of her head. Her long black hair spilled down over her shoulders. She seemed to be forming her thoughts, like a witness about to give testimony. Taking her time, she sat up, spread her hair evenly behind her, and leaned back in her chair. "I was young when my parents died. They owed Jimmi money," Mei explained. "I had to repay the family debt by working for him."

"As a translator?"

Her dark eyes studied him, as if trying to discern whether the truth would be a mistake. "No. Not as a translator."

Jack got up, went inside, and returned with the bottle of Hennessey. He topped up her glass and poured two more fingers into his, and sat back down. "So how did you end up in the states?"

"Jimmi made me a karaoke girl in his club in Chinatown."

"The place where they called you 'Bunny.'"

"Yes."

"Why did you go there and do that?"

Mei smiled at him indulgently, and then her face darkened. "When Jimmi wants you to do something, you have no choice."

Neither of them spoke for a while.

"I guess that's what you think I am," Mei said, staring off toward the Kachin ridge, the corners of her mouth quivering. "A karaoke girl."

"Wait a minute," Jack said, leaning over to look her in the eye. "I think a lot of you. Anyway, it doesn't sound like you had much choice."

"Thank you," she whispered.

They sat without speaking in the balmy air.

"Jimmi Zeng is a bad man. I'd give anything not to go back to that life." Mei shuddered.

"You don't have to," Jack said.

Her eyes widened as she took the measure of his words.

In the fading light, he couldn't help staring at her, following the curve of her mouth, up her cheekbones to her eyelashes and over to her girlish ears where they poked out of her hair. When she was about to turn away, embarrassed, he said, "And you don't owe me any explanations."

She considered that as she took a tiny sip of cognac, her lips glistening. "All right."

Jack leaned back in his chair. It was getting dark. The jungle, a warm, living thing behind them, was shedding its daylight languor, rustling and twitching, preparing for night, wrapping the two of them in its earthy grasp.

"What is the private equity business?" Mei asked.

"Why do you ask?" Jack answered.

"I'd like to learn about what you do," she said.

"Sure," he said, pleasantly surprised. "I try to invest in businesses that I can improve. Especially in remote places where I can buy in cheap."

"Is that what you're doing here?" Mei asked.

"In a way," he said. "It's a little more complicated."

"Why would you invest here, and not in America?"

"That's a good question."

She looked at him and then glanced at the sky. From up at the temple, the monks' chant reached them on the wind. "I can't see the big bird anymore; it's too dark."

"He's still up there, I'm sure."

"Will you stay here long?"

"My guess is I'll have to."

She regarded him dubiously. "You'll probably go back to America soon."

"I don't think that's in the cards," he said. "I guess I'm no better than those fools down at the casino."

"Someday, you will go back." She waited a long time, as if choosing her next words carefully. "Am I truly doing a good job?"

Jack exhaled, and took a long drag on his cigar. "Look, that first day? All I could do is form a quick conclusion about you."

"I know," Mei said. "It's OK."

"And I was wrong," Jack said as sincerely as he knew how.

"If you like my work, I could do the same thing for you in America," she said.

He laughed, trying to disguise his disappointment. "OK, OK—I get it. Butter up the boss, and get a ticket to the good life in the states."

"No, no," she said, frowning, her eyes serious as she looked at him. "I was there once, remember? That was not a good life for me."

"So why go back? To the states, I mean," he said.

"Maybe I could learn enough to be good at something. Maybe something that could be helpful to you," she said.

It was then that he admitted it: he had indeed allowed himself some hope about her in the last weeks. But only at the time he risked thinking about such things, in the night before he drifted off to sleep. As he sat there in the easy darkness, the cognac soothing his throat, the monks' chant echoing over the land, the warmth of the girl pulsed around him. He tried to think when he had ever felt as good, and couldn't.

"I should get to bed soon," she said.

Jack stood up. "You shouldn't go home alone here. I'll walk you up to the dormitory."

He told Victor he'd be right back, and he and Mei started walking up the road together. A few times they bumped into each other, and she reached out and touched his hand to steady herself. Over their heads, the sky had turned a bluish purple and the first faint stars were beginning to flicker in the eastern heavens.

Jack looked over at Mei, and she smiled back at him. He told himself not to get stupid, and fumbled for something to say. "It'd be nice to get back stateside, but for that to happen, I've got to figure out how to make some serious money here."

"You mean in the smelter business?"

"Any business—as long as it's legal."

She nodded.

As they walked up the road, he reconsidered his words. "You know, I take that back. As long as it's *moral.*"

"Yes," she agreed. "There is no legal here."

As they came around the corner of the smelter, Tao was carrying a box of parts toward an old pickup truck sitting jacked up in the feedstock yard.

They said hello to Tao and started to walk past, but then Jack stopped. "Just a second," he said to Mei. "I need to ask Tao a question." He turned to Tao. "*Taozong,*" Jack said, "what are you doing with that truck?"

Tao put his box of parts on the ground. "Fixing transmission," he said.

"You can do that yourself?" Jack asked, his face showing he was impressed.

Tao said, "I fix anything."

"And I'll bet you can make things too," Jack said.

"Yes…" Tao said in a questioning tone, paying more attention now, as if trying to figure out where Jack's words were going.

"You said sometimes you need a gun in Burma, and I was wondering where you'd get one. But I'll bet you know how to make them," Jack said, forcing a casual smile across his face. "Right?"

Tao took a breath, and nodded. "Yes. But only have one shot," he said.

"In many places, that's enough," Jack said. "Goodnight, *Taozong.*" He and Mei resumed walking toward the dormitory.

"Why did you ask him about guns?" Mei said.

Jack said, "You never know. With all the crazy stuff going on around here, I might need one someday."

They kept walking up the hill toward the dormitory.

"What do you think Tao and Chin and those guys are up to?" Jack asked her.

"I don't know," Mei said. "Whatever they're doing, you must be careful. It's not safe."

At the dormitory steps, he looked at her one last time, gestured goodnight, and turned to start walking back down the road.

"Mr. Davis?" Mei said behind him.

He turned around and looked at Mei, her face slightly raised, arms down by her sides, and took a few steps back toward her. "It's Jack, remember?"

"Goodnight, Jack," she said.

"Goodnight, Mei." He stepped close to her, leaned over, kissed her on the cheek, and walked away again.

CHAPTER 9

The next morning, Jack lay on his cot. The dripping, oily stillness of the jungle hung in the air, leavened by the whir of the angry bugs clustered up near the ceiling of his room. Out the bedroom window, the mountain ridge loomed, its dark outline of wind-bent foliage beating a grudging retreat before the dawn. Above the treetops, the gray morning's feeble sun barely outlined the spires of the temple, offering inhabitants little hope for the day.

Jack fought the urge to wake up. As he gained consciousness, he felt the heaviness return as he recalled what he had been worrying about when he fell asleep.

After he had walked Mei home, Victor had taken Jack through their financial situation. Any remaining optimism was tantamount to denial: they were screwed. They had been operating the smelter for over two months, enough time to learn the patterns of the factory and the business. Thanks to Tao, things had improved, but they were still losing money every day, and were almost out of runway. Paying down the Metalclad loan was no longer their biggest problem. They were running out of cash.

From his cot, Jack looked over at Victor, who was already up, sitting in bed and smoking.

The tobacco smelled earthy. "Do me a favor and hand me a cigar," Jack said to Victor.

"It's a little early for you," Victor remarked, and leaned over and fumbled in the duffel bag next to his cot. He passed Jack a cigar under the mosquito netting.

"Nothing else I can do," Jack said. He bit off the smoking end of the cigar and lit it. Clenching the cigar between his teeth, he punched his pillow in a ball and lay back against it. He blew on the lit ember until it glowed orange. Then taking a big drag, he blew several clouds of smoke up toward the bugs, futilely trying to scatter them.

"It's going to take more than smoke to scare that bunch," Victor said.

"They'll see. Today belongs to us," Jack said, willing himself out of his funk. He put his cigar down on the concrete floor and went into the bathroom. He washed his face in the sink, not needing the cold water to sober him, the whites of his blue eyes brighter in the darkness, tanned face lined with crow's feet. He brushed his teeth, and then checked himself once more in the mirror. He looked like he felt: defeated. He stared into his pupils where he lived, hating to find himself in a position like the one he was in. He called out to Victor, "What are the chances of us paying down a small slice of the Continental loan? Stay in their good graces."

"Are you kidding?"

Jake couldn't stand to look in the mirror any more. He shifted his gaze out the bathroom window at the parrots flitting through the tops of the trees. "Humor me."

"In the near term?" Victor asked. "Slim and none. The world market for silicon's got to improve. A lot."

"Say it did. Say world commodity prices stabilized. Given the way this place operates, how much cash do you think we can grab annually to amortize that loan?"

Victor took his time with the answer. "Now that we know the real numbers, as opposed to Metalclad's fabrications? If I were an optimist, I'd go ahead and say something stupid, like three million a year."

"That's all? But we've got to produce seven million a year just to pay the bank back on time, and that leaves nothing for us."

Victor said, "But I'm not an optimist."

"We're fucked, then," Jack said, "unless we can refinance." He came out of the bathroom. "Your turn," he said to Victor, picking up his cigar.

"I've watched you for years," Victor said, picking up his towel and retreating to the bathroom, shutting the door behind him. "You'll think of something."

"You should only smoke a cigar in the morning if you expect good things to happen," Jack said through the door.

"Better put it out, then," Victor intoned from the bathroom.

Jack took one more drag. "What do you think this place is worth in a quick sale?" he asked Victor. "I used to think seventy million. Now I'm guessing thirty to forty."

"Twenty," Victor said through the door, running the water harder.

"That's less than we owe," Jack protested.

"Sorry."

"I'm putting it out," Jack said, stubbing his cigar out on the floor.

Victor came out of the bathroom, toweling off his face. "Save it for when Tao and Chin come back from their charcoal run and we catch those guys in the act."

"What do you expect to learn at that point?" Jack asked.

"I'm not sure, but I'm tired of guessing," Victor said. "I'd like to know the score. It sounds like everyone in Dehong is moving stuff across the border. Chin and Tao; those guys in the casino…Costa."

"But the funny thing is, they don't have the trucks: we do," Jack said. "And if we just stuck to jade, we wouldn't get arrested."

"No, just get our ass shot off by the *Tatmadaw*," Victor said.

"Goddamn bugs," Jack said, getting up and opening the door of their bedroom. He grabbed a flyswatter and swung hard at the cloud of bugs clustered up at the ceiling of the room. He splattered some of them, and knocked more to the floor. He swung again and again, forehand and backhand, and herded the remaining swarm out the doorway. They'd be back, but it made him feel better in any event. He slammed the door and sat down on his bed. "I don't know. Maybe there's some other way out of this mess," he said to Victor.

Victor was silent for a moment. "There's not. The market for silicon's not going to improve for years. It's Tao's way or the highway. It's just slightly better than robbing a bank, that's all," he said.

"Listen, just because I can talk myself into anything doesn't mean you need to be involved," Jack said.

"I'm already involved," Victor said.

"Yeah, but this wasn't part of the plan."

"You don't have a choice, Jack. You made me a partner, remember?"

Jack paused. "You sure?"

"Positive."

When Jack and Victor arrived at the office, Mei was already there, preparing some papers at the end of the table. Hair up on her head and held with a silver pin, she had on a blue blouse and a pair of jeans. Fresh and clean, her skin glowed.

Spellbound by the memory of kissing her the night before, Jack couldn't take his eyes off her.

She smiled shyly and looked down at her desk.

Jesus, she was gorgeous. But all that did was make things worse. With disaster looming, Jack couldn't allow himself to get emotionally sidetracked. And who was he kidding? She was a temp. They had finished the translation of the documents—he should have sent her home weeks ago. Jack took a seat at the table. It was early; outside the office, the roosters were crowing. "Are the guys still down in Burma buying charcoal?" he asked Mei.

"No, they came home very late last night," she replied.

"Last night?" Jack looked out the doorway toward the feed-stock yard. "I'll be back in a minute," he said as he got up to head out the door.

And practically bumped into Tao, who was just walking in, Chin shambling along behind him. Covered in oily charcoal dust, the men carried blackened canvas bags, the kind the smelter deployed when it sent out silicon samples to customers. They dropped the bags on the floor. Amid the thuds, Jack heard clacking sounds.

"We talk now," Tao said.

"It's about time," Victor said as he pulled out a pad and pencil and opened his computer. "Let the due diligence begin."

Wide-eyed, Mei got up and scrambled for the door.

"Wait a second. We may need you to translate," Jack said to her, getting up to block her escape.

"They won't want me to hear this," she said, and ran out of the room.

Jack sighed. "All right, *Taozong*," he said as he plopped back down in his seat. "We're all ears."

Tao picked up one of the bags. He turned it over and emptied it in the corner. Greenish brown stones banged on the concrete floor. "Jade," Tao said. "Grade A."

Jack and Victor walked over to the dusty pile of rocks. Jack picked up a stone the size of a ping pong ball and examined it. "Doesn't look like much," he said. He looked inside another bag and shook it. "How much have you got in here?" he asked Tao.

Tao sat at attention, none of the usual reticence remaining on his face. "One bag five kilos. Maybe ten, twenty stones," he said.

"So when I saw you guys rooting in the charcoal pile, this is what you were up to," Jack said.

"Liu was boss." Tao shrugged. "We do what he say."

"Whatever. I'm not blaming you. But why are you telling us this now?" Jack asked them.

The room turned quiet. Outside, the smelter, which had run without interruption all morning, shut down. The silence of the jungle descended over the factory.

Tao said, "Now you boss. You good to us, but you got problems," while Chin, sitting quietly next to him, assumed his best hound-dog expression. "We same. Maybe we fix together."

Jack couldn't help it—he laughed at the absurdity of his situation. For lack of a better survival plan, he was actually considering what two guys who had crawled out of the Chinese bush were telling him. "Well, we know about our problems. Tell us about yours."

Tao said, "Jade man say use your trucks. I tell him we must ask you first."

"I assume Costa's the jade man," Victor said to Tao.

"Yes," said Tao, his lips pressed together. "Costa."

"But Chin, you told me the KIA controls the jade, right?" Jack asked.

"Yes," Tao and Chin answered together.

"So if we wanted to get involved with jade, we can make a deal with them," Jack said to the men. "Who needs Costa?"

Chin shook his head. "Kachin don't like Chinese. Don't trust us. And Costa has charcoal too. Can't smuggle jade in trucks without charcoal."

"But the Kachin trust Americans, right?" Victor said.

"Trust Costa," Tao said. "Maybe you meet them, they trust you."

"Where'd you get this jade?" Jack asked.

"Costa get," Chin said. "From Kachin mines at Hpakan. Best in the world."

"Can anyone else buy it?" Jack asked.

"Not at good price," Chin said. "Costa get best price from KIA. Good friends."

"So Costa's been doing this for a long time," Jack said to Chin.

Chin began to nod, but Tao interrupted him. "No," Tao said, "just short time. Before, smuggle drugs. But now, China don't like drugs. People die. Like back there," he said, pointing behind the office to the jungle where the gun battle had taken place. "Costa must change. He can get jade from KIA. You have trucks. Many stones, many trucks: big money. Everybody happy. Smelter profitable," he said, and leaned back, out of breath.

Victor murmured, "I don't think the auditors would agree with that assessment."

It was the most anyone had heard Tao say at one time. The room stayed quiet.

"Why come to us now?" Jack continued. "You guys have already been using our trucks behind our back."

"No, boss," Chin said. "Before you come, Mr. Liu use trucks two, maybe three times. He very afraid; must hide from Metalclad. But now trucks yours. You say OK, we can use many trucks," he said, as Tao nodded beside him, "many times."

"Who the hell are we going to sell the jade to?" Jack asked. Tao and Chin were silent.

"For starters, who buys it now?" Victor asked them.

"Costa sell," Chin said, shrugging his shoulders.

"So we're stuck with him," Jack said to Victor.

"You knew that was going to happen," Victor said. "But it's just for now. We make the first deal with Costa and get to know the Kachin?" Victor said as he lit a cigarette. "After that, who knows?"

"Yes, yes," Tao said, his gray eyes bright. "Maybe KIA need new friends."

"Let's turn this around," Jack said. "What makes you guys think Costa wants to do business with us?"

"Costa need money," Tao said, squinting his eyes.

"He call you, boss," Chin added emphatically. "That night in restaurant." Chin went over and picked up one of the bags. "He told us to bring you jade, show you."

Jack fought the urge to feel more comfortable. "What's the connection between the jade and the gun fight in the forest the other day?" he asked.

"Gunfight about drugs, boss," Chin said, "not jade."

"Why makes you say that?" Jack asked.

"I tell Costa many times: no drugs," Tao said, spitting, betraying emotion for the first time. He pounded his fist on the table. "Jade enough."

"Are we really supposed to believe there'll be no trouble with the Chinese police at the border?" Jack said to the two men.

"No problem," Tao said, waving his hand back and forth, dismissive. "Jade just like charcoal."

"Why even bother with charcoal then?" Jack asked.

"*Tatmadaw*," Tao said, his face grave. "On roads in Burma. Looking for jade. Very bad guys."

Jack asked, "Where's Costa keep his jade?"

Tao shrugged. "We get from him in Laiza, KIA place."

"Right past Mai Ja Yang," Chin said.

"I'm looking at Hpakan," Victor said, a map displayed across his computer screen. "It's way up north. I can't imagine it would be much fun to run a truckload of jade all the way across Kachin."

"Hold on a second," Jack said to the Chinese men. "Is it Costa's jade or the KIA's?"

But Tao and Chin, out of their depth, just stared blankly back at their interrogators.

"Huge difference in the splits," Jack said to Victor.

The expressions of the two Chinese didn't change.

"My guess is he's a finder," Victor said.

"That's going to make for a bitch of a negotiation," Jack warned.

Victor nodded. "I can't wait. OK, now for the fun part, guys," he said to the two Chinese men, holding a pencil and his pad. "How much do the Kachin want for the jade?"

"Chinese in Hpakan must pay four thousand RMB per kilo," Chin said. "Kachin sell to Costa for less."

"For one kilo, Costa pay KIA two thousand RMB," Tao said. "Grade A."

Victor made some notes and punched some numbers into his computer. "That's a little more than three hundred dollars," he said, looking up at Jack. "Not a lot of money."

"And what does Costa sell a kilo for?" Jack asked the two men.

Tao shrugged. "Five thousand?" he said, sounding like he was guessing.

"Nice margin if it's real," said Victor to Jack. "The other question is how many kilos one truck can carry."

Tao laughed. "Dump truck carry many, many kilos."

"How many?" Jack said.

Tao showed his white teeth. "You say. Just need money to buy jade," he said. "As many kilos as you can buy."

"So can a dump truck carry a thousand kilos?" Jack asked.

"Easy," Tao said. "KIA also have big jade stones. Only dump trucks can carry big stones."

"Jesus," Jack muttered under his breath as he glanced at the numbers on Victor's pad. "If those numbers are right, one truckload could yield well over half a million to the home team."

"Dollars," Victor said, and put his pencil down. "But before Costa's cut," he cautioned.

"That's the sixty-four-dollar question," Jack said. He turned to Tao. "So this is how one makes money in the Chinese smelting business."

Tao just nodded his head. As the smelter belched, he shuffled his feet, ready to go back to work.

Victor stubbed out his cigarette.

Jack made up his mind. The deal was right there, sitting in front of them. They had the trucks and enough cash to ante into the game. Once they were dealt their cards, he would figure out the rest. "Sounds like we need to pay Mr. Costa a visit," Jack said, standing up to signal the meeting was over.

"Yes, boss," Chin said, nodding. "I call him."

"So we're in business," Jack said, looking each man in the eye.

"No," Victor said. "As they said at the casino, we're in *the* business."

Everyone trudged out of the office without speaking.

Mei hadn't gone far. She was standing right outside where she could hear everything. When they filed by, she wouldn't look at Jack.

As the other men moved on, he stopped next to her, wishing he had something better to say. "I told you I needed to make a lot of money fast," he said in a low tone. "As long as it was moral. And this is probably as moral as it's going to get."

"Who cares about morality? You'll be killed," Mei whispered.

"I don't have a choice. But it's way too dangerous for you to stay here," he said. "I'm going to have to send you home."

She still wouldn't look at him.

The roosters had stopped crowing. A torturous sun baked the land, smothering anyone foolish enough to be there.

CHAPTER 10

The next day, after a sleepless night, Jack woke early. Stumbling into the bathroom, he stared out the window at the last of the night fleeing before the dawn's ivory fringe. He washed his face in the sink and made an attempt to comb his hair. He was emerging from the bathroom as Victor came in.

"You look terrible," Victor said to Jack.

"Same to you," Jack said. He walked onto their balcony to sample the morning. "Does that flight to Kunming run today?"

"Every day. Why?"

"I'm putting Mei on it."

"Who else can we trust around here?"

"There's no way she can stay," Jack said, lying down on the floor to do his exercises. "Too dangerous."

"Maybe so, but I doubt she'll come to the same conclusion," Victor said.

After breakfast, one of the rock crushers made Jack a second cup of coffee, and he took it back to the office to wait for Mei. The early morning sky, initially blue with promise, was overwhelmed by the day's rising heat, and turned a dull white.

Tao came by to take pictures of Jack and Victor for fake IDs, and then left. While Victor played with his computer, Jack sat alone, waiting for Mei to show up. He wondered if she was still sleeping… what she did with her long hair at night…what she slept in…what she dreamed about. She didn't pick up when he dialed her phone.

He waited a few minutes more, and then walked up the road to the dormitory. "Mei?" he said to one of the rock crushers as the woman emerged from the front door.

The woman shook her head and walked past him on her way to the factory.

Mei was nowhere to be found. Jack returned to the office. Victor was camped out at the table, punching numbers into his computer. "I'll have a model for our new line of work shortly," he said. "But depending on what Costa's cut is, crime may not pay that well in Dehong."

"It's got to beat being a smelter monk," Jack said.

"My mother won't like hearing I've strayed even more from the priesthood," Victor said.

Jack didn't feel like laughing. He slumped in his chair, waiting for Mei, unable to think of anything else. In the stillness, he stared up at the corner of the ceiling where the spider webs were heavy with dead bugs. Peering out the window, he could see the spires of the temple fighting off the burning sun.

Jack swore to himself, and headed back to the kitchen for some more coffee. Passing by the car parked outside the office, he was looking ahead at the dormitory when he caught the smell of Mei's hair and a hint of perfume. He glanced over at the car and saw her sitting in the shotgun seat, her tinted window partially down, ignoring him, looking straight ahead.

"I've been looking everywhere for you."

"You said I was to leave, Mr. Davis—where'd you expect me to be?"

So she was going to be like that. "You packed?"

"Of course."

He walked back to the office and told Victor he was taking her to the airport. Getting in the car, he looked over at Mei. Lipstick glistened on her mouth, mascara highlighted her eyes, and something sparkly shone from her eyelids. Her hair was piled on her head and held with a tortoise shell pin, and her silver earrings dangled down the nape of her neck. He had never seen her in a skirt: the tight hem rose halfway up her thigh as she sat in her seat, her hands twisted in her lap, nails painted like a showgirl's. He stared at her, bewitched.

"What is it?" she asked, probably thinking his leer made him just like all the other perverts from her karaoke past. Her face registered something he hadn't seen from her before: distaste.

"Might as well get this over with," he managed to say, sure he had lost her as he put the car in gear and drove out the gate.

They drove in silence down the mountain road into the sunny farmland of the river valley. Mei put on a pair of sunglasses with large dark lenses that covered her face. Turning toward the side window, she pulled out her mobile phone and began sending a stream of text messages.

Jack tried to convince himself he was glad to see this different side of her. His first impression had been correct after all: she was just a spoiled Chinese chick. Probably making arrangements to see her boyfriend up in Kunming. Some punk with spiked hair.

She finished with her phone. Sunglasses obscuring her face, she stared straight ahead. A minute later, she raised the back of her wrist across her mouth. And then he heard her sniffle.

"I have some money for you," Jack said to her in what he hoped was a helpful tone.

She shook her head. She sniffled again, louder, and stared ahead.

"Please," he continued. "I want you to have it."

"No," she replied, her voice rough. "I don't want your money." She hiccupped and caught her breath. "You told me I was doing a good job," she stammered, and started to sob.

Jack pulled over to the side of the road. When he stopped, Mei jumped out of the car and walked into the grass. She turned her back to him and held her hands to her face, shaking her head back and forth and crying.

Jack walked around the car to where she stood. "Mei, listen to me," he pleaded, standing behind her as she sobbed, feeling like an idiot. "You are doing a good job—I couldn't be happier. I just don't want anything to happen to you." He stepped closer to her and put his hands on her shoulders.

She whipped around, her nose red. "I thought you were my friend," she wailed. "You told me you wouldn't send me back to Jimmi Zeng's."

Jack was dumbfounded. He hadn't given that a second thought. "Look, Mei. I am your friend." He searched for words. "I'd like to be more than that. This isn't about sending you back to Jimmi Zeng."

"He'll find me. You don't know him. He always does. Don't you understand? I'm his slave!" She removed her sunglasses. Her eyes were soaked with tears, and mascara streaked her cheeks. She took some tissue from her purse and wiped her face.

Jack stood in the grass, the sun beating down on the top of his head. He took a deep breath, and then got in the car and wheeled it around so it was pointed back up the mountain.

He rolled down the window. "Hop in," he called. "We're going back."

She stood uncertainly in the grass.

"Come on before I change my mind," he said, reaching over and opening her car door.

She ran around to where he sat in the car, pulled open his door, and threw her arms around him, hugging him, her cheeks smudged, breathing hard and tightening her grip around him.

He awkwardly accepted her embrace, and then—her face soft and sticky next to his, wet eyelashes blinking alongside his temple, the hot smell of her body pouring over him—slid his arms around her and pulled her closer. "It's all right," Jack whispered.

"You'll see," Mei said. "I'll be good for you."

"I hope you get the chance," he replied.

———

Tao showed up again at the office at the end of the day. He handed Jack and Victor their fake passports and headbands. They examined the documents. The photos were dark and grainy. Jack didn't think his photo made him look Chinese, but he didn't look American either. The paperwork was decent. "Tell me again why we need these?" Jack said to Tao.

"*Tatmadaw* no let Americans in," Tao said.

"So now we're Taiwanese, right?" Jack said, thumbing through the fraudulent visa pages.

"Chinese in Burma have Taiwanese passports," Tao said, gesturing to them to follow him. "Need guns too," he said.

Jack and Victor followed Tao across the road and down into the basement of the smelter. A light was on in one of the cavern-like rock crushing rooms. Inside, Tao had set up a shooting range. A table was stationed at one end, and targets were arrayed on wooden posts at the other.

"Three kind," Tao said, gesturing at the collection of pistols laying on the table.

One pistol looked store-bought. Victor picked it up, hefting it in his hand. "Looks like a regular gun."

Tao shook his head. "For running," he said.

Jack examined the gun in Victor's hand. "I think he means it's a modified starter pistol. Right?" he said to Tao.

"Yes," Tao said.

"Is it loaded?" Victor asked Tao, who nodded. Victor aimed the pistol at a target and pulled the trigger. The gun made a popping sound.

"I don't know if that's much protection," Jack said.

"Small. Twenty-two rimfire," Tao said. He picked up the crudest-looking gun and handed it to Jack. "This one better."

The gun was nothing more than a six-inch pipe with a firing pin and a wooden block for furniture. "What is it?" Jack asked.

"Four-ten bore," Tao said, grinning slyly.

"A bird gun?" Victor said.

"It must be a slug," Jack said. "A twelve-gauge slug will stop a car at close range." He aimed the pistol at a target and pulled the trigger. His arm was wrenched backwards. The explosion reverberated in the underground room, the cordite claustrophobic. Down at the end of the gallery, the target and its post were obliterated. "I'm taking one of these," Jack said.

"Me too," Victor said.

"Only one shot," Tao cautioned them, waving his hand over the table of weapons. "Must take two." Grinning, Tao pulled up the right leg of his pants to reveal a snub-nosed gun in an ankle holster. "Same gun, just small."

———

The next morning, Tao drove the big blue Forland dump truck they had picked out of the fleet down to where Jack and Victor waited in front of the office. He stopped the truck, letting the engine idle, and climbed down.

Jack and Victor climbed up into the cab.

Jack sat in the driver's seat, studying the dust-covered dials on the dashboard, and checking the tightness of the clutch and the brakes. He rolled down the window. "Smells like peasants have been living in here," he said to Victor over the growl of the engine.

"I'm sure they have," Victor said.

Jack got out and looked underneath the chassis. "How long would it take you to weld an iron box that swings down from the undercarriage?" he asked Tao. "About three feet square, and a foot deep, with a locking device."

Tao crawled underneath the truck and examined the undercarriage. "Three hours," he said.

"OK, get it done and then we're out of here," Jack said to Tao, who crawled out from under the truck and drove it away. "For money," he said to Victor, "and guns. The last thing we want is to be caught carrying a gun in China. How much cash do we have on hand?"

"We're down to about twenty million RMB," Victor said. "I pulled three million out of the bank."

"Christ," Jack said. "Only twenty million? If this doesn't work, we're done."

Behind them in the doorway of the office, Chin emerged. He was speaking to someone on his mobile phone, nodding his head. "*Dui, dui.*" He listened for a moment. "*Hanhou,*" he said again, nodding his head up and down. "*Hada, hada; ha, ha, ha,*" he said, and clicked off the phone. "Everything OK, boss," Chin called over to Jack. "They wait for us in Kachin tonight."

────────

They would be up high, crossing through the southeastern foothills of the Himalayas, so Jack wore a pair of khaki cargo pants and a tee shirt under a denim long-sleeved shirt. He carried his fake passport in his back pocket and the real one in the compartment sewn down the shin of his pant leg. He packed socks, underwear, and extra shells in a small overnight bag with his toilet articles. Their guns were locked in the compartment under the truck.

As Chin drove the Forland out of the smelter compound in the late afternoon, Jack tried not to think of Mei, but it was impossible. He hadn't been able to make up his mind whether or not to say goodbye to her, and in the end had decided to simply leave. Who was he kidding anyway? He had no standing with her for anything more significant. But as much as he tried to push her out of his mind, he couldn't. He thought about how spectacular she had looked in the car, then wondered what she would look like lying underneath him, seeing right into him with those dark eyes of hers. He cursed himself. At this point, she was the last thing he should be thinking about.

────────

The four of them—Chin driving, Tao riding shotgun and Jack and Victor less conspicuous in the middle—sat jammed across the seat of the big dump truck, the windows open, the night air rushing in. Jack looked out into the sky, his headband itching his scalp. In the black, moonless night, he could see the Milky Way.

At the customs gateway to Ruili, the truck inched down to the check point. Backlit by vehicle headlights, they could see the same group of customs and immigration agents sucking on their cigarettes under the banyan trees. Jack looked for the captain, but didn't see him.

Chin pulled into the permitted vehicle lane, pulled on the emergency brake, left the truck idling, and jumped down to the roadway. Quickly, he walked over to the group of guards, calling out in a friendly tone as he approached them and handing out cartons of cigarettes. Then he scrambled back to the Forland. The barrier lifted, and they drove through. No one even glanced at the truck.

"So Tao," Victor said as they began to roll down the road, "I was watching the traffic coming the other way, trying to figure out which of the trucks are smuggling."

"No way can see," Tao said, his white teeth shining in the dark.

Victor persisted. "But they can't be smuggling. Most of them are empty."

"Empty truck means no permit," Tao said. "Must have permit to bring goods into China. Like us."

"But what about the trucks with people in them?"

"Those trucks maybe have drugs," Chin chimed in. "If pregnant women in back of truck, then maybe drugs. Burmese women get pregnant, and then eat little balloons with drugs. All get on back of truck, go China. Leave drugs, get paid, turn around, and come home."

"So a lot of the smuggling is drugs?" Victor asked.

"That kind. See women in truck, is drugs," Chin said.

"Why do the women have to be pregnant?" Jack asked.

"Not all, but Chinese rule. Women pregnant, guards no can touch."

As Chin spoke, they noticed a transport truck headed toward China on the other side of the road, off on the shoulder. Women were climbing down from the rear deck of the truck.

"What'd they do wrong?" Victor asked.

"Not pay enough," Chin said.

"What happens now?" Jack said.

"Sometimes make wait until women get tired, turn around, go home."

"But having a baby's expensive. They must be getting paid a lot of money," Victor said.

Chin said, "Sometimes Burmese lady stay in China, become wife. Chinese men pay big money for Burmese women—thirty, forty thousand RMB. Ladies sell babies in China too."

"So foreigners adopt the babies," Jack said to Chin.

"Adopt?"

"You know; take the babies home to America."

"No. Most times can't sell baby. Then just kill baby."

"Jesus Christ," Jack muttered to himself, wondering how people in what they considered the most civilized country in the world could be so barbaric.

"Where do we go now?" Victor asked Chin when they had cleared Mai Ja Yang's duty-free guard booth and were bouncing down the road.

"Meet Costa's guys now," Chin said, "across bridge."

It was the middle of the night. The streets of Mai Ja Yang were deserted, and there was no other traffic. The Forland coasted up to the border patrol guard booth on the Lwegel Bridge where it sat astride the river. A transport truck sat idling on the other side.

Chin reached down from the window of the Forland and handed their documents, including Jack's and Victor's fake passports, to the guard, chatting with him. A minute later, the guard stamped the documents, Chin traded them for a carton of cigarettes, and they rolled across the bridge into Burma.

The transport truck waiting for them resembled an army troop truck, but lacked insignia. In the rear, a group of guerillas sprawled lazily on the deck in faded camouflage fatigues. Some of them carried automatic weapons. The men stared back at the visitors from small eyes set in brown faces. They didn't look Kachin, or even Burmese.

"I've got a hard time believing those guys are going to protect us," Victor said.

"Mercenaries," Jack said. "Where are these guys from?" he asked Tao.

"Costa's guys," Tao said. "Thai people."

Pulling away from the bridge, the two trucks entered Burma. A full moon hung over the feudal land. Jack peered out the windshield as they followed the troop truck down the dusty road. The place felt different immediately. There was no belching line of trucks waiting to pass the other way through customs. There was no mechanized traffic at all, only a wayward pedestrian in a *longyi* and bare feet. His scraggly hair looked like someone had chopped it off with a machete. There were no stores, commercial buildings, or billboards. No lights. As the moon moved through the dark swatches of trees on the hills, he could see scarecrow-like fields of brushy crops in the low country along the river.

Jack looked out the side window and caught a glimpse of himself: he barely recognized the guy in the headband bumping down the Burmese lane, carrying guns and three million RMB, going to pick up some stones. He couldn't say who it was.

CHAPTER 11

Jack sensed there was someone there. "Hey Chin, is that you?" he asked as he lay on the floor of the bamboo hut where the guerillas had dumped them late the previous night.

No one answered him.

"Chin?"

"He's next to me sleeping," Victor mumbled from off to the right of Jack.

A surprisingly chilly breeze swept through the teak-planked lanai, the room open to the jungle air. "Christ, it's freezing," Jack said.

"Don't move," a voice warned from behind him.

Jack smelled mosquito repellent. Lying on his back on a grass mat, he slowly propped himself up on his elbows to look around. The three others in his group were spread out around him, sleeping in their clothes. Dawn was breaking. Looking beyond where they were situated, he could see a considerable distance in the gray light. Presiding over the high ground and ringed by forests, the hut and its compound of buildings felt remote but protected. An elephant carrying a man and a boy lumbered by in the morning mist. Frost sparkled on the grass.

Jack's scalp itched. "Can I turn around now?"

No one answered.

Jack heard the animal before he saw it. Beyond where Chin and Tao lay, a slithering, scratching ruckus exploded in the darkened corner of the room.

"Got 'im!" the voice behind Jack exclaimed.

Jack peered into the corner. He could see two eyes set in a large, rat-like head. The animal, about the size of a small cat, had something in its paws and was killing it on the floor.

"You want to tell me what that thing's doing in here?" Jack said.

"Protecting you," said the man behind Jack, the smell of mosquito repellent stronger as he emerged from the shadows. "She's a mongoose."

"What's it eating?"

"A snake," the man said, walking past Jack to inspect the animal and its prey. He returned and looked down at Jack. "We eat snakes around here."

Costa didn't look like any senior officer Jack had encountered during his ROTC days. Short and chubby, and clad in a plain white tee shirt and a blue plaid *longyi* hitched up dress-like around his knees, he was in his late sixties. His eyes were bloodshot and beady, his complexion splotchy and pink. Not ruddy, just pink; it didn't look like he got outside much. As if to compensate for his inadequate physical stature, he had had an eye job, and his fingernails were manicured. Costa's *longyi* appeared to have been ironed, and his bare feet were shod with fancy crocodile loafers.

Expressionless, Costa leaned down and extended a mackerel-like hand to Jack. His freckled, wrinkled skin contrasted with the silvery luster of his Rolex. "Colonel Dennis Costa, US Air Force, retired," he said in a Southern accent.

Jack and Victor stood up, towering over Costa as they shook hands. Off to one side, Tao and Chin woke, and sat up on their grass mats.

"Where are we?" Victor asked, looking around.

"Laiza. Headquarters of the KIA," Costa said, growling his words in what Jack figured was supposed to be his tough-guy tone. Costa walked to where Tao sat and leaned over, whispering to him and clapping him on the back. Tao just grunted, while Chin nodded his head up and down, agreeing with whatever Costa was saying.

Jack looked out along the perimeter of the grass-covered compound. Guerilla soldiers in fatigues with automatic weapons were stationed at intervals, while another group sat at tables cleaning their guns. A trench mortar sat in a corner, a pyramid of grenades stacked next to it. Earthworks behind a rampart of logs surrounded the parade ground. Beyond, cliffs and steep embankments dropped into jungle ravines. The compound was unfinished. One of the outlying trenches was being improved; Jack watched the man and boy on the elephant direct the animal as it pulled a log into place along a section of the redoubt.

Even if his host's used car salesman appearance didn't fit, it appeared to Jack they were in the right place. "Is this a military installation?" he asked.

"I guess you could call the CIA a *quasi*-military organization," Costa replied.

Jack's instinct was to tell Costa to drop the charade. But he played along, choosing not to disrupt things for the moment. "How's the CIA involved?"

"I can't describe our affiliation with the Company; it's classified," Costa said. "But make no mistake—you're not on a due diligence trip for one of your candy-assed investment deals."

The narcissistic, pear-shaped little man was the one who seemed misplaced. His thinning hair was plastered in a comb-over across the top of a dissolute face, the big tire around his midsection plopped on skinny legs sticking out from under his *longyi*.

"Ban; where are you?" Costa called. A young man in a dark *longyi* appeared, his head swathed in bandages. "I believe you may have seen Ban before," Costa said as Jack and Victor found themselves face-to-face with the truck driver who had escaped the army's clutches on the Stillwell Road. "He used to have a brother with us until a mishap up your way."

"We've bumped into him a couple of times," Jack said.

Although his face was boyish, Ban's Thai eyes were hard and appraising. He nodded wordlessly to Jack and Victor.

"Take Chin and Tao over to the kitchen, and fetch us some coffee in the study," Costa said to Ban. "Follow me," he said to Jack and Victor, leading them out of the hut through a latched gate in a white picket fence and down a long stone-covered walkway bisecting a walled inner garden. While outside the gate the compound resembled a military barracks, inside was a different story. Ridiculously nice, Jack thought to himself: the only kind of person with a place like this in the middle of the jungle was someone with no way out.

Lined with coconut palms and beds of pink impatiens, the inner garden's walkway led toward a house as out of place as Costa himself, looking like it had been moved piece-by-piece from Beverly Hills. The building's first floor walls were hand-cut stone, the second story fashioned from long teak planks, and the roof was lined with clay tiles.

As they made their way along the walk, guerilla soldiers appeared, inspecting behind the bushes and trees of the walled garden, AK-type assault rifles at the ready. Incongruously, a worker weed-whacked the grass.

"Snakes," Costa explained loudly over the whine of the machine as they walked by. "If we didn't cut the grass, there'd be hundreds of them crawling around—never get anything done."

"This place has got to be a huge nut for him," Jack said to Victor, his voice drowned out by the weed-whacker. "No wonder he needs money."

Reaching the house, they walked up wide stone steps into a front room consisting of an open lanai. Further inside a second living area, ceiling fans whirred above their heads. The floor was dark mahogany and covered with patterned rugs. The walls were lined with bookcases. A large and airy space, one side of the room was a sitting area filled with bamboo and wicker furniture, while the other was office-like, dominated by a large desk covered with maps and papers. Jack looked twice at a Glock service revolver lying on the desk, doubling as a paperweight.

The three of them stood awkwardly in the middle of the room.

"So. The internet says you're from the DC area," Costa said to Jack.

"That's right," Jack answered. "How about you?"

"Little place called Lexington, Virginia," Costa said. "And you went to Georgetown. That's right up Route 29."

Jack nodded.

"I read you played football for the Hoyas," Costa said.

Here it comes, Jack thought.

"Me, I was a tailback for VMI," Costa said, his eyes flickering.

Not on those bird legs you weren't, Jack thought. Victor's internet search had mentioned nothing about Virginia Military Institute. But football had a way of making liars out of some American men.

"I always thought of Georgetown as a sissy school," Costa said, without animosity, as if for some stupid reason he expected Jack to agree.

"Except when it comes to football, I guess," Jack said, smiling back at Costa. "I can't recall ever losing to the Keydets."

"Take a seat," Costa said, the pleasantries over. He selected a bamboo chair next to the big desk and motioned to them to sit down as Ban re-appeared from a side door carrying a service tray loaded with pots of coffee and tea, and cups and saucers. "Not that one," Costa said to Jack as he started to sit down. "I can't hear so well out of my right ear. Gun side," he said as Jack switched chairs.

Ban placed cups and saucers in front of them. He poured the three men coffee, took some tea for himself, and sat down off to the rear of Costa.

Wondering if Ban spoke English and whether or not it was his brother on the grill of the Forland, Jack stirred some raw cane sugar into his coffee. As the sun began to beat down on the land, a warming wind rustled the palm fronds outside, buffeting the pair of dragonflies playing in the air at the edge of the lanai.

"All right then," Costa said, clearing his throat, "let's get started. Ban will take your passports."

Their coffee cups in midair, Jack and Victor just stared at him.

"This is a military compound," Costa growled. "Standard operating procedure." He pulled a pair of tortoiseshell glasses out of the breast pocket of his tee shirt, breathed on the lenses, and started polishing them with his *longyi*.

Jack pulled his Taiwanese passport out of his pocket and handed it to Ban, wondering why Costa didn't ask for guns instead, and then realized Costa didn't imagine he would be carrying one. Victor did the same.

Ban took their passports and handed them to Costa, who opened Jack's, examined it, and then tossed it back at Jack in disgust. "The real one, goddamnit."

"No way," Jack said. "I don't give my passport to anyone."

"I'm not going to keep the fucking thing," Costa said, irritated. "I just need to look at it."

Jack handed him his real passport.

Costa put on his glasses, examined Jack's passport, and handed it back to him. He did the same with Victor, glancing at Victor's red travel document with a smug expression. Then sitting back in his wicker chair peering through his thick-lensed bifocals at his two guests, he screwed up his face into what Jack figured was his best badass expression. "All right. Chin told me you wanted to talk. What the hell do you guys think you're doing?"

"You invited us, remember?" Jack said.

Costa scoffed. "How's that?"

"That night in the casino. You mentioned selling us some charcoal."

"Cut the crap."

Jack shrugged. "We just thought you'd want to continue using our trucks."

"What's that supposed to mean?" Costa asked.

"Just what I said," Jack said. "It took us a while, but we finally figured out that a smelter with a hundred permitted Forlands is a useful thing."

Costa faked a laugh. "Why would I want to do anything with you?"

"Tell me why you approached us that night," Jack said, looking past Costa's shoulder across the lanai where the morning fog was lifting, the sun cutting through the dry, cold air under a cobalt sky.

"I'll ask the questions around here," Costa snarled. "Who do you think you're talking to?"

Jack couldn't help himself. It was something he needed to say. "All I know is, you don't have anything to do with the CIA," he said evenly.

"Listen motherfucker, I can have you wiped off the face of the earth," Costa said, "just like that," snapping his fingers. Behind Costa, Ban sat listening impassively.

Jack's face flushed and the top of his scalp buzzed, the way he felt when he knew he had made a big mistake. From their phone conversation with Costa that night in the casino, they had already concluded he was a jerk. But catching his act in the flesh was enough to destroy any notion of teaming up with the guy. "We understood from Tao and Chin you wanted to do some business." Jack shrugged. "I guess we were wrong." There was no point in saying much more. The ceiling fans whirred slowly above their heads.

Then Costa surprised Jack. "What do you have in mind?"

"We're planning to run jade in volume," Jack answered, not interested in beating around the bush, and thinking maybe the guy really did need money.

Costa scoffed. "Not with me."

"I guess not, but it added up for us," Jack said, hoping that beyond the bravado the guy possessed a little common sense. "You've got the jade, and we've got permitted trucks and capital."

Costa glared at them. "You see all this?" He turned and swept his hand around the compound. "I built it myself. This place; the casino; my business here. No one helped me, and no one is going to take it away from me," he said, "though some fool may die trying."

"You don't want to team up with us," Jack said, "your guys smuggling drugs can keep getting gassed in General Dong's death wagons. In any event, you're not freeloading with our trucks anymore. We'd like to do business with you, but it's your choice. We can find someone else."

"Like who?" Costa bellowed, his mosquito repellent redolent as his face ran with sweat. "You think the KIA's going to talk to you?" Costa snorted. "The jade belongs to us—me and the KIA," he said, pointing his thumb at his chest. "Any son of a bitch who tells you different is a liar."

"You're making my point, Costa," Jack said, his tone stable, trying to calm the guy down so they could get a deal done. He repeated himself, what he did with stupid people. "You've got the jade, but we've got the trucks."

"Colonel Costa to you," the man barked. Then he paused a long time. "It'll be cash on the barrelhead," he said, surprising Jack again. But now he knew: Costa definitely needed money.

"We thought you'd give us until the end of the month," Jack said, trying to break the ice, see if the guy could handle a little humor. Costa stared at Jack through his coke-bottle lenses until Jack grinned. "Just kidding," he said.

"We'll see if you're still a comedian by the time you're finished here," Costa muttered, a fleck of white spittle perched on his lower lip. "Still alive, for that matter. So how much jade do you want to buy?"

"What are you offering?"

"You said volume. Anything less than five million RMB, you're wasting everyone's time."

"Sorry," Jack said, shaking his head, "that's too much for starters," not wanting Costa to figure how much cash they were carrying. "No way we can do that first time out. Later, maybe. What price per kilo are you talking about?"

"Five thousand RMB gets you a kilo of Grade A stones," Costa said, wiping his lip.

Jack looked over at Victor. "When do you want to head out?"

"What's that supposed to mean?" Costa sneered.

"You just quoted us the retail price," Jack said, keeping his tone casual.

"You think you've got a choice?" Costa scoffed.

Jack shrugged. "I guess we'll make our way over to Hpakan and find out."

"You'd never get through. There are *Tatmadaw* checkpoints—tax gates," Costa said, his nostrils flaring—"all the way to the Uyu valley. They'd skin you alive."

"If we've got to pay five thousand RMB a kilo, we'll take our chances," Jack said.

"How much you have to spend?" Costa demanded.

"I'm surprised at you—that's the oldest trick in the book," Jack said, forcing himself to grin again at Costa. "What works for us today," he said, putting his game face back on, "is to pay you a million RMB for jewelry-grade jade at two thousand RMB per kilo."

Costa snorted. "You're dreaming. I won't do a deal for anything less than three million RMB."

"Three million might work," Jack said, "depending on the splits."

"That's easy. Two-thirds, one-third," Costa said, his right eye twitching as he tried to stare back at Jack.

"Two-thirds our way is generous," Jack said.

"Stick it up your ass," Costa growled.

The longer Costa argued, the more Jack felt a deal could happen. "The only thing that makes sense to us—and it's fair—is fifty-fifty," Jack said. "You've got the jade, and we've got the trucks and the capital."

Costa sat in his chair, his combativeness beginning to ebb, as if he was ready for a morning nap. "I'd have to see your money first," he said.

Jack looked over at Victor. "Give us a minute," he said to Costa, and he and Victor walked outside onto the front lanai.

"It doesn't matter what we agree to," Jack said to Victor when they got outside. "He'll be trying to skin us alive as long as he's breathing."

"Agreed. But for right now, he'll do fifty-fifty for three million," Victor replied. "Even though it's all the cash we've got, if Tao's right and we can sell this stuff for anywhere close to five thousand RMB a kilo, we've got to do it."

"Subject to a caveat," Jack said. "We're doing one transaction with this pig, and that's it."

"Amen," Victor said.

They walked back inside. "At two thousand RMB per kilo and fifty-fifty, we're good spending three million," Jack said.

Costa's pointed, lizard-like mouth twisted into a grin. The man actually seemed relieved. "All right, then. Hand over the cash to Ban. You boys relax here for the day, I'll fetch the stones, and then you'll be on your way."

The tops of Jack's ears started to get hot. "Wait a minute. It's your jade, right? Don't you have it here?"

"I don't keep jade in Laiza. This is a goddamn war zone," Costa replied.

"It doesn't look like a war zone to me," Jack said. "More like a place to hide from the law."

Costa ignored him, got up and walked over to a map of Burma on the wall and picked up a pointer, looking like a professor as he peered through his glasses at Jack and Victor. "Let me explain a few things to you idiots. We're here," he said, placing the tip of the pointer to the left of an orange dotted line, "in Laiza, just west of the Chinese border. Because this is the KIA capital, the *Tatmadaw* has the place surrounded. Meanwhile, the jade mines are up in northwest Kachin, in Hpakan, here," he said, pointing at the map again. "The Kachin control most of the province, especially the rural areas, while in the dry season, the Burmese army hunkers down in the towns in the valleys where their armored vehicles can maneuver. But since the truce between the two sides, the Chinese have come in, and now it's a free-for-all to control the jade." With the pointer, Costa indicated a spot on the east bank of the Irrawaddy. "So whatever jade the KIA controls, they want to keep it in a safe place: here, at their depot in Waingmaw, east of the Irrawaddy from Myitkyina," he said. "Then they cut the big boulders into pieces, clean and bag the stones, and sell the stuff. So if you want my jade, I've got to go there to get it," Costa said.

"And that would be the last we'd see of you and our money," Jack said. "I've got a better idea: you go get your jade, we'll wait here and pay you when you get back."

"You think I'm going all the way up there when I don't know if you've got the money?" Costa sneered. "Pay me now, or there's no deal."

"Victor?" Jack said, and the two of them went back outside.

"There's no way we can show him the money before we get the jade," Jack said to Victor.

Victor lit a cigarette, sucked on it, and exhaled. "It's just like we figured," he said. "Costa's a finder. He needs our cash to close."

"I hear you, but try telling him that," Jack said.

"Happy to do so. I'm used to playing the bad guy, remember?"

"I can't ask you to do that. He's going to take it out on the messenger, that's for damn sure," Jack said. "Whatever happens, we're all going to need to go to Waingmaw together to get the jade."

"At least we get to meet the KIA," Victor said as he followed Jack back inside.

As Jack and Victor sat back down, Costa began pacing the floor. Ban sat like a wooden Indian in the corner.

"We were under the impression you controlled your own jade supply," Victor said, starting things off.

"And your point is?" Costa didn't appear to enjoy being questioned by Jack's second-in-command.

"Let me see if I can clear up the confusion," Victor persisted. "Your role with the Kachin is?"

Costa clenched his jaw. "The fuck's that supposed to mean?" he said, stopping his pacing in front of where Jack sat.

"Come on now," Jack interrupted, not wanting Victor to take any more heat, trying to appeal to Costa's practical side. "You're a finder here. The KIA owns the jade; you're introducing us; and we're buying it from them. Fair enough. But where I come from, that entitles you to a ten percent commission," he said as evenly as he could, "not half the deal."

"Who the fuck you think you are?" Costa shouted. "Talking to me about a fucking commission!" He grabbed the Glock off the desk and, neck-tying an arm around Jack's head, leaned over on top of him and jammed the barrel into Jack's mouth. Costa's wet, fleshy stomach slid against the side of Jack's face. Jack's chair tipped over, spilling the two of them onto the floor, Costa sprawled on top, his *longyi* riding up around his ass.

For a split second, Jack held still and waited to die. He didn't, at least not from a bullet. But he was going to choke to death on his tongue unless something happened fast. He struggled to wrestle Costa off him, and tried to get to his knees.

In a gruesome dance, Costa knelt in tandem with Jack as he hung on to his hair with one hand, keeping his pistol jammed into Jack's mouth with the other. As the men swayed to and fro, Costa's fingernails scraped the back of Jack's neck, his sweaty hands reeking of mosquito repellent. "Call me a fucking finder?" Costa bellowed, the pistol barrel banging hard against the back of Jack's throat. "I'll tell you what a finder is—someone they'll send looking for you."

Victor and Ban stood by helplessly.

Costa and Jack staggered as they stood up together, both breathing hard. At loggerheads, they stared at each other along the length of Costa's gun arm, both gasping for breath. Jack breathed in hard, snorting air through his nose, drooling down the metal gun barrel, his mouth dripping blood on the floor. Costa's pressure on the pistol in Jack's throat started to wane.

"You piss your pants yet, fuck face?" Costa yelled, his cheeks dripping with sweat. "That'll teach your ass," he barked, and faked a laugh. A strange look—disgust, or perhaps self-loathing—crossed his face as he jerked the pistol out of Jack's mouth, threw it across the room, and stomped out the side door.

Jack collapsed on his knees in the middle of the room, alternatively spitting blood and sucking in air.

Ban ran after Costa while Victor knelt down next to Jack. "You OK?" he said.

Jack nodded but didn't say anything. After a minute, he stood up, walked over to the corner and picked up Costa's pistol. He checked the magazine. It wasn't loaded. He flung the gun back into the corner.

A minute later, Ban returned and handed Jack a cloth napkin. "Sorry. He get crazy some time. That gun never have bullets," he said. He leaned over and helped Jack wipe his face. "OK?" he said.

"Thanks. Don't worry about it," Jack managed to say. So the guy did speak English.

"You should blow his goddamned head off," Victor said.

"He wasn't going to shoot me," Jack said, struggling to speak, still breathing hard. "He needs the money." He stood up, leaned over, and spat some more blood on the floor. His saliva had a metallic flavor, and he could taste the blood running inside his mouth where his teeth had cut his tongue. He pulled his chair upright and plopped down.

Ban handed Jack a glass of water. He didn't say anything to Jack, but studied him.

"You want to leave?" Victor asked.

"Hell no," Jack said. "That had to happen. I was counting on it."

Ban left the room. A moment later, they could hear Ban and Costa arguing down the hall. After five minutes, Costa returned alone, as if entering the room for the first time. His tee shirt soaked with sweat, he walked over to a sideboard cabinet, pulled out a flask, and offered it to Jack. "*Baiju?*"

Jack took a swig. The alcohol burned his throat, but numbed it too. It felt as good as bad can feel. He took another pull of the firewater. Ban returned, and handed Jack another napkin soaked in cold water. "Didn't they teach anger management at VMI?" Jack said to Costa, forcing himself to grin as he cleaned the blood off his face.

Breathing hard, Costa ignored him, and sat down in a chair. Except for the fans, the room was quiet. "You're going to need buyers for your jade," he said out of the blue a moment later. "You don't have distribution, you're playing with yourself."

Still grasping for breath, Jack said, "Chin and Tao say you can help with that," trying his best to show Costa his generous side.

Costa leaned back in his seat. "I've got the guy, all right. He's in Kunming." He took a swig of *baiju* himself. "If I'm delivering the buyer as well as the seller, I should get a lot more than ten percent."

Jack glanced over at Victor. "I guess we can double that," he said, "even though it's a lot of money for introductions. But the only way you collect is for us to go to the jade depot together," he said.

"Fine with me," Costa said with little enthusiasm. "Anyone hungry?"

"So we've got a deal?" Jack asked Costa.

"I guess so," Costa said, avoiding eye contact.

No one made a move to shake hands.

"Make sure she's got breakfast working in the kitchen," Costa said to Ban, "and then get the men ready."

Ban looked happy to be dismissed as he left the room.

"There's just a couple more things," Victor said.

"You're out of time," Costa said, getting up and starting to walk toward the kitchen.

"How long have you been running jade?" Victor asked.

Costa stopped in the doorway. "You're kidding, right? How the hell do you think I paid for all this?" he said.

"With something other than jade, I'm pretty sure," Victor said, his face calm. "We're just trying to make sure we leave Burma with a cargo of stones."

"Romanov," Costa said, "I don't like you."

Victor acted like he hadn't heard him. "And we haven't discussed the charcoal."

"What about it?" Costa asked.

Victor shrugged. "That's the other reason we're here."

Costa appeared confused. "You pick it up after we get the stones," he said.

"What's the water content?"

Costa raised his eyebrows. "What?" His decibel level increased.

"What's the quality of the charcoal?" Victor asked. "We've got a smelter business to run."

"Are you fucking nuts?" Costa exploded, his face turning red. "Who gives a shit about the smelter? Crazy Polack," he said. "Charcoal's charcoal. I'm getting some breakfast."

CHAPTER 12

Costa led them down a hallway. Suddenly starving, Jack smelled food cooking. Entering a large working kitchen, they found Tao and Chin eating breakfast with Ban, who had traded his *longyi* for combat fatigues. A crone-like Burmese woman, face so lined her age was indeterminate, sat mute on a stool in the corner, while a handful of cats dozed on the stone floor alongside an iron stove.

As the three men sat down shoulder-to-shoulder on one side of a long board table, Ban served Costa and the two visitors bowls of congee laced with shredded lumps of chicken, chives, and breadcrumbs.

The congee burned Jack's throat but he ate as much as he could. He could see that Tao, sitting across the table, had noticed the scrapes and bruises on his face, but wasn't saying anything. Shoveling food into his mouth, Chin was oblivious.

Costa farted. "You guys got mosquito repellent?" he asked.

"Nope," Victor said.

"Jesus Christ, Chin," Costa exclaimed, "you're going to get these guys killed," a smirk on his face. He farted again. "At least keep them alive until I collect my money," he cackled.

The others ate in silence. The old woman came over to the table, put a plate of thin pancakes in front of each man, and then gave Jack a clean napkin to wipe the blood from his mouth.

"Had enough to eat?" Costa said a few minutes later. "Could be your last supper." He laughed as he left the room.

When they were finished eating, Jack and Victor followed the others outside to a gravel parking area where the vehicles waited. The sky was cloudless and the sun was out, although the air remained chilly. The four of them climbed up in the idling Forland, exhaust curling out of the tailpipe. Six men sat in the back of the troop truck next to them. Ban sat at the wheel of a shiny new Jeep. Army green with an encircled white star painted over the hood, it could have passed for a US armed forces vehicle.

The kitchen screen door slammed.

"Check out Kemo Sabe," Victor said to Jack.

Emerging from the kitchen, Costa was clad in full camouflage regalia. A pistol was strapped in a holster around his thigh, and a pair of Ray Ban sunglasses perched on top of his Ranger beret. A bird colonel's silver eagles were emblazoned on either side of his military blouse.

He climbed into the shotgun seat of the Jeep and it rolled out of the yard, the troop truck and the Forland trailing behind. At an iron gate on the edge of the compound, guards snapped to attention and saluted as the vehicles rumbled through. Their commanding officer offered them a desultory touch of fingers to his forehead.

Outside the gate, Costa's world ended, replaced by a narrow track of damp hardpan that wound down out of the mountain jungle and through the outskirts of Laiza. They passed bamboo huts clustered under tall banyans where women tended cooking fires while babies scrambled on packed earth. Wiry brown men looked after water buffalo in the fields.

"What the hell is that?" Jack said, gazing ahead.

"That golf course," Chin said.

It *was* a golf course. The dirt road travelled alongside a sandy fairway, half grass and half weeds. On a jaundiced green, a ragged ensign hung limp from a crooked flag stick.

"KIA golf course, boss," said Chin. "Colonel Costa and KIA make. KIA officers play here. You play next time with Colonel Costa."

"I don't know about that," Jack said. "He'd probably want to put money on the match, and I don't have eyes in the back of my head."

They bumped down the muddy byway, leaving civilization behind. Rutted by runoff, the road dropped straight downhill, descending into a thick forest. Majestic conifers, tall and green and dark, stood close together, blocking out the morning light and leaving the land cold. In the shadows along the road, puddles were scrimmed with ice. The caravan rolled through pockets of chilly mountain air and mist. Ahead of the Forland, Jack could see the men in the back of the troop truck swaying shoulder-to-shoulder, puffs of vapor rising from their breath.

Curling around the side of a rocky hill, the vehicles emerged from the forest and gathered speed as the road flattened out along a ridge running above the surrounding land. On the high ground in the sun, frosted tips of grass sparkled like diamonds. Looking north as they approached an intersection with a well-traveled highway, Jack could see the foothills of the Himalayas in the far distance. To the east down a cliff below them, a rushing river ran parallel to the road.

"Across river is China, boss," said Chin. "Up that river one mile, Costa's charcoal place."

As the road dropped down out of the mountains, the temperature climbed and the foliage changed. The conifers disappeared, and the land became lush and dotted with groves of hardwoods. Water from melting frost dripped onto their windshields from limbs arched over the road. Chin turned on the wipers, and their rhythmic squeak broke the silence inside the cab. The trucks rumbled across a creaky iron bridge, the stream below a deep blue-green. Jack looked up at a craggy mountaintop and watched two guys sliding down zip lines toward the road, lying prostrate on loads of fresh-cut timber.

"Where are we? It's beautiful country," Jack said.

Chin craned his head to look at the men on the wires dropping down through the forest. He said something in Chinese to Tao, who answered with a few words.

"South of the clouds," Chin answered Jack.

"What does that mean?"

"*Taozong* say is where we are. Special place."

"South of the clouds," Jack said. "I like that—it sounds like a place I could be."

Tao said something else to Chin and they both laughed, Tao looking sideways at Jack.

"*Taozong* say here you called Lord of the Sky," Chin said, his eyes on the road, head bumping up and down. "Burmese name for warlord in the mountains, boss."

"Like you," Tao said to Jack, his eyes looking straight ahead.

———

Two hours later, the road descending thousands of feet and the temperature climbing, they came through stands of bamboo into the broad central valley of the Irrawaddy. Villages sprouted up, inhabited by hungry-looking people. Mounds of trash and garbage sat like geographic landmarks, as if they had been there for decades. Dogs wandered in the road, noses down, ignoring traffic as they searched for food.

"Almost there," Chin said. "This Waingmaw." He gestured north as they paused at the end of the rural road and waited for a break in the traffic to merge onto a large highway. "Up there, across big river, is Myitkyina, biggest city in Kachin."

"No checkpoint yet?" Victor asked as they threaded a gap in the highway traffic and chugged north.

"Not this side of river," Chin said as Tao waved his hand back and forth in agreement. "From here to mountains, Kachin place. *Tatmadaw* start at Myitkyina."

Up ahead, Costa's Jeep slowed down and turned off the road, the two trucks following them. High on a pole, a red and green flag overlaid with two white machetes moved listlessly.

KIA soldiers in forest green uniforms and scarlet berets rolled back an accordion-like metal gate stretched across the driveway entrance. As his Jeep broached the gate, Costa snapped a salute at the soldiers standing at attention, holding antiquated carbines.

Ahead of them, a rusty complex of metal sheds squatted in the midday heat. Three uniformed men in bush hats stood waiting at the edge of a dusty parking lot. The taller officer in the middle, sporting a bushy mustache with red epaulets on the shoulders of his forest green uniform jacket, appeared to be in charge. As soon as Ban parked the Jeep, Costa bounded over to the man and saluted.

Jack and Victor climbed down from the truck and made their way toward their hosts.

"Meet Major Maran of the Kachin Independent Army," Costa said, introducing the tall officer, "my partner, and the big boss here," he said, hamming it up.

Jack and Victor shook hands with the three military men. Major Maran began speaking immediately in Kachin to the visitors, his teeth stained brown. His eyes were lizard yellow, and his face, spotted with moles, was covered with sweat. Wordlessly, the two other officers stood next to him in shirtsleeves, blinking like a couple of iguanas in the hot sun.

"What's he saying?" Jack asked Chin, who along with Tao had walked up behind him.

"He welcome you here," Chin said. "Hopes you buy jade so they get money to fight the *Tatmadaw*. He ask for business card."

Jack and Victor gave the major their cards. "Does the major have one?" Jack asked Chin, who shook his head. "Do me a favor then, exchange phone numbers with him."

As Chin was recording Major Maran's number in his mobile phone, the major seemed fixated on Tao. His face hard, he barked a question at him, and then seemed to relax when he heard Tao's answer.

"What was that all about?" Jack said to Tao.

"He ask I Chinese," Tao said. "I tell him I am Tibetan."

The introductions over, Major Maran removed his jacket and handed it to one of the junior officers, and led the way into the building. Costa scrambled alongside the major, yakking in his ear. Passing through a linoleum-floored reception area, the group entered the dark inner work space of the main facility, a cavernous, barn-like structure.

The building had no windows. Lengthwise, the center portion of the building's roof was raised, letting in light and air. The atmosphere inside was damp and earthy. Dirt and rock littered the concrete floor of the facility, which ran on a slight incline from one end to the other. Down the middle of the barn, a dump truck lurched along the floor, spilling a brown swathe of earth and rocks across a ten-meter-wide expanse of concrete. Behind it, a squad of men in camouflage pants, naked from the waist up, followed with rakes and shovels, culling stones to the side. Others picked through the stones, putting them in bags they carried around their necks. Off in a corner, men with hammers and chisels broke large boulders into chunks.

Jack stopped and knelt in the alluvial earth. He ran his fingers through the sand and gravel, looking for jade. A few yards away, Victor turned over a greenish slab the size of a small boy, Tao helping him. "This thing's got to be four feet long," Victor called over to Jack.

Major Maran turned around and saw that his visitors had become distracted. He barked an order across the barn. A worker with a rock hammer came over to Jack and knelt beside him. Picking through the stones, he selected one the size of a lemon, whacked at it a few times with his hammer, rubbed the loose dirt off the stone, and held it up in front of Jack. A bright green gash ran the length of the rock with the brownish skin. Inside, it looked alive, like the innards of a ripe kiwi.

Costa walked up and peered over Jack's shoulder. "You're looking at jadeite," he said, playing tour guide. "The Cadillac of jade. Hpakan's the world's only true commercial site for the stuff. 'Stone of heaven,' the Chinese call it. They call the green color you see *fei-cui*; it's the same as a kingfisher's neck feathers. Before the eighteenth century, the Chinese had never seen jade like this. Once they did, the emperors wouldn't accept anything else," Costa waxed on sociably, smelling the money.

Jack stood up and brushed off his hands. "Time to see the inventory."

Costa signaled to the major, who began walking down the middle of the barn to a cage-like gate at the rear. He opened it, turned on a light, and went inside.

Jack followed the major into the dark inner sanctum, adjusting his eyes in the dim light. Running the width of the barn, the storage room was lined floor-to-ceiling with shelves of brown stones.

Major Maran sat down at a long table, his fellow officers and Costa joining him. He didn't waste any time. As soon as everyone was seated, he spoke forcefully in Jack's direction.

As the major finished, Chin seemed dismayed. "He happy to see you, boss," Chin said, "but he say very sorry: price of jade go up."

"What a surprise," Jack said. Costa avoided his gaze. "What's his price today?" Jack asked.

Chin said something to Major Maran, and then they bantered for a minute. "He say you pay four thousand RMB per kilo, help KIA win war," Chin said with no conviction.

"I'm sympathetic, but not enough to pay the *laowai* price. Tell him if he keeps that up, we'll drive up the road to Hpakan and cut a deal with the Chinese," Jack said, watching Chin's face flinch.

Chin spoke to the major, who responded angrily. Chin protested in return, and they spent another minute arguing. Major Maran spoke emphatically, then stopped abruptly. The room was quiet while everyone waited.

Chin turned to Jack, frustrated. "Boss, Major Maran say you have no money."

"Where'd he get that idea?" Jack asked.

Chin said, "He say every time Americans come, have no money."

"I see your reputation has preceded you," Jack said to Costa.

Costa yelled at him, "Show him your cash, you stupid motherfucker."

Jack turned to Victor. "Got a minute?"

They walked outside.

"These guys barely know Costa," Victor said.

"Yeah, but the major seems desperate for money," Jack said. He stuck his head back inside the door of the jade room. "Hey, *Taozong*," he called in Tao's direction, motioning for him to come outside. "I thought the KIA needed friends," Jack said to Tao when he stood in front of them.

"*Dui*," Tao said, his face untroubled. "You have money, you good friends with KIA," he said, his lined eyes crinkling.

"Better friends than Costa?"

"Costa not KIA friend," Tao said.

"All right," Jack said to Victor, knowing it was time to play their cards, "get everyone to keep their seats, and I'll be right back." Victor and Tao filed back into the jade room while Jack walked quickly across the barn floor and out the building to the Forland in the parking lot. Crawling under the rear of the truck, he removed the big bag of cash, and their guns for good measure, and headed back inside.

When he entered the jade room, conversation ceased. Wordlessly, Jack plunked the bag on the table, opened it, and pulled out a pink slab of hundred RMB notes wrapped tightly in white tape. On the Kachin side of the table, no one spoke, their eyes fixated on the cash. Major Maran sported a big grin, Jack noticing he had two front teeth growing one behind the other.

Jack said to Costa, "Tell them we've got three million RMB, less your commission, for Grade A jade stones at the Costa price. Two thousand RMB a kilo."

Costa smirked. "Tell them yourself," he said. "I'm just a finder, remember?"

Chin had heard enough and didn't wait, shuffling around the table behind Major Moran, leaning over and whispering to him.

The major spat words back at Chin, glared at Costa, and then turned to stare at Jack, his yellow eyes flashing.

Chin hesitated, and then stammered, "Major say there's no Costa price. Save money; don't pay Costa commission."

"That's a nice idea, but not very helpful at this point," Jack said. He looked over at Victor and said, "I guess we're going home empty handed," as he leaned across the table and grabbed the satchel.

Jack and Victor walked out the door.

Behind them, they could hear chairs scraping the floor and people shouting.

"Not very Chinese of you, refusing to negotiate," Victor said to Jack as they walked across the barn and passed through the reception area, startling a clerk at the front desk. They blinked in the afternoon sunlight as they stepped out of the office building and crossed the parking lot to the Forland.

"No peeking," Jack joked with Victor who was looking over his shoulder. He willed himself to believe that things would turn out all right. They climbed up in the Forland and waited, Victor cradling the big bag of cash in his lap.

"Here come the guys," Victor said a minute later. They watched Chin and Tao emerge from the building and march toward the Forland. Costa chased behind them, his face red as he ranted, Ban trailing after him. "I don't see any jade."

"Does one of you guys know the way home?" Jack asked Chin and Tao as the two men clambered up into the Forland.

Eyes glazed in semi-shock, Chin started the truck and began backing it up to turn around.

"Davis, you stupid son of a bitch," Costa yelled across the parking lot. "Take the deal, for fuck's sake," he shouted over the noise of the idling Forland. "I can get five thousand a kilo in Kunming."

"We'll try the Chinese down the road," Jack called to Costa.

They couldn't hear the rest of Costa's words as Chin gunned the accelerator, wheeled the truck around, and headed toward the gate. Costa ran behind them as his Thai contingent scrambled to follow in their vehicles.

Chin was pulling up to the guard booth when his mobile rang.

"Bingo," Victor said.

Chin fished his phone out of his shirt pocket. "*Wei? Dui; dui,*" he said, giving Jack and Victor the thumbs-up sign, holding his phone to his ear. "Major want talk."

Jack peered at the side mirror as Major Maran and the two officers exited the office door and walked toward the gate, the major speaking into his mobile phone. The major approached Chin's side of the Forland and harangued him through the open window for several minutes.

Costa got out of his Jeep, waddled over, and started kibitzing with Chin and the major.

Ignoring Costa, Chin said to Jack, "Major say want to be friends. Have many stones for you at good price."

"Don't keep us in suspense," Jack said. "What's his price?"

Chin said something to Major Maran, the major replied, Chin raised his voice, and then they kibitzed some more. Then Chin said, "Three thousand RMB."

"Take the deal, goddammit," Costa carped over the noise of the truck.

"Our limit's two thousand," Jack said to Chin.

"Don't tell him that, Chin," yelled Costa.

With Costa still screaming, Chin spoke again to the major, who sneered back. They argued some more.

Jack tapped Chin's shoulder. "Kick this rig in the ass, and let's go see the Chinese."

As Chin gunned the Forland and signaled the guard to lift the gate, the major thumped his hand several times on the truck's fender, loud and insistent, yelling at Chin over the engine noise.

Chin dropped the Forland back into neutral, listening to the major's words over the din. "Major say maybe one time for low price," he said, turning to Jack, his eyes hopeful.

"Two thousand a kilo this time," Jack said, "and…" he said, gauging the major's face, seeing he was close, "…next time we'll buy ten times as much."

The prospect of a big payday "next time" did the trick. The major stuck his hand through Chin's window to grab Jack's. Then he pulled his phone out of his pocket and punched some buttons. A few minutes later, a phalanx of guards banged out of the front door of the office, lugging dozens of bags of jade across the parking lot. Tao climbed out of the Forland and dropped its tailgate, and the men began loading the jade into the back of the truck. After checking everything ten minutes later, Tao peered in the window of the truck and gave Jack and Victor the thumbs-up sign.

"It's put up or shut up time," Costa said, standing next to Tao, a couple of his Thai guerillas mustered next to him for intimidation. "Hand over my cash," he said. Ban gave a backpack to Tao.

"Go ahead and pay him," Jack said to Victor.

"No," Tao said. "Pay now, but KIA must come to border," Tao called to Jack, his eyes earnest.

"Fuck that," Costa shouted, "you don't need those guys."

"We OK, boss," Chin chimed in.

"No," Tao insisted. "KIA important."

"Sounds right to me," Jack said. "Chin, tell the major he's got to throw in an escort."

Chin spoke to the major, Jack heard him say "OK," flashing his brown teeth at Jack, giving him the thumbs-up, and then waving at some of the guards. A minute later, a Jeep loaded with young Kachin soldiers pulled up behind the Forland.

Victor separated out Costa's commission of six hundred thousand RMB, dropped it into Ban's backpack, and handed both bags out the window to Tao. Tao gave the backpack to Ban, passed the big bag over to Major Maran, and then climbed back into the truck. The major took the bag, handed it to an aide, reached in the window, and shook Jack's hand with both of his. Everyone made a show of saluting each other, and the caravan rolled out the gate.

Chin took the Forland through the gears. As the big rig picked up speed and they settled in for the highway ride, Chin stole a glance at Jack sitting next to him. "You know Chinese at Hpakan, boss?"

"No. Why?"

A sloppy grin formed on Chin's face. "You told them we go buy from Chinese." He started to laugh.

"What, you think just because we're a couple of *laowai* we don't know any tricks?" Jack said.

Chin didn't say anything, but just grinned to himself as he kept driving. At an intersection, he slowed down to study the signs.

"You want me to show you the direction to the charcoal pits?" Jack asked Chin, kidding him.

"I know boss," Chin said, smiling, the truck rolling ahead. "Past your home, at south of the clouds."

CHAPTER 13

With Ban leading the way in Costa's Jeep, the caravan retraced its morning journey, rolling along the Irrawaddy bottomland through bamboo groves, their thin silvery leaves shimmering like the rippled surface of a lost ocean.

An hour south of Waingmaw, they turned east onto a steep track and headed upland. The road rose out of the Burmese plain into the Kachin piedmont. The air soon felt brisk and clean. Broadleaf foliage fell away, hardwoods and then conifers marking the higher elevations. The last of the afternoon sunlight sliced through gaps between the trees, dappling the surface of the land. Parallel to the road, streams poured off the hillsides, cascading spray down rocky ravines, running clear and fast.

"South of the clouds again," Jack said to Chin, Victor and Tao asleep, their heads bobbing up and down.

"Not for long," Chin said.

As they neared the Chinese border north of Laiza, everything changed. The temperature plummeted. Ahead of them, tall mountains loomed, their peaks obscured by dark thunderheads. The sun disappeared. At the end of a long climb, the Forland's engine gasping, they entered a dank forest.

The trucks bumped around a corner and the trees ended. On both sides of the road, the forest was clear-cut, the mountainsides denuded. Like dead soldiers, remains of trunks and stumps lay on the ground as far as the eye could see, the last testament of a now-barren land. Dotting the forlorn plain, charcoal pits smoldered, wisps of smoke escaping from their rounded hillocks into the gloaming.

The vehicles struggled, the muddy path full of potholes and littered with boulders. Then in the dim light, Jack spied the dark shapes of guards in camouflage with automatic weapons, and they came upon a camp.

Penitentiary-like, the gated compound was laid out in sections separated by high fencing topped with concertina wire. A low wooden office building sat out front. Behind it huddled a cluster of bamboo huts. Further back in the woods, Jack could hear the throb of electric generators. Most of the human activity was centered on corrugated metal sheds illuminated by strings of naked light bulbs. From one of the sheds, a heat source vented steam up a tin chimney into the sky, while in the next building a dozen men were busy stuffing white powder into plastic bags. Next to the sheds in a feedstock yard piled high with charcoal, a front-end loader chugged back and forth, loading a line of trucks.

Under a grove of trees, rows of canvas tents ran perpendicular to the buildings, separated by another barbed wire fence. Fluttering inside the tented area like rabbits in a cage were at least a hundred barefoot women in raggedy clothes.

As the caravan rolled up to the gate of the compound, headlights shone on the inmates. Jack tried to see their faces, but the women turned away as if curiosity could kill. Finally, one glanced up, affording Jack a clear view of her face. She looked terrified.

Ban eased the Jeep into a parking space and Costa got out, not saying a word to anyone as he strode through the gate of the pen and disappeared into the wooden office building. Chin cut the Forland's ignition and headed toward an outhouse, while Tao stood next to the truck, not willing to let its cargo out of his sight.

"I thought we were going to a charcoal business, not Don Corleone's operations center," Victor said.

An old woman herded everyone to a collection of wooden picnic tables laden with bowls of food. The young KIA soldiers huddled together by themselves, looking intimidated. It was only then that

Jack realized they were not armed. They concentrated on their food, and didn't make a sound.

Sitting on the ground inside the pen just yards away, the women were eating too, in silence, like animals in the forest. It was as if they were holding their breath.

The old woman fussed over the newcomers until they sat down. Jack was famished, but couldn't eat. Tao chewed a few bites, and then went back to stake out the Forland. Chin wolfed his food. Victor strolled through the open gates of the tented area, picking his way between clusters of girls gathered around their cooking fire. He pulled a burning stick out of the fire, lit two cigars, returned to the table, and handed one to Jack.

"Thanks," Jack said, taking a drag from the cigar. "I'm not sure how to handle this."

Victor shrugged. "We're outnumbered. Up close, you can see them shaking."

Jack said, "I guess they're the cheap labor for his casino."

"Those would be the lucky ones," Victor said.

"Hey Chin, where do those girls come from?" Jack asked.

Chin looked up from his rice bowl. "Slaves? Most from Burma," he said, slurping some more rice. "Some look for work, then Thai guys steal them. Others, parents sell."

"Has it always been this way?"

"No," Chin answered. "Only since truce between *Tatmadaw* and KIA in 1994. Then border open with China and big business start. Chinese men come here, build mines. Need sex. Too many men in China. They want slave for karaoke girl—sometimes wife. Pay big money. China right over there, down that road across river," he said, pointing beyond the charcoal feedstock yard.

Jack said, "But surely when they get to China, they can escape."

"Not so much, boss. No papers. No papers in China, go to jail."

Next to them, Costa's guerrillas had finished eating. Their tables were littered with beer bottles. All the men appeared to be Thai, and were dressed in unmarked combat fatigues similar to the men from Costa's place in Laiza. But unlike Ban and those men, these camp soldiers were rowdy and boisterous. Many of them were drunk, yelling and swearing at each other. The smell of marijuana was pervasive.

"Must be Costa payday," Victor said as the noise level from the guerillas' tables escalated.

The women behind the fence stole glances at the Thais, dread in their eyes. One of them—barely a teenager—looked across the way at Jack, her soft face flawless, eyes like a fawn's.

A group of charcoal tenders and wood cutters, done for the day, traipsed through the camp. Their dogs scampered underneath the tables, searching for scraps. One of the guerillas threw some food toward the dogs, sparking a frenzy of yaps and yelps as the pack lunged for the prize. Another guerilla swung his leg at the noisiest offender, an animal no bigger than a squirrel, but missed. The dog kept squealing.

Jack was looking the other way when the man shot the dog. The gunshot exploded as if it was fired next to his head. Jack spun around. The gunman sat at the table next to him, his pistol dangling in one hand, glaring at Jack. The dead dog wriggled on the ground, the rear half of its body blown off, its open eyes wild and still blinking, front legs twitching in place. It was enough to cause Chin to stop eating.

"Let's get the hell out of here," Jack said to Victor.

"Ready when you are," Victor said.

The screen door on the wooden building slammed, and Jack and Victor turned to see the camp warden waddling toward them. Costa yelled their way, "Is this one stop shopping, or what?" He was back in his element, the mortification of the afternoon a memory. "Everything you could ask for: jade, women, drugs—to say nothing of charcoal," he said, chuckling. He grabbed a bowl of food, pushed Chin out of the way, and sat down at the table across from Jack and Victor.

Jack checked his mobile phone. Two bars of reception. Like Chin had said, China was close by. "If it's all the same to you, we're going to keep driving," he said to Costa.

"No can do," Costa said, his chopsticks shoveling rice from his bowl into his mouth, slurping as he sucked in every morsel. "There's a line of trucks in front of you. My loaders won't get to yours until early tomorrow morning." He farted.

Jack said, "You could take some guys out of that drug lab, get them to lend a hand."

Costa ignored him. He wiped his hands on his pants, removed a piece of paper from his shirt pocket, and handed it across the table to Jack. "Here's your jade buyer: Yao Chow Fook. Right across from Green Park in downtown Kunming. Best prices in western China," Costa said. "Call him, let it ring three times, and then hang up and call him right back. I've already told him you're coming." He turned around and pointed past the charcoal feedstock yard. "Take the back way. Ford the river there, and you're back in the PRC in less than a mile."

Jack examined the information on the paper and put it in his pocket.

The three men sat in silence, Costa wolfing down the last of his rice bowl. When he had finished, he wiped his mouth, leaned back, and looked across the table. "I try to stay close to my charcoal customers." He smirked. "You guys coming back next time?"

Jack exhaled. "To be honest, not if we can help it."

Costa leaned back and roared with laughter. "How the hell did you get so squeamish? Haven't you ever been to Las Vegas? This is no different: just meat on the hoof."

"Notwithstanding your previous comment, and just to be clear: you're saying we're invited back?" Victor asked.

The girl's shriek from the back of the camp served to bring the after-dinner conversation to a halt. Jack peered into the darkness, trying to see what was happening. Out of the pack of women huddled in the corner of the fenced-in yard, a Thai guerrilla emerged, a girl slung over his shoulder, pounding his back with her little fists. The guy carried his prey into one of the tents, a couple of his drunken friends following behind him and yelling encouragement.

"Oversexed Thai bastards," Costa said. "When there's no girls around, most of 'em fuck animals."

From the tent, they could hear the girl begin to scream.

At the next table, the weaponless KIA guys grumbled loudly, visibly disturbed. They stared across the way, powerless as they watched the rape scene unfold, their faces dark and troubled. The men—boys really—stamped the ground and milled around, raising their voices, angry and frustrated as they watched one of their own get physically abused.

"Can't you put a stop to that?" Jack said to Costa.

"How the hell you expect me to get these girls pregnant," Costa said. "Osmosis?"

CHAPTER 14

Jack kept his hand on his pistol all night, and didn't sleep a wink.

But the morning came like any other, and they took on their load of charcoal at Costa's camp without incident. They left by the back way, and passed through the remote border patrol post at La Zan. When they pulled up to the lightly staffed gate, Tao jumped out and handed some cigarettes to the Chinese guards, who waved their truck through without even looking in the cab. No patrols stopped them as they wound east through the city of Ying Jiang and back into Dehong.

It was Sunday. Nothing stirred in the factory yard when Chin drove the Forland through the front gate at seven that evening. Pots and pans clanged and banged as the dormitory's residents prepared dinner. Creepers whirred, anticipating the solace of the night.

The Forland groaned under the weight of its payload as it rolled along the factory road until Chin brought it to a halt next to the Land Cruiser in the feedstock yard. He raised the dump truck's bed, and tons of charcoal skidded through the swinging tail gate into a black mound on the ground. The pile grew two yards high before scores of canvas bags plopped onto the peak and the tail gate banged shut, the noise echoing across the empty yard.

The four men transferred the bags of jade from the charcoal pile to the back of the car. "Tao, you'll drive us up to Kunming tomorrow," Jack said when they were finished. "Find Mei and bring her along so the translation goes smoothly."

Tao and Chin went off to the dormitory, and Jack and Victor drove the car down to the office and left it locked out front. The two of them trudged up to their bedroom. As Victor lay down on his cot and lit a cigarette, Jack pulled off his boots and stripped off his clothes, black and oily with charcoal.

"How do you feel?" Jack said to Victor.

"Better than you smell," Victor said, taking a long drag of his cigarette. "Boy, am I whipped. And I didn't have to swallow a gun."

Jack went into the bathroom and turned on the shower.

Victor spoke through the door, "Did you think we'd get back here?"

"Never a doubt in my mind," Jack lied. "We're halfway to a payday." He soaked himself, scrubbing with a pumice stone. He washed his hair twice. After getting out and drying off, he looked in the mirror. He felt older.

"All yours," he said to Victor, who didn't answer. Untying his mosquito netting from the slide rack attached to the ceiling, Jack draped it over the length of his cot, pulled the netting over his head, and lay down. "Do you want to take a look at the stones?" he asked Victor.

The bedroom was silent.

"Victor?"

Lying on his back, Jack couldn't sleep. Through the bedroom window, he could see the sky. Stars winked in the moonless night. There was no breeze, and nothing stirred in the jungle.

He got up and went downstairs. He poured himself a glass of Hennessey, grabbed a chair from the office, and sat outside. Up in the black sky, the Milky Way began to unveil itself. The sweet Dehong air, still and heavy, wrapped around him.

He heard Mei coming down the road a minute later. He could barely see her. She was dressed in a flannel shirt and jeans, feeling her way along in the darkness, walking carefully toward him.

"Jack?"

"Hi," he said, his pulse quickening.

"Are you OK?" she asked, standing in the road. "Tao said you had trouble."

"I'm all right," he said. "C'mon over, have a seat." He brought another chair out of the office.

She sat down. Moving closer, she peered at him in the dark.

"You're a sight for sore eyes," he said, looking at her beautiful face.

"I am?" she whispered.

"You sure are," he said.

She put her hand up along the side of his mouth. "Tao said someone hit you."

"That didn't feel nearly as bad as what we saw at Costa's camp," Jack said.

"You mean the girls," she said.

"Yeah."

She stared at him, her eyes flat. "It's worse than you think," she said, her expression turning hard.

Jack changed the subject. "Did Tao tell you we're going to Kunming tomorrow? Is that OK for you?" he asked.

"Yes," Mei said. She took a moment before speaking. "I was so afraid for you."

Under the inky black sky, that was all Jack needed to hear. He leaned over and kissed her lightly on her mouth.

She kissed him back, and then raised her hands to the sides of his head. "Lean back and close your eyes," she said. "You need to rest." She began caressing his face.

———

The next day, they left Dehong early. When they hit the outskirts of Kunming in the late afternoon, Jack asked Tao to pull over to the side of the road. As the car idled, he punched Yao Chow Fook's number into his phone and handed it to Mei. "Costa said let it ring three times, and then hang up and call him right back."

She held the phone to her ear for a moment, and then redialed the number. The phone made a clicking sound as someone picked up on the other end of the line. "*Hey, ni hao Yaozong,*" Mei said, "*Wo shi Mei; Daviszong mi shu.*"

After a moment of silence, the person on the other end of the line spoke. Mei listened, spoke again in Chinese, and then listened some more, looking up wide-eyed at Jack as the line went dead.

"What'd he say?" Jack asked.

Mei stammered, her face losing color. "He…he sounded surprised you weren't alone."

"But you told him we're coming, right?"

She just nodded and put her phone back into her bag.

Riding shotgun next to Tao, Victor punched Yao's address into the Toyota's GPS system. "His place is less than an hour away," he said to Jack. "What do you want to do?"

"Let's get over there before he has second thoughts and leaves," Jack said. "*Taozong*, let's go," he said, tapping Tao's shoulder as he saw the concern remaining on Mei's face. "What?"

"Nothing," she said, "just the way he sounded."

"Let's be real careful, OK? Tell *Taozong* to expect the worst."

Mei spoke to Tao in Chinese as he pulled the car back out on the highway, and he muttered something back to her, weaving with the traffic, scanning the road in front of him. "He does," she said.

Tao navigated through Kunming's busy city center to an older, low-rise section of town. Urban dust, grayish and dead, covered the buildings. The Yunnan sky, which had been bright and blue on the drive from Dehong, was now overwhelmed by an angry pack of clouds.

They rolled down a hill to a T-shaped intersection controlled by a traffic light, and gazed over a city park centered on a large pond choked with lotus plants. Tourists strolled up and down, taking photos and buying trinkets from street vendors. Fat raindrops began to plunk the windshield. Tao turned on the wipers.

"If this is Green Park, it should be right down there," Victor said, pointing to show Tao the way as they sat at the light waiting for it to turn. The light changed, and Tao turned onto the road past the Green Park Hotel, nestled under a dense grove of banyans. "He's got lucky eights: eight hundred eighty-eight Green Park Road," Victor said to Tao.

Tao drove halfway down the block and pulled up to a decrepit storefront. In both Chinese and English, flaking gold lettering was set across dusty glass windowpanes: *Yao Chow Fook's Fine Jade and Jewelry.* The place appeared abandoned. No wares were visible in the display window, only lifeless venetian blinds.

They climbed out of the car and locked it as each of the men carried a sample bag across the sidewalk to the front door. Jack tried the buzzer. Nothing. The rain picked up. People passed by on the sidewalk, stealing glances from underneath their umbrellas at the strangers. The traffic along the road was heavy. Jack waited for a lull in the flow of cars, and then pushed the buzzer again. He listened for the ring inside, but couldn't hear anything. Jack was about to tell everyone to head back to the car when the front door cracked open.

"*Wei?*"

Jack pushed the door open wider. "Mr. Yao; *Yaozong?*"

"Yes?" The man's voice came from the shadows.

"I'm Jack Davis. We called you earlier. I believe Costa told you to expect us?"

"Why…yes." He sounded flustered.

"May we come in?" Jack said, keeping pressure on the door.

"Oh, my goodness. Yes, please, come in," the man relented, opening the door.

When they had all crossed the threshold into the musty store, the little Chinese man shut the door and turned to them in the half light. As he examined the group in front of him, he held his hands together as if trying to compose himself. "You will have tea?"

"That would be fine," Jack said, the others standing mute, a strained expression on Mei's face.

Mr. Yao seemed nervous, and in a hurry. He marched into the darkened store interior, leaving his four visitors standing at the entrance. He got halfway across the room before he realized they weren't behind him. "Oh, sorry, sorry. This way." They followed him carrying the bags of jade, the old wooden floorboards creaking. The place smelled like an attic. Scurrying down the length of the display area, Mr. Yao disappeared through an open doorway into a back room.

Lit by a single fluorescent bulb hanging from the ceiling, the back room was half as big as the front display area. The space was not as musty—in the right-hand corner an open transom over a side door allowed in fresh air—but reeked of human sweat and garlicky food. A round table sat in the middle of the room, surrounded by bamboo chairs, the fabric of the seats frayed and ratty. Several paper cartons of Chinese takeout and a few half-consumed plates of food littered the table. On the left, a small sink stood along the wall. The water in the sink was running.

"Please sit," Mr. Yao said, offering Jack the chair next to the side door.

Instead, Jack walked around to the opposite side of the table and positioned himself so he could see both doors. "*Xie xie*," he said to Mr. Yao, setting his bag of stones at his feet and sitting down. The others did as well. Jack put his hands under the table. There was plenty of room to maneuver. He reached down in his pants pocket and felt his gun.

Mr. Yao continued to stand, looking confused, his nut brown face lined by a furrowed brow and a scraggly mustache, black eyes ringed with red. As Jack and the others seated themselves, he seemed to grow more edgy. Eyeing the four people and the bags of jade arrayed around the table, he hesitated, and then as if things were inevitable, sat down across from Jack and put his hands on the wooden surface. His knuckles were tattooed. "We are alone?"

Jack made himself grin. "Except for the person making that tea you promised."

"You have the jade?"

Before Jack could answer, the side door banged open and three Chinese guys in black leather barreled in, looking like they were late for a train.

Mr. Yao jumped up from the table and started barking Chinese at his visitors, his gold teeth flashing, a different guy with three thugs backing him up. Mei pushed her chair away from the table, her hands over her ears, terrified, while Tao yelled back at Mr. Yao.

The biggest Chinese thug pulled out a tile cutter and slashed at Victor as he stood up from his chair, raising his arms in defense.

Jack and Tao's guns discharged simultaneously, one shot smacking the man with the tile cutter in his chest and flinging him backward against the wall, the other spinning one of Mr. Yao's henchmen completely around, blowing off his arm.

The thug with the tile cutter, eyes shocked and mouth open, slid slowly down the blood-splattered wall and sat on the floor, chin on his chest, while the two other men scrambled out the back door. With Tao's empty gun trained on him, Mr. Yao tried to speak, mouth opening and closing like a blowfish.

Jack's eardrums rang. The close air in the room was full of cordite; a bluish cloud gathered around the light fixture at the ceiling. The thug sitting on the floor dropped his tile cutter. It rolled across the wooden floorboards until it stopped at what remained of the other guy's arm. The thug tried to raise himself to his knees, couldn't, and slumped over.

Jack looked over at Victor, whose right forearm was slashed lengthwise, the tattered sleeve of his shirt hanging down his arm, already soaked with blood. "You all right?"

"I will be," Victor said, standing up and examining his forearm as he walked over to the sink.

Mr. Yao chose the moment to make a move for the door, but Tao sprang up, tackled him to the floor, and then climbed on his back and stuck the barrel of his gun in the back of Mr. Yao's head. Tao smashed the man's face against the floorboards as he yelled at him in Chinese.

"Ask *Taozong* to see if he can find out what's going on," Jack said to Mei. "Fast. We've got to get the hell out of here," he said as he went to help Victor, turning on the hot water faucet in the sink and running water over the wound.

Mei spoke excitedly in Chinese to Tao.

"*Cui*," he said, yelling at Mr. Yao in Chinese as he kept his gun jammed into the back of his captive's head. When Mr. Yao struggled but wouldn't speak, Tao stuffed his gun in his waistband and hiked Yao's arms up over his head, one of his shoulders popping, Yao screaming in pain.

Mei picked up the tile cutter and went over to Victor at the sink, cutting both sleeves of his shirt off at the shoulder. She grabbed a cake of soap to scrub his forearm, Victor grimacing as the soap mixed into his wound. Then she tied the clean sleeve tourniquet-like above the wound. "Hold your arm up in the air," she said to Victor, the blood running freely out of the wound, dripping onto the floor. "We've got to get him to a doctor," she said to Jack.

"I'll be OK," Victor said over Mr. Yao's screams as Tao ratcheted his arms up further.

Jack stepped across the room to check the Chinese thug on the floor. He couldn't tell if he was dead or alive. He searched his pockets: no identification. Jack glanced down at Mr. Yao, moaning, his face smashed flat on the floor, Tao sitting on him. "*Taozong:* we've got to go. Ready?"

"*Dui,*" Tao grunted as he hoisted Mr. Yao up onto his feet, one arm hanging strangely, and then sapped the side of his head with the gun. Mr. Yao crumpled to the floor. Tao stuffed his gun back in his waistband, knelt down to check Mr. Yao's pulse, then rifled his pockets. "He OK," he said, standing up and nodding at Jack. Tao gathered up the bags of stones and nudged Victor ahead of him through the door back into the interior of the store.

While Jack circled the room quickly, picking up the two spent shotgun shells, Mei put the tile cutter in her pocket, and they followed Tao and Victor out.

Tao gunned the car down side streets, swerving to avoid potholes.

"Let me see that arm," Jack said to Victor, sitting next to him in the back seat and examining the wound.

"Look at the good side of things," Victor said, holding his arm upright, blood oozing onto his lap. "This is the last time we pay Costa a buy-side commission."

The car bumped down the street. Jack tried to steady Victor's arm. The cut was deep—Jack could see all the way to the bone—and needed expert care. He looked at the back of Mei's head. "What happens if we go to a hospital?"

"No," she said. "It's not like the US. He'll bleed to death before they get to him. And then they'll turn us over to the police."

"Do you know any doctors in Kunming?" Jack asked.

"Most would report this to the police," she said, "except for one I know."

"I'll be all right," Victor said, and then winced as Tao couldn't avoid slamming over a pothole.

"You're going to have to call the guy," Jack said to Mei.

She reached in her bag for her mobile, punched one of the speed dials, and waited. "*Hey, Zengzong. Ni hao, ni hao,*" she said into the phone. She spoke in Chinese for several minutes, and listened for a minute longer. "*Hada, hada,*" she said, and clicked off her mobile.

"Was that the doctor?" Jack asked her.

"Jimmi Zeng," she said. "He's calling his doctor. The man will be at Jimmi's office by the time we get there. He's an excellent physician."

"Christ," Jack said, gulping. "Sorry, Mei. That's the last thing you needed."

"It's all right," she said, feigning cheerfulness. "Getting Victor fixed is what matters." She spoke in Chinese to Tao, giving him directions to Jimmi Zeng's office.

"Thank you very much," Jack said.

"Thanks Mei," Victor croaked.

Ten minutes later, Tao pulled up in front of a small office building. Everyone piled out. The security guards called out to Mei like an old friend, but she shushed them and led the way inside to an elevator. They got off at the second floor and quickly followed Mei down an inner hallway to a luxurious office.

"Please," Mei said, holding the door open to admit them.

"Good evening," said a handsome Chinese man standing behind a desk. He sounded American. He had been conferring with another Chinese man standing next to him in an overcoat and holding a briefcase. He started to move around to the front of the desk to welcome the two *laowai*, but then saw they were covered with blood and stopped.

"Mr. Davis, this is my boss Jimmi Zeng," Mei said, putting on a brave smile.

Jimmi Zeng stayed behind the desk, evaluating Jack. He gave Mei a curt nod, said something in Chinese to Tao, and then turned to Jack. His face ageless but probably fifty, Jimmi was almost as tall as Jack. His skin was smooth and golden, with long, layered hair swept back from his forehead and trailing down his neck, a look only available via a beauty salon. He wore expensive clothes and shoes.

Jack had thought that if he ever met Jimmi Zeng, he'd strangle the man. "Thanks for helping us," he managed to say.

Mei said, "And this is our patient, Mr. Romanov."

Jimmi didn't respond to Jack, but instead motioned to the other man next to him. The two of them took Victor by the shoulders and led him to a wet bar in the corner. The man shucked off his overcoat and set his medical valise on the conference table. "This is Dr. Tong," Jimmi said to Victor. "He'll be looking after you, but unfortunately he doesn't speak English."

Dr. Tong didn't say anything. After examining Victor's arm for a moment, he washed his hands in the sink. He sat Victor down at the conference table, removed Mei's makeshift tourniquet, and straightened out Victor's arm over the surface of the table so it lay flush. The doctor poked at the wound as Victor grimaced. Then he spoke to Mei for several minutes. It was obvious they knew each other well.

She pulled the tile knife out of her back pocket and showed it to the doctor.

Victor eyed the knife, his face turning blue.

The doctor extracted a small flashlight, a pair of tweezers, and some flat wooden tongue strips from his bag. Sitting down next to Victor and shining the light on his forearm, he used the tweezers and tongue strips to carefully pull bits of the torn sleeve away from the wound.

Dr. Tong pulled and poked at the cut. Victor's face muscles clenched. Jack forced himself to look over the doctor's shoulder, while Mei looked away. At the same time as he treated Victor's arm, the doctor started speaking to Jimmi.

"He says your friend should go to a hospital," Jimmi said to Jack. "He needs to be stitched up."

"No can do," Jack said.

"And why is that?" Jimmi asked pleasantly, as if they were speaking about stock prices.

"We got into an altercation a half-hour ago, and I've got a feeling one of the opposition didn't make it," Jack answered.

"Ah, yes. That would make a hospital inadvisable," Jimmi said. "Let's see what we can do here." He spoke to the doctor, who, with no change in his expression as he heard Jimmi's words, started addressing Mei again.

"The doctor says he must repair the wound now," Mei said to Victor. "Since we cannot go to the hospital, he must do it here in Mr. Zeng's kitchen. If that's all right with you."

"Fine by me," Victor said, "as long as I get that guy's tile knife as a souvenir." He stood up from his chair to go with Mei, but the doctor gently held Victor's shoulders, urging him to re-take his seat. Then the doctor searched around in his bag, pulled out a plastic package with a syringe, and extracted a small vial. Holding it up in the air and eyeing it in the light, he spoke again to Mei.

"He says he should give you a painkiller before you move," Mei said, "and asks if you are allergic to any medicines."

"No," Victor said. "As long as we're covering the housekeeping, does he take Blue Cross?"

Jimmi laughed, while Mei managed a smile for Victor's sake. After the doctor injected the back of Victor's bicep with the local anesthetic and a minute passed, Mei led the two of them to the kitchen.

"Sit down," Jimmi said to Jack, saying something in Chinese to Tao and motioning to them to take seats at the conference table in the middle of the room. Overhead lighting provided warmth to the surroundings. Off to either side, groupings of upholstered chairs were partially hidden by broad-leafed plants. Next to the wet bar, a glass cabinet above a sideboard was stocked with wine and liquor. A bag of golf clubs sat in the corner, next to the Chinese businessman's obligatory accessory, a large aquarium.

Tao remained standing until Jack pulled out a chair at the table and gestured to him to sit down.

Leaning back, Jack took a deep breath and told himself to relax. "Does the doctor think he's going to be all right?" he asked Jimmi.

"Another inch and it could have been a lot worse. But then again, we must thank Lady Luck anytime she can help us. I understand you're from New York," Jimmi said.

"Who told you that?" Jack asked.

"My agency," Jimmi said, smiling as he eyed Jack quizzically. "Remember? How's the smelter going?"

"It's a struggle," Jack said, uncomfortable even speaking to the guy who had made life so miserable for Mei.

"Things are off for me in New York as well," Jimmi said.

"Things are off there for everyone," Jack said as he eyed the cigar humidor on the conference table. Jimmi pushed the humidor toward him, but Jack put his hand up. "*Bu yao, bu yao.*"

"So you've been in China before?" Jimmi asked.

"A while back," Jack said.

"Who did that to your friend?"

"A very excitable boy," Jack said.

"A dead one?"

"Probably by now."

"That's not good."

"No."

"And he worked for?"

"Some guy named Yao."

"Yao? What's this Yao do?"

"He's in the jewelry business."

Jimmi's eyes opened wide. "Hah? Yao Chow Fook?"

"That's him."

"What are you doing fooling around with a guy like that?"

"What kind of guy is he?" Jack asked.

"A very bad guy. Seriously, what the hell were you doing?"

"I appreciate your help with Victor. Thanks very much," Jack said.

"You're way over your head," Jimmi said as he stared at Jack.

Jack looked over at Tao watching the two of them talk. He had heard and understood most of the words, and his eyes remained steely. "Thanks again," Jack said to Jimmi. "Really."

"Yao Fook shut down his legit jewelry business a while ago," Jimmi said, half talking to himself. "Last I heard he was buying raw jade from Burma. You're not running stones, are you?"

Jack forced himself to scoff. "What would make me stupid enough to do something like that?"

"It wouldn't necessarily be stupid at all. Especially not if that smelter of yours has trucks permitted to go to Burma." Jimmi studied Jack's face. "I've just never seen a white guy with the balls to do it."

"But in the end, running jade is stupid?" Jack asked.

"The problem is, it's never just running jade," Jimmi said.

"Meaning?"

"Look, jade is beautiful. And running stones is beautiful. Hell, everybody wins. But it leads to other things. Things way beyond your control. Beyond your understanding. You're a foreigner, for God's sake."

"What things?" Jack asked.

"Drugs, slaves. Bad things," Jimi said, his golden face betraying nothing.

"Ever run any jade yourself?"

Jimmi laughed. "I grew up in New York's Chinatown. What do you think?"

Jack shrugged. He wanted Jimmi to talk.

"If there's an angle, I've done it: loansharking; gambling; girls. Running jade too."

"What's your main thing now?" Jack asked.

"Girls. The world loves girls," Jimmi said, but not affectionately, as if he were a rancher speaking of beef or pork. "Karaoke clubs. Casinos. That kind of thing. Great cash businesses. China would collapse without them," Jimmi said, studying Jack's face for any reaction as he spoke.

"So, no interest in running jade," Jack said.

Jimmi said, "You need a clear line of supply. I do a ton of business in Burma, but I've never had the right relationship with the Kachin to get involved with jade. They control a lot of the stones, and most of the highways, and they're not high on Chinese these days."

"Fair enough," Jack said. "Speaking of Burma, have you ever run across a white guy down there named Costa?"

"Who hasn't?" Jimmi said, his face impassive. "Costa's the man to see in Burma for drugs—and girls." Jimmi raised his eyebrows and winked. "One of Burma's best exports."

"He's the one who introduced me to Yao," Jack said.

"You're probably buying your charcoal from him," Jimmi guessed. "He's got a monopoly on the stuff down there. The girls too."

Tao had been sitting and listening, but was starting to fidget. He tapped Jack on the shoulder, leaned over and whispered in his ear: "Jade still in car." They had left the jade in the back of the car, not knowing they would be inside for so long.

Jack had little choice. He threw the poker chip into the pot. "Want to see the jade Mr. Yao tried to steal from us?" he asked Jimmi.

Jimmi appeared surprised, but only momentarily. "Why not?"

Jack nodded at Tao. "*Dui*," he said. "Go check, and bring a bag back up."

Tao hurried out of the office.

"How about a drink?" Jimmi asked when Tao had left.

"No thanks," Jack said, not interested in drinking with Jimmi Zeng.

"How's Mei working out for you?"

"Fine; thanks for sending her," Jack said.

"When can I get her back?"

Jack tried not to pay attention to the twinge in his chest. "I guess that's up to her," he deadpanned.

"Hardly," Jimmi said, standing up and going over to his golf bag. He pulled an iron out of the bag and took a few half-swings. "It's not her decision. She's yours as long as you need her, and then it's back to the salt mines."

Jack found it difficult to stay conversational. "What's that supposed to mean?"

"She owes me," Jimmi said, not looking at Jack as he dropped the club back into his golf bag. He took out another club and glanced up at Jack. "She's mine," he said, as he studied Jack's face. "Mei belongs here. I've got big plans for her."

Jack wanted to break the club over the man's head.

As Jimmi swung the club toward him, he read the expression on Jack's face. "Ah, another love-smitten white guy," he said, not smiling. "She does it to everyone. That's why I had to get her out of New York," Jimmi said, examining Jack to gauge his reaction.

Jack knew better than to say anything.

Jimmi shook his head back and forth. "Don't do it," he warned. "This is China, remember? It's best to stay out of things you don't understand."

Jack was about to tell the slimy bastard to shut the hell up, that Mei would return over his dead body, when he heard footsteps in the hall. A moment later, Tao lugged in a bag of stones and dropped it next to the conference table.

"Here, take a look," Jack said, bending over the bag and extracting a handful of stones. He laid them out on the conference table.

Jimmi put his club back in the golf bag, picked up a stone, and eyed it. His nails were manicured. Poker-faced, he put the stone down on the table, and walked over to his desk. Fetching a pair of black-rimmed glasses, he returned and picked up another stone. He examined the second one, put it down, and selected a third. Then he opened the bag of jade and studied several more stones. He exhaled as he sat back down at the conference table. "Where'd you get these?" he asked Jack.

"From the KIA."

"Through Costa?"

"That's what he would tell you, but not really."

"They're jewelry grade. What'd you pay for them?"

"A good price."

"What are you going to do with them?"

"We were supposed to sell them to Yao," Jack said.

"Costa arranged that?"

"Supposedly," Jack scoffed. "I'm thinking now that's as phony as his story about the CIA. I didn't see bags of cash at Yao's place, that's for sure."

"Did you ask Yao for the money?"

"We didn't get that far," Jack said.

"He just decided to relieve you of the stones," Jimmi said.

"Something like that," Jack said. Feeling his face flush, he leaned back in the chair and stared up at the ceiling for a moment before plunging ahead. "There's no point in beating around the bush. What can you pay me for them?" he asked Jimmi.

Jimmi eyes remained flat. "I told you; I'm not in the business anymore."

"I heard you."

"You lost me, then."

Jack wondered for a second what Mei would think about what he was about to say. He told himself he was right, and she would agree. He had no choice but to make a deal with the scumbag. "I can't sit on these stones. Give me a price to take them off my hands."

"For me to consider doing that, you're going to have to tell me what this is really all about," Jimmi said.

Jack had to make a sale; otherwise, they'd be out 3 million RMB. "You want supply? We've got a direct line to the KIA," he said, speaking loudly and slowly so that Tao could hear and understand. He knew no Chinese guy ever accepted a white guy's opinion for anything, but hoped that when Jimmi buttonholed Tao he could pick up the script and run with it. "And we've got a hundred permitted trucks."

Jimmi picked up one of the stones, turned it over in his hand, and placed it back on the table. The stone was gashed open, the jadeite inside sparkling in the beam of the ceiling light, floating on the tan wood of the table like a green stalk of life on a windswept plain.

Jimmi went over to his desk, sat down, pulled out a pen, and made some notes. Without apologies, he started peppering Tao with questions in Chinese, as if Jack wasn't even in the room.

"*Dui,*" Tao answered, doing his part. "*Dui.*" When Jimmi was done with his questions, Tao went on the offensive, speaking firmly, pressing more points to Jimmi.

Finished, Jimmi looked back at Jack. "Okay; I get the picture. It looks like you've got things lined up, coming and going. That could be a different situation."

"I'm glad you agree," Jack said.

"I said maybe." Jimmi paused for a moment, fished an abacus out of a desk drawer, and did some calculations. "How much jade is in your car?"

Jack said, "There's two hundred and fifty of those bags. Twelve hundred kilos."

Jimmy pushed around the beads on the abacus. "I can take this lot off your hands for three thousand RMB a kilo," Jimmi said, the words trailing behind him as he stood up and walked over to his golf bag again.

"I'm told the going price in Kunming is five thousand," Jack said.

"That may be, but this is a fire sale," Jimmi said clinically, pulling out his putter. "You've got to make it worth my while." He held the putter with both hands down in front of him, and eyed an imaginary line down the carpet.

"Four thousand RMB per kilo today, and you're my permanent outlet," Jack said.

"At the same price?"

Jack thought about it for a moment. "Not quite. After this, five thousand a kilo for the first ten million RMB. After that, it's a jump ball."

"And Mei returns on the next plane," Jimmi said.

"Forget it," Jack managed to stammer, about to blow his cool and smash the guy's too-pretty face, Tao watching him disapprovingly.

"Just kidding," Jimmi said, having sized up his adversary. "For me to pay a price like that in the future, it will be imperative that we use your trucks for girls as well."

"Not interested," Jack said.

"Don't be so quick to say no to doubling your money. We can talk about it some other time," Jimmi said.

"Right now, I need to know about this time," Jack said.

Jimmi swung his putter toward the imaginary cup, his eyes following the line of the ball, ending up on Jack where he sat across the room. "Deal," he said, as if the ball had dropped into the hole.

———

An hour north of Dehong, Jack woke up. Tao was driving. Victor, his arm trussed in bandages, was sleeping next to him in the back seat. Jack yawned, then realized Mei was turned halfway around in her seat, waiting for him to open his eyes.

"Did he talk about me?" she asked.

"Not a word," Jack lied.

She seemed relieved.

"Do you think Jimmi Zeng buys any of those girls down at Costa's camp?" Jack asked her.

"Are you kidding?" Mei said. "All of them—except the ones who go to work in the casino. Jimmi's the market in Yunnan, and Costa's his main source of supply."

"Jesus," Jack said, "no wonder you didn't want to go to the casino. Why didn't you say something?"

"I tried," Mei said, "but it wasn't my place." She brushed the hair out of her eyes.

Jack thought carefully about his next words. "He didn't seem to view you as just a—you know—karaoke girl."

"That's because I'm not," she said, shaking her head back and forth. "He's a god and I'm…I'm…" she exhaled, frustrated, "whatever he wants me to be that day. Think about it," she said.

"I don't want to," Jack said.

Mei said, "While you were sleeping, Tao was telling me what Jimmi told him."

The high beams of a big rig going the opposite direction whitened Mei's face like the sun shining on the moon. As soon as the truck was gone, Tao pulled out in the passing lane on the straightaway, hit the accelerator, and gunned the car down the highway, passing a half-dozen farm vehicles.

"He said he likes the deal, but warned Tao he could get killed working with amateurs."

Jack leaned back in semi-consciousness, trying to forget what Mei had just told him. With a little less than five million RMB stuffed in a bag at his feet and having just cleared close to four hundred thousand bucks in his first jade transaction, it would be nice to feel good about something for a change.

Like he used to feel back in his glitter days in New York. After one of his closings, everyone gathered around the Four Seasons bar and laughing at Jack's stupid jokes. He knew he wasn't funny but he enjoyed those times, laying steps in the stairway he was building to the top of the world. Knowing in truth he might not get there, but at a point in his life where he could still fool himself in the process.

But Jimmi's words rang in his head. An amateur. The man was right. Forget any savvy and experience he might have garnered in other venues, that's all Jack was ever going to be in this part of the world. He remembered how sympathetic he had felt when some likable bumpkin stumbled into his investment firm in New York, pitching a deal he was utterly incapable of accomplishing. Jack felt as much empathy for those few souls who realized their true odds as the scorn he held for the rest, the majority of supplicants who assumed just because they had read about a transaction in *The Wall Street Journal* they had what it took to pull off the same thing themselves. Already fooling themselves, thinking they could fool him too.

Jack wasn't fooling anybody. They had just risked their lives for a lousy four hundred thousand bucks.

CHAPTER 15

Dawn arrived Tuesday morning as Tao wended his way through the outskirts of Mangshi and up the mountain to the smelter, going slow for Victor's sake. Cocks were crowing when they arrived at the gate of the compound. In front of the office building where Tao and Mei dropped them off, Jack held Victor up straight, wrapping one arm around his shoulder, and then guided his friend upstairs to bed.

Jack lay down on his cot, pulled his mosquito net over him, and tried to sleep. But the roosters wouldn't shut up, a dog started barking, and he had too much on his mind. He checked on Victor. Out cold.

Jack got out of bed, did his exercises, and stepped into the shower. Goosebumps formed as the icy water chilled his skin. Scraping at his face with a razor, he craned his neck around the door of the washroom to verify that Jimmi's bag of cash was still where he had left it under his cot. He dressed, wandered over to the dormitory kitchen for a cup of watery coffee, and came back to the office.

As he sat alone, the morning fog began to burn off, and patches of blue opened up. A scent of jasmine wafted through the open door, and he could feel the warmth of the dry season's sun. The elements were conspiring, telling him he should feel good. But he knew better.

He had figured running jade would be an acceptable gambit. No one was going to jail, and the cash flow would bolster the smelter's basic business until things improved. But they had just narrowly missed being killed, at least one man was dead in Kunming, and

SOUTH OF THE CLOUDS

the agents they had been forced to use on both sides of the transaction were human scum. It wasn't worth it. Not for a few hundred thousand dollars, when people he cared about could have been badly injured or worse. And if running jade wasn't a good idea, he had no idea what was.

———

That afternoon in the cafeteria when they were finished with lunch, Jack told Tao and Mei that since Monday's Kunming trip had displaced the smelter's monthly business meeting, they'd do it that afternoon, and asked them to be in the office in an hour.

A short time later, he wasn't surprised when the screen door of the office screeched open and Victor limped in. "How do you feel?" Jack asked.

"Better than yesterday," Victor said, collapsing in his seat. "Did everything work out all right with Jimmi?"

Jack exhaled. "Look, he bailed us out bigtime. You, and us."

"So what's wrong with that?" Victor said, eying Jack as if he knew there was more to come.

"Do you know what Mei told me? Jimmi's the one buying Costa's girls."

"She would know," Victor said. "No wonder he has a competent medical staff on call."

"You sure you should be up and about?" Jack asked him.

"We've got some sorting out to do," Victor said.

Jack said, "You're reading my mind," finding Victor's ashtray for him.

Tao and Mei arrived. Mei set a thermos of hot water and a brace of empty mugs on the table, and passed around teabags.

"Ready?" Tao asked, looking like he wanted to get down to business.

"Just a second," Jack said, gathering his thoughts. "You guys were incredible yesterday. All of you," he said, looking each of them in the eye as he spoke. "And I was wrong about this."

"The only thing you were wrong about," Victor said before Jack could say anything more, "was that one truck of jade isn't nearly enough." He took a long drag of his cigarette and blew the smoke out the open doorway. "But let's hear Tao's report first. I think he's going to make my case."

"Take it away *Taozong*," Jack said.

Tao referred to handwritten notes. For the majority of his presentation, he spoke in Chinese to Mei, who translated to Jack and Victor. He breezed along, reporting routine smelting regimes, no machinery problems, and stable raw material costs. He pulled out his computer and took them through the production runs. They were managing their costs while experiencing adequate demand for smelted products, but profitability wouldn't occur until they received much stronger orders. After ten minutes, he finished and looked across the table at Jack and Victor, waiting for questions.

"Well, that's a nice operating report," Victor said, fishing another cigarette out of his pocket with his good hand, "but meanwhile, we're hemorrhaging cash."

"What can I say? You were right," Jack said, taking Victor's cigarette and lighting it for him.

"About?" Victor asked, standing up and walking to the open door.

"Your prediction for the business a year ago."

"Hardly. I projected we'd be able to pay down Continental in three years," Victor said from where he stood in the doorway. He took a drag on his cigarette and then tossed it outside and returned to the table.

"One drag?" Jack said. "That's a pretty expensive smoke."

"I'm trying to stave off cancer until the next knife fight does me in," Victor said. "I don't know why you're in such a good mood. Monsoon season will be back before you can sneeze. After that, the roads will become impassible and the quartz mines will shut down. Meanwhile, without the pop from the jade run, we'd be out of working capital by the end of the year."

Raindrops plopped on the roof. "I hate the goddamn rainy season," Jack said, glaring at the morning sky, willing the clouds away.

"We're going to the bank tomorrow to deposit our cash. We can try to hit them up for a loan."

"All that means is we'll be working for two banks, not one," Victor said.

Tao leaned over to Mei and began whispering, his eyes blinking like an all-knowing sea turtle.

Mei said, "Tao said he heard that while the roads are still dry, the *Tatmadaw* will launch an offensive to cut off the KIA's ability to sell jade."

Jack said, "So let me guess: the KIA probably would like to do another deal sooner rather than later."

"Want to sell many stones now," Tao affirmed.

"And that could also mean we don't have to worry about the *Tatmadaw* wasting time on us," Victor said, clearing his throat.

"Is this the part where you suggest a really big run?" Jack asked him.

"No, this is when I *insist* on one really big, *last* run," Victor said. "Then we get the hell out of here."

———

At sunrise the next morning, Jack walked in the door of the kitchen. Standing in an apron next to the stove, her back to him, Mei was the only person in the room. As she heard the door open, she turned and looked over her shoulder, smiling when she saw him.

"What are you doing here?" he asked.

"Sit down and find out."

He did as he was told, happy to watch her. Mei went outside and returned with an armful of wood, stuffing it into the firebox. She drew water from the pump into a kettle, poured some of it into a couple of pans on the stovetop, and put the kettle on another burner. At the prep table, she chopped and diced things with a large kitchen knife. The pans started to boil, steam rising to the ceiling. Mei ladled something from one of the pans into a white porcelain bowl and, carrying it with both hands, walked over to where he sat at the table and set it in front of him. "Rice soup," she said.

He tasted it. "It's good; like cream of wheat." He ate some more.

While he ate, she chopped more things at the prep table. She brought over a bowl of cut fruit—strawberries and kiwis and apples and oranges—covered with yoghurt and sprinkled with chopped nuts. Returning to the stove, she ladled something else out of a second pan and then placed another steaming bowl in front of him.

"Pear soup. With herbs from Tibet," she said. "It's good for you." A minute later, she brought a mug of instant coffee and a small pitcher of milk and sat down across from him.

"So you cook too."

Perspiration from the heat of the stove glistened on her forehead. "All Chinese women cook. I can teach you if you like." She smiled.

"I can boil water. That's as much as I need to know," Jack said. She laughed. "You could cook if you wanted to," she said.

Jack ate a spoonful of fruit, and drank some of his coffee. "Not everyone can do what you've done the last few days."

"It was nothing," she said. "I'm used to it."

"That's a lot to get used to," Jack said.

Mei said, "I'll bet your wife was the same."

Jack took a deep breath. "Yes, she was," he said, reminiscing, automatically expecting guilt to kick in, as if he was violating a trust by talking about Hadley with Mei. But it didn't happen. That's when it struck him: given the circumstances, Hadley would have approved.

Mei said, "You could teach me something."

"What?"

"How to invest money."

"So you've come into a fortune recently?" Jack joked.

"I could help you," she insisted.

"*Teach me how to invest money.*" That's the same thing Tie Liu had said to Jack when they had started the hydroelectric company in China. "Should I tell you what happened with the last person who asked me that?" he said.

"As you wish," she said tentatively.

Jack said, "It was a Chinese guy named Tie Liu. I asked him and another man named Lin Boxu to be my partners when I established my hydroelectric company here. Tie was a country bumpkin from Henan, and extremely unpolished. But smart, and ambitious. He asked me to teach him how to invest in hydroelectric projects, so I did."

"I've warned you about people from Henan," Mei said, unsmiling as she stared back at Jack. "What happened?"

Jack shrugged. "Tie tricked Lin Boxu, who was a Princeling but very weak, into a plan to steal the company from me. Tie convinced Lin that the two of them should control the company, not a *laowai*. They arranged for a group of Chinese investors to back them, buy a majority of the shares in the open market, and take over. The day they told me I was out was the last time I ever saw them."

"Men from Henan are liars," Mei said. She got up to clear the table, and then walked back over to him. "Not like you." When he tried to say something more, she held two fingers to his lips, not letting him, and kissed him on the forehead.

He wanted to say more to her. A lot more. She wasn't just beautiful, she was smart, diligent, and tough as nails. He could sit in front of her forever, watch her full lips when she spoke to him, her eyes when she smiled, the casual way she brushed the hair out of her face. He liked being close enough to smell her. He wanted her, and was tired of fighting it.

After breakfast, he went back to his room to check on Victor. Then he fetched Mei and Tao and the three of them drove into Mangshi to deposit the winnings from their jade run at the bank.

The Farmer's Bank offices were located on the town's main street right across from Mangshi's open air market. As they entered, Tao got the bank manager's attention, all smiles when Tao told him Jack was there to make a significant deposit. The man motioned for them to follow him up to a large, sweat shop-like room on the second floor where a dozen women were at work.

Between the sounds of the marketplace coming through the open windows and the clack and whir of bank machines, it was very noisy. The manager leaned over and said something to Mei, motioning toward a Steelcase table in front of them. "Please," Mei said to Jack, taking his satchel of hundred RMB notes and pouring them out onto the table. A sour-looking lady—the head clerk—eyed the pile of money, spread it out with her hands, selected a random note, and held it up to the light. She tossed the note back on the pile and repeated the process with another note, and then repeated it again.

Jack looked at Mei and raised his eyebrows: with the racket, it was difficult to have a conversation.

Mei said loudly toward Jack over the din, "Checking for counterfeit money."

Satisfied, the head clerk regarded Jack like a human being for the first time, said something to the bank manager, and then she and her team of clerks fed the money into machines that counted and stacked, wrapping the pink blocks of notes with white paper tape into hundred thousand RMB packages.

"It's a miracle they're taking this loose cash. We'd never get away with this in New York," Jack said to Mei, the background noise obscuring his words. "Money laundering," he said when she looked at him with a puzzled expression.

They followed the manager downstairs to his office and took chairs around his conference table. His milkmaid accomplice appeared, smiled at everyone, and sat down without a word, followed by a woman in an apron serving green tea.

"Is this where they get bribed?" Jack asked Mei as they sipped their tea.

Mei ignored Jack's joke as the manager, an obsequious smile on his face, presented Jack with a receipt for his deposit.

"Tell him business is good, and I'd like him to lend us twenty million," Jack said to Mei, maintaining a pleasant expression for the manager's benefit. "US dollars, not RMB. We'll do him a favor and pledge our receivables."

As Mei delivered the pitch, the manager maintained the same dumb expression, doing what Chinese culture dictated that all men do, sit there and look stupid while trying to act smart. He finally asked Mei a question.

"He asks what you will do with the proceeds of the loan," Mei said to Jack.

"General purposes," Jack said, a calm expression plastered on his face, knowing that any banker anywhere in the world says no when asked for a loan that will be used solely to pay off the previous sucker.

Mei replied to the manager, and the conversation went around in circles. Finally, the man offered what sounded like final words to Mei.

"Sorry," Mei said to Jack, "he says he can't do a big loan now. What about a smaller one?"

"Ask him what he can do," Jack said to Mei, "but he's not getting our receivables."

"He doesn't care about that," Mei said, "just his bribe." She spoke to the manager for a minute, who responded with some words and a greasy smirk.

Mei said to Jack, "He can do fifty million RMB."

Jack sighed. "It's better than nothing," he muttered.

Mei went back to completing arrangements with the manager. Shortly, the meeting sounded like it was coming to an end. "*Hada, hada,*" Mei and Tao both said as they stood up together with the manager and his milkmaid, the four of them nodding like bobble-head dolls, smiling, adding more "*hada, hadas*" and finally shaking hands, ending the ritual with a chorus of "*ha, ha, ha's.*"

"The fifty's done," Mei said to Jack as they got up to leave. "Subject to Tao taking care of him later," she whispered under her breath as everyone smiled their goodbyes to the manager and his paramour.

"I'm glad you're on my side," Jack said to her.

Mei said, "It would help for you to be a little more Chinese."

"Victor's right; it's time to get the hell out of here," Jack said.

———

"I got some cash from the bank, but not enough to refinance our way out of this mess," Jack said to Victor in the late afternoon when they returned from the bank.

"You knew that was going to happen," Victor said, getting up from his computer.

They fetched the bottle of Hennessey and some glasses and sat outside in the early Dehong evening, the geckos chirping in the grass and butterflies floating on the thermals.

Victor sipped his cognac. "According to my calculations, a big jade run—twenty-five trucks—gets us half way to the same place."

Jack lit a cigar. "Jesus Christ," he said, "twenty-five trucks? It'll look like Macy's Thanksgiving Day parade out there. And that only gets us half-way home? I was hoping we could do one more run and be done with this goddamned place." He tried to blow a circle of smoke, but couldn't. "But forget fifty trucks. The spy agencies would spot us from the satellites if we tried that," he said, and laughed.

"At least you've still got a sense of humor," Victor said, tossing his cigarette.

"On a serious note, whatever we do, we're going to need KIA protection this time," Jack continued. "All the way: going in, and coming out."

"Especially in and out of Costa's," Victor said. "We're stuck buying charcoal from that fat bastard, and he'll be looking to get even. I don't trust him as far as I can throw him. Do you think Jimmi will spring for the jade again?"

"That's the other thing," Jack said. "I don't see how we can look ourselves in the mirror unless we try to help those women. But if Jimmi's involved, that compounds the problem. He's already told me he wants the girls in the trucks," Jack said as he drank some Hennessey. "You know what I'd love to do to that smartass? Pitch him a curve. Somehow get him salivating over the girls, then fool him with an off-speed delivery and shut him down."

Victor said, "If your pitch involves luring him to Costa's, I wouldn't worry. Twenty-five trucks full of girls? He won't be able to say no."

"The trick is," Jack said, "to get him up there, and then bush-whack him somehow."

Victor said, "I'll bet the KIA would be game."

"You might be right," Jack said. "Did you see those KIA soldiers when the Thai guy was raping that girl? They were furious. Costa's no partner of theirs." Jack snorted. "He's just an AWOL serviceman holed up in the woods making heroin, trafficking slave women, and selling charcoal. Major Maran has been so occupied with the *Tatmadaw*, he's had no idea what's going on right under his nose."

"The problem is, it's an even fight at best," Victor cautioned. "Costa's mercenaries are killers. Meanwhile, did you see the KIA guys in our escort? Kids. Those Thais would have to be taken off the field if we're going to get in and out of there safely."

"What we need is a distraction," Jack said. "A big one."

Victor said, "If you want a guy who ought to care about blowing Costa out, it would be that Chinese general in charge of stopping drugs. General Dong. With some of that artillery of his, he could launch a *very* big distraction."

"I think I see a plan coming into focus," Jack said, pouring the last of the Hennessey into their glasses.

"I'll make some notes," Victor said, getting up to go into the office.

"Look at it this way," Jack said when Victor returned with his pad and pencil. "If all we can pull off is another run like last time, that's not the end of the world."

Victor said, "I don't know about you, but at this point, I'm feeling like a horse headed to the barn."

Jack took a drag on his cigar. "You know what Jimmi told Tao we were?" he said, looking across the Mangshi valley toward Burma. "Amateurs."

"It's good he's thinking that way," Victor said.

———

The next morning when Jack walked into the office, Victor looked up from his computer screen with a grin on his face. "We got an offer from the Spaniards last night."

"FerroAtlantique?" Jack asked.

"The largest silicon smelterer in the world," Victor confirmed. "The offer sucks, but still—it's an offer."

"What would they want with this hunk of iron?" Jack asked.

"Hey, give yourself a little credit," Victor said. "Maybe the timing was off, but you had the right idea here. No one is going to be able to run silicon smelting operations in the West anymore. Between the electricity costs and the environmental rules, that's over. And the market's moving here too."

"So what'd they propose?" Jack asked.

"A lousy price," Victor said, "for the equity. But they'd assume the debt."

"Thank you, Jesus," Jack exhaled.

"Don't get too excited," Victor said. "They're bottom fishers."

"Hold on, though," Jack said. "If, God willing, this deal were to work out, not only would the bank be off our back, but we might be able to use a loss on our equity to shelter any gains from selling the jade."

"Exactly. We sell the smelter at a loss, write down the gain, and come out way, way ahead," Victor said.

Jack said, "Let's stop talking about it."

The next day, Jack called Chin to ask him to get ahold of Costa, tell them they were coming back soon for more charcoal, but Chin was out. Jack and Victor were closing the office up for the day, everyone else already up at the cafeteria having dinner, when Chin finally showed up. His face was mottled and discolored.

"There you are," Jack said to him. "We need you to give Costa a call, let him know we'll be coming back soon for more charcoal." He took a closer look at Chin. "Have you been drinking?"

Blocking the doorway, Chin mumbled something.

Jack and Victor said nothing, waiting for Chin to spit it out.

"Jade run because of me," Chin finally stammered, not able to look at either one of them. "I need bonus."

SOUTH OF THE CLOUDS

"And you're going to get one," Jack said, trying to be reassuring. But he couldn't clear his mind of how much Chin reminded him of Tie Liu, the chubby little scumbag with the equally misshapen face. "A big bonus," Jack repeated. "December starts next week, and Spring Festival is two months away. Everyone in China gets their bonuses then, and we're going to show you our appreciation, you can be sure of it."

"I need bonus now," Chin whined. "I know Costa. You don't know him. I negotiate with Major Maran too. Jade deal nothing without me," Chin said, raising his voice.

"You know better than that," Jack said to Chin as gently as he could. He could smell baiju on Chin's breath. "You'd be better off to drop the subject."

"Liu gave me ten percent," Chin said. "I know everyone. My job very difficult; very important."

"I see," Jack said. "So this is one of those Chinese deals where the stupid *laowai* are supposed to pay a finder to find a finder, right? I don't think so. Don't be a fool; you're part of a good team. But if you're unhappy with your job, I'm sure there's someone else who would love to have it."

Angry, Chin marched out.

"There's your Chinese Judas," Victor said.

"You never know," Jack said. "It could be. Here's how to tell. Rather than cut him out, we keep him close to us. Feed him some misinformation, and then watch him like a hawk, see what he does with it."

CHAPTER 16

When everyone showed up in the cafeteria for breakfast the next morning, Jack asked Tao and Chin to contact Major Maran and let him know they wanted a meeting.

"How much jade this time?" Tao asked.

"No jade now. We just need to talk, make a plan for a big run," Jack said. "Maybe we could do it in Laiza?"

Chin pulled out his mobile and searched for the major's number.

"What's the Burmese expression for hello?" Jack asked Tao.

"*Min ge la ba*," Tao said.

"*Min ge la ba*," Jack said, repeating the words to himself. "Major Maran deserves a friendly greeting."

Chin reached the major and made arrangements. A day later, the four men headed to Laiza in a permitted Forland transport. Chin shepherded them through the customs booth at Ruili and the border patrol gate at Mai Ja Yang with no issues. Curling around the hills west of the border, they kept their eyes peeled for *Tatmadaw*, but saw no patrols. They reached the tiny KIA stronghold an hour later, and the Forland lumbered down Laiza's dusty, potholed main street. Perched on the side of a mountain, the ramshackle settlement, jammed with shops and Chinese peddlers, seemed as if it might begin rolling down the hill at any moment. Reaching the opposite end of town, they passed through the gates of KIA headquarters.

Major Maran and his two sidekicks were waiting for them in a non-descript office.

"*Min ge la ba*," Jack said to the major when they sat down.

Major Maran flashed a smile of appreciation, but otherwise appeared disgruntled. True to character, he began spouting Burmese to Chin before his aides had served tea.

"He say sorry. No sell jade," Tao whispered in an aside to Jack and Victor while Major Maran was lecturing Chin. "He very, very upset about Costa's camp. About women." Tao's jaw tightened as the major kept talking.

"Hey Chin, doesn't the major know we don't have anything to do with that?" Jack said while the major was still speaking.

"If not, please tell him," Victor added.

But Chin was unresponsive. Sullen, he wasn't going to make their case, let alone translate. When the major was finished, Chin slumped in his seat.

Tao shook his head. "I tell him," he said, and launched into a discussion with the major.

A few minutes later, Major Maran's frown disappeared. He asked Tao a couple of questions, appeared to get the answers he needed, and leaned back, more relaxed.

"No problem," Tao said. "Costa tell him you good partners. I say no," he said. "Now major understand. He say jade OK…" Tao said, starting to give Jack and Victor a thumbs-up sign.

And then Major Maran interrupted Tao before he could finish.

Tao listened, and then nodded. "Last time you tell him buy ten times more jade next time," Tao said, his white teeth exposed. "That make him very happy. Ten trucks this time, he give same price as before."

"Tell him we're going to do even better than that," Jack said. "We're sending twenty-five trucks," he said, emphasizing the words.

Major Maran didn't know much English, but he knew what twenty-five meant. He smiled broadly.

Chin started to pay attention.

"But," Jack said, holding up his forefinger for emphasis, "only if we get protection."

Tao spoke to the major, whose face once again soured. His words were terse.

"He say no can do," Tao said, shaking his head. "He need men next month for fighting."

"We want to do it next week, not next month," Jack said. "But without his help, with that many trucks we'll be jumped by the *Tatmadaw* for sure. No escort, no cash."

Tao spoke to the major, who laughed. "He say no problem next week; *Tatmadaw* only come next month," Tao said.

"We're talking next week," Jack emphasized.

Sitting up, Chin couldn't disguise his surprise.

Tao and Major Maran spoke to each other a minute more.

Tao said, "If you bring twenty-five trucks next week, he give you full protection. Also make special deal for you in Bhamo. Friend has Imperial jade there, but he leave soon. Very, very best jade. Special green color."

Chin's eyes widened.

"Like the color of apples in springtime," Victor said, as if he was reciting the words. "I've read about Imperial jade. They say it turns the Chinese insane."

"As if we haven't got enough to deal with," Jack said. "How much does he want for it?" Jack asked Tao.

Tao spoke to Major Maran. "He say twelve stones worth thirty million RMB in Hong Kong. His friend sell to you for ten million."

Jack and Victor glanced sideways at one another. Maybe they could finish with one big run after all. With the upside from a haul of Imperial jade, the profits from the run could total close to the twenty million they needed. But they said nothing.

"We're not saying no," Jack said, "but we'd need to see the stones. How do we get ahold of this guy?"

Tao translated to Major Maran, who pulled out a piece of paper and wrote a name and number on it. As he handed it across the table toward Jack, Chin reached for it, but Jack lunged and grabbed it first.

"Thanks Major," Jack said, as Chin tried to wipe the embarrassment off his face. "We'll think about it. But whether we buy the Imperial jade or not, we need an escort—in and out—until we leave Costa's."

After Tao translated, Major Maran started talking, his face hard. Tao said, "Major ask: why you need Costa?"

Jack said, "There's nowhere else to go for twenty-five truck-loads of charcoal. But that's our only involvement with Costa going forward."

Tao conferred with the major some more. "He say OK. But only put charcoal in trucks at Costa's. No women. He very, very angry. He send troops to stop Costa."

"An excellent idea," Jack said, Victor nodding for emphasis. "We were planning to suggest that ourselves. He should send those men right behind our trucks. We get the charcoal, and the major's men take care of Costa. Just to confirm, the major's talking next week, right *Taozong*?"

Tao said something to Major Maran, who with a serious expression gave Jack the thumbs-up sign: "Next week," the major said in English.

———

On the way home when they were a few miles north of Ruili, Jack's mobile showed bars. He called Mei.

"Where are you?" she asked as soon as the call went through.

"On my way back from Laiza. Everything's fine."

"The *Tatmadaw* are down there. I was worried."

"Don't be. We're China side now."

"When will you be home?"

"An hour or so. You need anything?"

"What do you mean?"

"You know what I'm saying. This is what American men do when they've had a good day at the office: call home and ask if you need anything. Like some milk from the store."

She didn't say anything, but he could tell she was pleased.

"So, you need anything?"

"A coffee pot and some real coffee."

Early the next morning, leaving Victor behind to recuperate, Jack flew to Kunming to pay a visit to Jimmi Zeng. At noon, he sat across from Jimmi at his desk. Jack had called ahead and was expected. But after inviting him to sit down, Jimmi seemed intent on playing a silly mind game, acting as if he was otherwise occupied. With Jack at the desk in front of him, Jimmi furrowed his brow as he fooled around for several minutes with a couple of pieces of raw jade and a magnifying glass. A man served green tea.

"What kind of reception did you get with the stones?" Jack said when he figured he had waited long enough to be polite.

Jimmi looked up as if Jack had interrupted him. "I figured you'd ask me that," Jimmi said, setting aside the things on his desk. "My guess is you're thinking you survived your debut, so you'll be going back to Burma soon. Probably do a big run, pay off your banks, and get out of here," Jimmi said, probably imagining he sounded to Jack like a fortuneteller, not realizing he was merely confirming that he and Chin were talking.

"We're taking twenty-five trucks down," Jack said. "Next week."

"Costa involved with the jade this time?" Jimmi asked.

Jack said, "We're dealing direct with the KIA."

Jimmi said, "He's not going to be too happy about that. Where you getting your charcoal?" he asked. "Costa's the only large player down there."

"We'll hold our nose and buy his charcoal. Letting him make a few bucks isn't the end of the world," Jack lied.

"Who's going to buy all the jade?" Jimmi asked, a smug expression on his face, as if convinced he was the obvious solution.

Jack surprised him. "I understand that amount of jade might be a tall order for you. But with twenty-five truckloads, we've got takers," he said. "The buyers at the Ruili jade market are very interested."

Jimmi frowned. "Wait a second. I thought we were a team on this," he said.

"Of course we'd like to be," Jack said. "We're just keeping some irons in the fire in case you get cold feet. We'd love to sell the jade to you. Subject, of course, to the price we agreed on." He stopped talking, and began slowly counting to twenty.

Jimmi picked up one of the jade stones on his desk and examined it through his magnifying glass. "A *laowai* who doesn't say what's on his mind makes me nervous," he said a minute later.

"Where does it say the Chinese are the only ones allowed to be inscrutable?" Jack said, forcing a laugh.

"The difference," Jimmi said, getting up from his desk, "is that for the Chinese, it's not learned behavior."

"Don't kid yourself."

Jimmi walked over to his golf bag and began fooling with his putter. "What price do you have in mind?"

Jack just looked at Jimmi.

After a few moments, the golden boy smiled. "Are you going to tell me?"

"I don't need to. We already agreed on a price," Jack said.

"You mean five thousand RMB a kilo?"

Jack nodded.

Jimmi said, "But this is a different situation."

Jack said, "Right you are. This isn't a fire sale."

Jimmi's face soured. "What about those empty mules of yours?"

"The charcoal trucks?" Jack asked, doing his best to answer casually. "I'm surprised. You're the one who warned me to stay away from the dark side of jade. Like trafficking girls."

Jimmi said, "I might consider doing five thousand a kilo, but I said the deal depended on the girls being in the trucks." He walked back to his golf bag and traded his putter for an iron. "You've got a distribution channel: take advantage of it." He forced a big Hollywood smile on Jack. "You'll see. The girls—and the drugs they're carrying—make the deal twice as good." He took a practice half-swing down the carpet.

"Do this deal," Jack said, "and I'll think about it," he lied, watching Jimmi feign a laugh at the *laowai's* effort to negotiate, the skin around his eyes crinkling. "And one other thing," Jack said. "We're not bringing the jade to Kunming. You're going to need to meet us at Costa's with the cash." As Jack studied Jimmi's face in the light of day, he realized that the golden boy had undergone a facelift.

It was Jimmi's turn to be inscrutable. "I heard the KIA are trying to unload some Imperial jade. That would be really interesting. Can you get your hands on any of that?"

"I don't know if we'll have time," Jack said. "We're on a tight schedule."

Jimmi swung the club directly at Jack. "I'll pass for now. What day did you say this was happening?"

———

"Jimmi tried to tell me he's passing," Jack said to Victor when he got back from Kunming that night.

"Do you believe him?" Victor said.

"Nope," Jack said. "He definitely wants the deal. My guess is he's sitting in Kunming now, already counting his money, racking his brain figuring out how to sideline us."

"There's only one way for that to happen. He's going to need to collaborate with Costa," Victor said.

Jack said, "Can you imagine the two of them? Like two cats in a bag. Two cats who are both talking to Chin."

Victor was silent for a moment. "I'm not sure that's a bad thing," he said. "So your money's on Jimmi to show up?"

"Count on it," Jack said. "He wants the girls. And you should have seen him salivating over the Imperial jade."

They sat outside the office, smoking in the twilight.

"Jimmi says the only way to make money on a jade run is by trafficking girls," Jack said.

Victor said, "Did you tell him you're no good with women?"

———

"I need to find General Dong," Jack said to Tao at breakfast the next day.

Tao just looked at Jack.

Jack said, "I was just thinking I could give the general some help solving his drug problems."

Tao understood. His face lost its lines, and his teeth appeared. "General Dong find you. We need quartz," Tao said. "You come, see General Dong too."

An hour later, Tao and Jack climbed into a dump truck and rolled out of the smelter yard, down the hill through Dehong and north along the Mangshi River bottomland toward the quartz quarries. Under the hot December sun, the air in the cab was stifling. Jack rolled down his window and surveyed the unfamiliar landscape on either side of the narrow, two-lane road. They slowed down and waited for a boy leading a pair of water buffalo to move out of the way.

"Ying Jiang way," Tao said about the road they were on. "Back way to La Zan. Many drug smugglers here. They think no army," he said, smiling cynically.

Barely five minutes later, creeping cautiously down a narrow lane lined with ten-foot-tall stands of sugar cane, the truck came around a corner and almost collided with a Chinese half-track sitting in the middle of the road. A squad of soldiers stood off to one side, partially hidden in a cane field. Two helmeted men in tan camouflage strode into the middle of the road, automatic weapons slung over their shoulders. One held up the palm of his hand.

Tao downshifted, his eyes fixed on the scene in front of him. As its tires scraped the road, the Forland creaked to a halt amid a whooshing chorus of air brakes. The Chinese soldiers appeared fit, but very green. Their uniforms were new, their gear still shiny. Behind beardless faces daubed with eye-black, the youths wore serious expressions, as if that would be enough to transform their security game into a battlefield skirmish.

Beyond them in a short-sleeved bush jacket and a set of gold wire-rimmed Ray-Bans, a hatless General Dong stood watching. His thinning hair was swept back over his head, and his skin seemed darker and browner than what Jack remembered. The general said something to the aide standing next to him. The man pulled a silver metal Zippo out of his pocket, whipped it open, and lit the general's cigarette.

It was as if they had been waiting for Jack.

General Dong began walking toward the driver's side of the Forland. His aide accompanied him while the other soldiers stopped milling around and came to attention. The general kept walking toward the vehicle, coming even with the truck. He sauntered past the driver's side, glancing up briefly as he walked by, seeing Jack but ignoring him, continuing alongside the truck. Jack looked in the driver's side rear view mirror and followed the general's footsteps until he disappeared out of sight.

A few moments ticked by. Jack stared straight ahead out the windshield, fighting the urge to look to his right.

"I didn't know you could use sugar cane for charcoal, Mr. Davis," the general said, standing next to Jack's open window.

Jack took his time, and then turned and looked down at the general, who was holding his cigarette in his palm as if he was playing a musical instrument.

"We're on a quartz run today, General."

The general took a drag and blew the smoke Jack's way. "I would appreciate it if you would come down out of there."

Jack opened his door and climbed down. He followed the general over to the side of the road, under the shade of a tree.

The general gazed over the land. "It looks like California, don't you think?" He took another drag on his cigarette as his eyes surveyed the sea of lime-colored cane waving in the morning breeze.

"Or Hawaii," Jack said, standing next to him, smelling the combusting tobacco, and glancing down to see what the general was smoking. It was a cigarillo, a thin, brown cigar made with imported tobacco, and much more expensive than a Chinese cigarette.

"I lived in California for many years," the general said, taking another drag, still contemplating the cane fields. "I think it is America's most beautiful land." He turned to look at Jack, his eyes brown and clear. "And you?"

"Hawaii is. But I'm from New York."

"Ah, yes. Of course. I looked you up on the internet, you see. And I wondered—why not California?"

"I love California. I just never got around to living there," Jack said.

"And why would that be? A man of your taste. Why would you not live in the best part of America?"

"It just wasn't where the money was—for me anyway," Jack said.

General Dong took one last drag, dropped his cigarillo, squashed it under his heel, and turned to look at Jack. "And running a smelter in China is where the money is for you now? I don't think so."

"Just trying to make a living, general."

"Please. I know exactly what you are doing." He was silent for a moment. "I have no problem with you bringing jade into China," General Dong said. "But if you're involved with Costa, I won't be able to help you." The general's eyes widened, stark white against his freckled, brown skin. "Do I make myself clear?"

"Yes sir, you do," Jack said. "All I plan to do with that guy is buy his charcoal."

"I'm glad to hear it. I have harsh measures in store for Mr. Costa," General Dong said, "and I can't put them off."

Bingo. Jack wanted to shake the man's hand.

General Dong said, "It would complicate things considerably to find you in the line of fire. The last thing I need is—how do you say it—an international incident next Wednesday."

"Next Wednesday. Right," Jack said. "We'll do our best to make sure that doesn't happen."

The two men walked back to the idling truck.

———

In the morning, Mei was standing by the stove in the kitchen monitoring the launch of her new coffee pot when Jack walked in. "What are the chances you could be packed before noon?"

She looked at him, alarmed.

"No, no," he said as she turned away from him. He stood behind her, putting his hands on her shoulders and reminding himself that he still needed to be careful with his words around her. As good as Mei's English was, it was still her second language. "Sorry, that came out wrong. I just thought that before things heat up, it'd be nice to get away for a weekend. That's all. There's a plane to Kunming we could take. Victor can cover for me."

Mei's anxiety tapered off. She moved away from him, not wanting the rock crushers at the other end of the kitchen to spread gossip.

"What would we do?" she asked.

"What normal people do," Jack answered. "You know; relax, eat dinner, go sightseeing."

"No, no," she said, directing him to sit down at the table. "I must work."

"Really?"

"Yes," she said, conveying the smelter's first mug of real coffee to him.

"So you want me to go by myself?" he said, taking the coffee from her. He watched her move around the kitchen preparing his breakfast, not speaking while her brain processed what he was saying, trying to assess whether it was a good thing or a bad thing.

She looked up at him, her eyes calm now. "Where would we go?"

"The coffee's excellent," he said. "I thought we'd go to Teng Chong."

Now she was disappointed. "That's just an old village."

"What did you expect me to say, Paris?" Jack said. "Look, I know Teng Chong's not much, but it's nearby, and it's supposed to be interesting. I heard many people—foreigners too—go there. We could stay in a little inn, walk around and look at the historic buildings, go into the shops. Sleep in real beds and have someone clean your room for a change. Like I said, what normal people do."

"Someone will clean my room?"

———

Chin drove them to Mangshi's airport terminal, the profile of the orange tile building in the shape of a peacock, the sacred bird of the

Dai. The flight to Kunming took off on time, turning north over the temple on the mountain and heading up the long Dehong valley, the high peaks of its eastern flank obscured by thunderheads.

Mei sat in the window seat, looking out over the clouds below, her face pressed up against the window. In her travel attire—the same clothes she had worn when she had been on her way to the airport weeks earlier—she looked as beautiful as she did that day, the tight skirt halfway up her thighs, her hair on her head, silver earrings sparkling along her cheeks. But happy this time.

"Why don't you wear clothes like this more often?" Jack asked her, looking over her head out the window, smelling the perfume in her hair.

"I don't like men looking at me," she said, still gazing out the window.

"I look at you."

"You're different."

They changed planes in Kunming for the connection to Teng Chong. As they passed through the central plaza of the terminal, Jack stopped at the flower stand and bought Mei some pink lilies. She stood in the middle of the airport's swirling crowd, her knitted brow not able to hide her happiness. She smelled the flowers.

"They smell good, don't they," Jack said.

"No one's ever given me flowers before."

Jack said, "There's a first time for everything. Bring them to Teng Chong; they're for your room."

"I have my own room?"

"You're going to like it."

"What about you?" Mei asked.

They arrived in Teng Chong in the early evening. As the plane's engines shut down and the seat belt sign blinked off, the passengers got up and began to disembark. Mei collected their unopened water bottles and put them in her bag. Eying another unopened bottle in the seat forward of theirs, she confiscated that one too.

Amused, Jack watched her. "What are you doing?"

She looked back at him, a serious expression on her face as she moved up the aisle to the plane's exit door. "We will need the water."

"We can't just buy some?"

"Too expensive," she hushed, the two of them walking past the flight attendants dressed in traditional Dai garb.

It was a tourist crowd, and everyone was excited to be there, including Mei. He watched her, glad she could enjoy herself, wondering if she had any idea that the two of them were the subject of the crowd's attention, everyone stealing glances at the beautiful Chinese girl with the only *laowai* on the plane.

The inn had sent a car. Mei read the makeshift sign in Chinese held up by a man smoking a cigarette, took Jack's bag together with hers and handed them to the man, and they got into a tiny aluminum-sheathed van and headed into town. The thunderheads in Dehong had followed them to Teng Chong. The last light of the afternoon was disappearing over the hemlock-covered mountains as rain clouds moved in. It was going to be a race to the inn and dinner.

After a few miles of countryside, they passed through Teng Chong's dusty suburbs and entered Heshun, the old town. The buildings—houses, pavilions, memorials, archways—were primordial, crudely constructed of shale-like stone and chestnut-colored wood. Lotus ponds gurgled, and a kaleidoscope of flowering plants—bougainvillea, hibiscus, and oleander—cascaded everywhere.

Bumping down a narrow, cobbled lane lined with high stone and plaster walls, their driver navigated through scattered tourists and street vendors pushing carts. After a quarter mile, the driver stopped, got out, and swung open a gate, and then guided the van under a wooden arch marked with red lanterns into a courtyard. Quadrangle style, the stone and wood-beamed inn was two stories, enclosed on all sides and topped with a gabled tile roof. Covered exterior balconies coming off the rooms on the second floor encircled a stone courtyard. A banyan tree filled one corner of the courtyard and shaded the entire compound, a granite fountain trickling at its base.

An old woman in an apron appeared, offering them a toothy smile. Greeting Mei, she leaned her head around the corner and called into the interior of the building for reinforcements.

"We'd better hurry to dinner," Jack said to Mei, "or we're going to get soaked. Ask them to take our bags to the rooms."

A girl walked out from a back room and questioned Mei in Chinese as she consulted her register.

"*Dui*," Mei said to the girl's question. "Two rooms?" she said to Jack, eyes curious.

"Two rooms."

Mei finished registering with the girl. Leaving their bags with her, they departed for dinner. The old woman, still smiling, her lined face in marked contrast to her white teeth, stood at the entrance to the inn and handed Mei an umbrella on their way out.

They found a restaurant just as the rain came. Rushing inside and grabbing the last two seats next to an open window, they watched dark clouds gallop across a navy blue sky. The wind gusted, blowing the napkins off the table. Pregnant raindrops plopped on the roof and rat-a-tat-tatted against the window sash; a few lobbed through the open window and splattered their faces. Waiters hurried into the room, and swung slatted wooden shutters across the windows. Mei let down her hair and shook out the rain.

"I could watch you do that every day."

Mei looked at Jack, smiled, glanced over at the people at the next table to see if they had overheard him, and then gave him a serious expression, holding her finger to her lips.

Jack laughed. "After spending two years in New York City, you're not very American."

"I didn't get out much," Mei said, intending humor. The waiter reappeared with a scroll-style menu in Chinese and handed it to her. "What would you like to eat?" Mei asked, reviewing the menu.

"Whatever you want. As long as it includes a vodka on the rocks." Looking at the beautiful Chinese girl across from him studying the scroll, like a scene in an ancient painting, listening to the drum of the raindrops and the rustle of the wind through the shutters, Jack didn't need anything else. Just a drink.

The waiter came to take their order. Mei ordered a vodka for Jack and water for herself, and asked for a wine list. The waiter shook his head, and they settled for a bottle of Yunnan's fruity table wine. Mei ordered food for them: crayfish, blackened trout, chicken stew, and greens.

The waiter disappeared, and returned a minute later with Jack's vodka and a carafe of wine, leaving it on the table. Jack poured Mei a glass.

"Do you know what the name of this town—Heshun—means?" Mei said as she took a sip of wine, enjoying herself. "Place of peace and harmony."

It poured walking home but they didn't care. The umbrella was serviceable, and the few raindrops that found their mark were as warm as bathwater. Mei's face glistened as she leaned her head alongside his. On the front of the wooden door marking the entrance to their inn, the staff had pinned a message for them: their rooms were on the second floor, next to one another. By candlelight, they found their way up the stairs and along the balcony. Above them, raindrops thrummed a staccato on the balcony's thatched roof. The fountain gurgled in the courtyard; snippets of people's voices floated up in the night air.

Mei reached the door to her room. She opened it, turned, and looked over at Jack standing at his door.

"Goodnight," he said as he opened his door and started to step into the room, aching for her, but telling himself not to make a stupid mistake.

Mei didn't respond. He stuck his head back out his door and looked over at her. She stood waiting for him.

And then he did what they both wanted, walking over and taking her in his arms. He kissed her a long time, tasting her mouth, her ribcage tight against him, feeling the beat of her heart, her hair covering his face, cheek warm against his. Her tee shirt rode up above her waist, and his hands felt her bare back, and then slid down inside her jeans. She pulled him into her room. Not letting go, they stumbled toward her bed. As Mei loosened his belt and tugged on his pants, Jack stripped her tee shirt over her head and they tumbled onto the bed. And then her legs were around him and he was inside her and nothing would ever be the same.

———

The next morning, they made love again, then slept late. Finally, Mei rubbed his shoulder, and kissed his forehead. "We'll miss breakfast if we don't hurry."

"It doesn't matter," Jack mumbled blissfully, not wanting the night to end.

"Yes, it does," Mei said. "It's free."

The inn served a breakfast of congee, toast and preserves, hard-boiled eggs, and tea. Afterward, they spent all day walking the streets of the old town.

That night after dinner when they returned to Mei's room, Jack went to take her but she held him off. "Wait, my tiger," she said. "I have a surprise for you. Lay down on the bed."

He did what he was told. As Mei lit a candle, he looked up at her. Her robe was open in front, and she held a vial of oil.

"Over on your stomach."

He rolled over on his stomach.

"I can't massage your back with your shirt on."

Jack pulled off his tee shirt and his pants and threw them in the corner.

Mei picked up his shirt and pants and hung them over the back of a chair, pulled off his underwear and then sat on the bed next to him and started rubbing oil on his back.

She started massaging his right foot and leg. By the time she got to the left one, he was asleep.

———

The next day at the entrance to a Buddhist temple, the man running the incense store tried to make a sale by holding up a selection of choices. "Pray? You wish to pray?" he asked through gold teeth.

Mei stopped, bought some incense sticks, lit them, and placed them in the sand of the offering vessel. She knelt down to pray.

The man gestured to Jack to join her, but he shook his head. "Just looking," he said to the man. He asked the man to take a photo of the two of them. Jack snapped another of a smiling Mei standing next to a purple cascade of bougainvillea. She looked as radiant as he had ever seen her.

"Are you interested in religion?" Jack asked Mei as they strolled along a few minutes later.

"I wasn't before," she said, "but now I need to pray for you."

That night, Mei gave Jack another massage, and then took off her robe and lay down next to him.

"When are you going to show me your paintings?" he asked her, fooling with the charm around her neck.

"My what?"

"You know," he started to say, turning on his side, but she put two fingers on his lips. "Shhhh. Do you know the last time I lay next to a man I loved?"

"I guess I don't."

"Never."

He propped his elbow under his head, and looked at her face, bathed in the moonlight.

"Working for Jimmi, I always wondered what it meant to love someone. I watched movies and television, and every one of them was about how wonderful it was to be in love. But because Jimmi put me into slavery when I was still very young, and the men were animals, I couldn't love anyone."

He watched her as she spoke, how the moon reflected in her eyes. He reached over for her, felt the warmth of her body and tasted the salty sweat on her skin. After making love, they fell asleep. In the night when he opened his eyes, she was awake, watching him, a serious expression on her face.

"What is it?" he asked.

"I just need to make sure you're still here," she said.

"Where would I go?" he said playfully, trying to put her at ease, his face resting on her bare shoulder as he tried to see her expression in the darkness.

"I know," she said, and exhaled a sigh. "I'm funny about that. I've been that way since my parents…"

He waited for her to continue.

"…left me."

"No, no, don't torture yourself," he said. "They were in the service—it was part of their job."

She shook her head. "That's what I told you. That would have been all right," she said, pushing her face into the pillow.

He kissed the side of her head and whispered in her ear. "It's OK. You don't have to explain."

She sucked in a breath. "They couldn't afford me," she finally said, rocking back and forth face down on the bed, her hands clasped in front of her face, "so…"

"Hey, it's all right," he said, putting his hand on her shoulder.

"…they sold me to Jimmi," she said, exhaling, barely intelligible.

She was quiet a long time, as if waiting for a verdict.

As she looked up at him expectantly, he gathered her up in his arms and held her. "I don't want you to worry about that anymore," he said to her, smelling the heaven in her hair.

"It doesn't bother you?" she asked. She kept watching him in the dark, as if waiting for a real answer.

"No. It doesn't bother me at all," he said, looking out the window at the moon, thinking about another time in his life—the only other time—when he'd been in love.

When he looked back at her, he wasn't sure what he saw in her eyes—it looked to him like she didn't believe him—but she wrapped her arms around him anyway, and squeezed. "I'm so happy," she said.

"The one thing that used to bother me doesn't anymore," he said to her. "I never thought I'd get over my wife."

Mei was in the bathroom when Jack woke in the morning. As the sun peeked over the eastern hills and its rays snuck through the gap in the curtains, he pulled on his jeans and tee shirt and stepped outside on the balcony.

The night's rain clouds were gone. The dry winter sky was clear blue, the air perfectly still. He could hear the sounds of the city waking, wagon wheels rumbling down the stone lanes, mothers calling their children to breakfast. The smell of pancakes drifted up. High overhead, a hawk circled on a thermal.

Barefoot, he walked along the balcony, following it around the quadrangle. He found a stairway to the roof, gained the top of the building, dragon dogs standing guard on the cornices, and looked out on a heavenly world—the same world where young girls were bought and sold like chattel—but appearing at that moment as the earth was meant to be, the bougainvillea climbing up the side of the building as purple and pure as the altar cloth in a cathedral. Ahead of him, below a wave of billowing cumulus, lounged the green foothills of the Himalayas. There in the ancient town—the skyline of tiled rooftops undulating like a lost fleet of schooners on a secret sea—he had found some answers.

CHAPTER 17

"I figure he's got to hit Costa's camp at the end of the day," Jack said to Victor when he returned from Teng Chong, discussing their hopes for General Dong's plans the following Wednesday.

Victor said, "Agreed. They're not going to invade a foreign country in broad daylight, I don't care how close the camp is to the border. But those green troops won't be able to fight at night. We'll just take our time, and arrive fashionably late." Victor consulted his notes. "For being such a jerk, Costa sure is a popular guy." He laughed. "Everyone—us, General Dong, Major Maran—is lining up to see him. We just need to make sure Jimmi Zeng shows up for the party."

Jack said, "This is what traitors are for. By now, Chin's told Costa and Jimmi all about our plan. They've probably already made their arrangements. All Jimmi's got to do is get his ass up to Costa's camp, pay the man for his girls and his drugs, and then deal with us. I'm sure he thinks we'll be child's play."

Victor said, "We just have to hope the KIA shows up on time to save the day. How do you feel about going after that Imperial jade?"

Jack said, "If we really want to punch our ticket with one run, it's the only way."

"And so…" Victor said.

"I already had Mei call the guy," Jack confessed, laughing.

"I figured," Victor said. "In that case, we're going to have to split up when we get to the Irrawaddy valley. You take Chin and head south to Bhamo for the Imperial jade. Tao and I can take the trucks north to Myitkyina and pick up the regular jade. Afterwards, we'll meet back on the highway and head to Costa's together."

Jack said, "You're going to need a separate truck just to carry all the cash."

Victor looked at his notes. "Looks like sixty million RMB, plus or minus, for Major Maran," he said, doing some calculations. "And with any luck, we turn that into…at least fifteen million dollars."

"Courtesy of Jimmi, or another lucky buyer," Jack said. "And that's before you factor in another five million from the Imperial jade. Then we pay off the bank, call up the Spaniards, and hand them the keys."

"No, then we sell that fine smelter to the lucky Spaniards for an excellent price," Victor said. "Good thing you've got me around."

They were interrupted by a knock on the office door. Chin came in, breathing hard. "Major Maran call many times. He must know if you want Imperial jade," he said to them.

Chin's lie didn't cause Jack to miss a beat. "We haven't made up our mind yet," he said to Chin. "We may not have time; we're on a tight schedule. We've lined up a big jade buyer at the Ruili jade market. We need to load up our charcoal at Costa's by no later than Wednesday afternoon in order to hit Ruili by the evening."

Chin stomped out.

"He didn't speak to the major," Victor scoffed.

"Guaranteed he didn't," Jack said. "That Imperial jade is like honey to bees."

"Too bad we can't get Chin hooked up with General Dong," Victor said. "Give him our coordinates and estimated time of arrival, tell him to schedule the disruption right before we show up."

Jack and Mei made love in her dormitory room under the moonlight streaming through her window. Afterward, Jack lay on his back, Mei's head tucked under his chin, raven hair spread across his chest. "Close your eyes," she said.

He closed his eyes, and felt her hand massaging his chest in a circular motion.

"When will you leave?" she asked.

"I'll be back soon," he said.

"Are you going to buy the Imperial jade?" she asked.

"We've got to," he said.

She said, "Everyone will try to take it from you."

"It's the only way out of here," Jack said.

Mei said, "I knew you'd leave one day," as she rubbed his body.

"I'm not leaving you," he said, lifting himself up to look her in the eye. "Do you trust Chin?"

Mei said, "You know better than that. Other than Victor, you shouldn't trust anyone here." Jack started to ask her another question, but she pushed him down on the bed. "No more talking," she said.

He felt her forefinger rub his eyelids.

"That feels good."

"Shush." She kept rubbing his eyes with her forefinger, and then sat on top of him and used both forefingers to massage the bones of his face, around his eye sockets and his cheekbones and along the brow of his forehead.

"Who taught you this?"

"My living Buddha. The one who told me I'd find you one day."

She finished with his forehead and rubbed his head behind his ears and his earlobes and came down his temples to his mouth, her fingers kneading his bones and caressing his skin, round and round, making it all go away, Jack forgetting everything except for the Chinese goddess purring over him, willing herself into every pore of his being. When she was finished, he brought her down to him.

She buried her face next to his. "You're the best thing that ever happened to me, but I don't deserve you," she said.

"Don't talk like that," he said, pulling her to him and holding her, feeling her ribs and her breasts pressing against his chest. He smelled her, felt her breathe, and felt her hips begin to find his.

"All right," she said, her breath warm in his ear. "For now."

"Forever," he said, rubbing his hand up and down her back, her heart beating and chest shivering, feeling all of her, his lips brushing her hair along her ear, wanting her again, knowing he would always want her, and that he had never wanted anyone like he wanted her, and never would again.

She grabbed his head with both hands, kissed him hard on the mouth, and moved herself underneath him. "After this, you must go," she said, eyes like a cat's, boring into his. "Leave me as much of you as you can."

———

On Monday morning, Jack and Victor ate breakfast with the roosters, and then prepared to shove off. Jack checked the action of his guns one last time, strapped his snub-nosed weapon around his ankle, and stuffed extra shells into his pants pocket. Closing up their room, he gazed across the factory yard. The last stars were winking out, and the husk of the moon looked down from the western sky. Like a herd of restless elephants, the line of Forland trucks waited at the feedstock yard, their engines idling. The smelter coughed and then started up, thrumming through its daily test runs. The de-dusting machine started to whine, right on time.

"Thank God for Tao," Victor said, standing next to Jack, the two of them listening as the sounds from the big machines banged out a crude rhythm.

"The truth is, there are some days when this place isn't so bad," Jack said.

"Until the monsoon season," Victor said. "And don't forget what you told me: the longer a foreigner owns a business in China, the poorer he gets."

They climbed aboard the two transport trucks in the front of the caravan, Jack riding shotgun with Chin at the wheel in the first one, and Victor and Tao in the second. The remaining twenty-three Forlands lumbered through the gate and down the mountain to Mangshi to pick up their cash at the Farmer's Bank.

At seven o'clock in the morning, Jack and Victor met the manager at the front door of the bank and followed him upstairs. With the manager looking on, women filled duffel bags with RMB.

When they were finished, Victor lit a cigarette as they contemplated the pile of bags in front of them.

"After all this, how much do we have left?" Jack asked.

"Ten million or so," Victor said, and paused. "RMB."

"Christ! That's it?" Jack exclaimed. "Including the proceeds of the loan we just borrowed?"

"I told you," Victor said. "We're broke."

"God almighty," Jack said. For the first time since they had arrived in Dehong, he was truly worried. He took a moment to concentrate. "I might as well take the rest of it to Bhamo," he finally said to Victor.

They grabbed the bank manager and withdrew the last ten million from their account.

"So this is what it feels like," Victor said.

"What?" Jack said.

"Swinging for the fences."

They helped the bank staff lug the duffel bags downstairs and into the trucks: sixty million RMB for Victor, and twenty for Jack. After Tao thrust a sack of cash into the expectant hands of the bank manager, the man slithered back inside. The men climbed up into their trucks and the caravan headed west through the Dehong hills to the border patrol post at Mai Ja Yang.

At the Lwegel Bridge guard booth, Chin got down from his seat and shuttled over to the booth, doling out cigarettes and, because of the size of the caravan, small amounts of cash too. The barrier was raised, and the fleet of trucks lumbered over the bridge into Burma. After driving west down the mountain ridge to the valley highway, they split up. They would rendezvous at the same point late that afternoon for the trip up to Costa's.

———

The guy Jack was supposed to meet in Bhamo had set up camp temporarily in a tent on a hill outside of town. Jack told a protesting Chin to wait in the truck.

"You're not Chinese," the skinny man said in a disappointed tone to Jack when he presented himself at the entrance to the tent. The man had a set of beaver-like front teeth, a pronounced nose, and a clipped British accent. If Jack had to guess, he would say he was from India. As two partially hidden bodyguards in combat fatigues held the flaps of the tent open, the man stood blocking the entrance, examining Jack. He was dressed in loose linen pants topped by a matching Nehru jacket buttoned up to his shirt collar. A floppy hat and a pair of big circular-lensed sunglasses obscured his face.

The skinny man shrugged, and invited Jack inside. He spoke to someone, in a turban and white robe, who ushered them into a sitting area. The turbaned man disappeared and then returned with a tray, setting it down on the table in front of Jack. On it were dishes, each filled with small polished jade stones. The green color of the stones was lighter than emerald but equally brilliant, and although they were almost transparent, their depth was endless.

The skinny man sat across from Jack, sunglasses removed, eyes closed. Taking controlled breaths, it appeared he was meditating. From across the table, his body odor was overwhelming. The turbaned man returned with a tea service, and poured Jack green tea in a porcelain cup and saucer with gold trim.

His host opened his eyes. "You must forgive my initial lack of hospitality, Mr. Davis, but I don't appreciate most white men. They remind me of the English. And they don't understand fine jade." He looked down his nose at Jack. "I still need to make up my mind about you."

"I should confess: I have no idea what I'm looking at," Jack said, peering at the stones.

The skinny man waved his hand back and forth dismissively. "That is no matter. I have already arranged your transaction with Major Maran. He said you would want to purchase a dozen stones. But as long as you are here, you should inspect your goods," the skinny man said. He extended his hand across the tray. A bony forefinger pushed one of the dishes closer to Jack.

Jack picked up the dish. It held a dozen stones of slightly differing sizes, each brilliant.

"Take one. You must feel them. And they need your body's warmth to perform," the skinny man said.

Jack selected a stone the size of a grape and held it up between his thumb and forefinger in front of the light. "It's beautiful."

The skinny man watched Jack. "When you shoot your gun, which eye do you squint?"

"My left."

"Here then," the skinny man said, taking a jeweler's loupe on a silver chain from around his neck and handing it to Jack. "Place it over your right eye, squint, and have another look."

Jack put the lens in front of his right eye, squinted his left, and re-examined the stone. The color was staggeringly pure. "*Jesus.*"

"We call it *feicui*. The best color you will ever see in jade."

"How much is it?" Jack asked, handing the loupe and the stone back to the skinny man.

The skinny man laughed. "Spoken like a true American. The better question is how much someone will pay you for this Burmese beauty in New York City, especially since your government has outlawed them."

"If you say so," Jack said, waiting for the answer.

The skinny man's lips, pursed as he studied the stone in his hand, were the same purplish color as his eyes. "It's just a small stone." He sniffed. "With the right setting? Four hundred thousand, I suppose," he said, tossing the stone back into the dish. "Dollars."

Jack said, "You've got my attention." He didn't speak again, waiting the man out.

The skinny man looked at his watch, and then turned and signaled the turbaned servant. "We will be breaking camp soon. Do you wish to examine more jade?" he asked Jack.

"Not until you answer my question," Jack said as he looked down one last time at the dish of green jade.

"I thought Major Maran told you," the man said, seeming exasperated. "That stone will cost you one hundred fifty thousand dollars," he said. "Or approximately nine hundred fifty thousand RMB." The skinny man looked at his watch again, and then over at Jack.

"Thank you. Time to go, I guess," Jack said, forcing a smile.

The man looked at Jack with a quizzical expression.

"The major advised me I could expect to purchase a stone like this for less than one hundred thousand dollars," Jack said.

"How disappointing." The skinny man waited for a minute while Jack remained comfortably silent. Then he beckoned to the turbaned man and spoke to him at some length. He turned back to Jack and sighed. "I must leave here tomorrow, and I don't want to travel with these stones in this wild land. For you, Mr. Davis, one hundred ten thousand dollars per stone."

Jack said, "In that case, I'll take two dozen."

———

Afterward, Chin pushed their Forland through the streets of Bhamo, dodging cars and bicycles.

As Chin drove, Jack studied his rearview mirror. The motorcycles they had first spotted a few miles back cruised several blocks behind them, riders incognito in their helmets, headlights weaving back and forth like the tentacles of a hydra-headed monster.

Bhamo's streets ended at the highway on the edge of town. In the afternoon's waning light, Chin pulled into the line of vehicles heading north and did his best to hide in the traffic. He and Jack peered into their rearview mirrors.

"They're gone," Jack said to Chin, who grunted back. An hour later, as they approached an intersection, Chin began downshifting. Jack recognized the crossing from earlier in the day. They were at the meeting place.

Chin slowed to a crawl, flipping on the low beams to pierce the lowland fog, and then sucked in his breath. Past the connecting road, the remains of one of their dump trucks lay smoldering, partially hidden in a stand of sugar cane. Acrid smoke rose from what was left of its front end, the ass-end of the truck bent perpendicular. A dead man's head hung out the window.

"Goddamn," Jack said under his breath, his chest pounding, looking around in the gloom for the other trucks, but not seeing them. There were no local onlookers anywhere.

Chin pulled across the side road closer to the wreck, keeping the headlights trained on the metal hulk, and stopped. As Chin climbed out of the cab, Jack grabbed a bottle of water and began swallowing the two dozen stones in his pocket. He chugged down the remainder of the bottle, and got out of the truck.

The two of them walked toward the smoking wreck. On its side, the Forland appeared to have been blown in two, the cab unhinged from the rear carriage. A sweetish scent of crushed cane hung in the air. The only noise came from the hissing wreck. Chin walked alongside the truck, shining a flashlight across the mess. Irregular patterns of bullet holes had pierced a door and a window.

Jack tried to see beyond the wreck to where the truck's load of charcoal had spilled over the ground. He didn't see any jade bags.

Chin's flashlight beam stopped on the dead man in the Forland. He uttered something, and was about to step toward him when a band of men sprang out of the cane patch and rushed them.

There were close to a dozen of them. Overwhelmed, Jack and Chin were wrestled to the ground. Jack couldn't see the men holding him from behind. Several of them pulled him down, and then jerked his arms behind his back. He glanced over at Chin, who was being throttled easily by a single man.

As the thugs realized their mission had gone as planned and no one had gotten their ass shot off, they called to each other, sounding half drunk, their bodies sweaty and rank. Jack smelled marijuana in their clothes. From the forest of cane behind the smoking truck, a guerilla emerged wearing a hat, a pistol strapped on his leg. He switched on a flashlight as he walked toward them, barking orders. It was Ban. What the hell did Costa think he was doing? And so much for General Dong's big distraction.

Jack yelled at Ban, but he didn't respond. Chin didn't utter a word. Ban gave instructions to two Thai guerillas, who searched Jack.

One of the men pulled Jack's gun out of his pants pocket, and kept searching, finding nothing else. Shining his flashlight into Jack's eyes, the man screamed at him, his breath like kerosene, using words Jack couldn't understand. Ban pushed the guerilla away from Jack apologetically, and then growled into his walkie talkie in Thai. Jack heard his name, and a response crackled. The motorcycles that had tailed them in Bhamo pulled up, Costa's troop truck right behind them, and Ban issued orders. The Thai mercenaries hoisted Jack and Chin into the rear of their Forland transport truck, cinched up their ankles with ropes, and everyone climbed aboard. A minute later, trucks and motorcycles pulled out onto the highway.

The night was pitch black. There was no moon, and no stars.

Bumping along in the truck, not knowing where they were headed, it wasn't fear Jack fought as much as anger—with himself. A similar black night from long ago loomed up in his mind, when he had been on a camping trip as a ten-year-old child. His father had gambled on a short cut and they had become lost. Jack had been terrified, but his mother was faring worse, until Jack took the road map from her and guided them out. He had never been lost again. But for someone who was supposed to know the way, he had blundered: he had counted on the Chinese, and underestimated Costa.

After an hour, the caravan turned off the main road, engines straining as they headed upland. Jack's head banged against the deck of the Forland. He raised himself up and looked over the metal railing of the truck bed. As they rolled and dipped along in the darkness, he recognized the denuded forest plain at the edge of Costa's camp. He looked the other direction, past Chin's bouncing head, trying to detect military activity in the woods. "Where the hell are the Chinese?" he said out loud in frustration.

Even so, when the first fusillade of rockets exploded in the sky, Jack was taken by surprise. He hunkered down in the truck bed, thinking someone was firing at them, expecting to be shot. Flattening himself out, he tried to stay low behind the railing. Then he heard the Thais yelling and shouting in the troop truck ahead, and realized they were as confused as he was. Orange and red percussions ripped across the sky. Rockets. It had to be the Chinese. Motorcycles and vehicles thrashed across the ground, scurrying for shelter. As blasts detonated uselessly off in the forest behind Costa's camp, Jack cursed the Chinese soldiers' inaccuracy.

The trucks lurched to a stop, and Ban and the guerillas jumped out. For a moment, it was quiet, except for the sound of Thai mercenaries digging trenches, and random gunfire spitting out of the woods. A minute later, a frenzy of shooting erupted closer to the vehicles. Jack raised his head up off the truck bed, and witnessed a slaughter. The invaders were clearly General Dong's Chinese soldiers, and they outnumbered the Thais. But the battle, taking place across the field in front of him, was no contest. The company of green Chinese soldiers—the better part of a hundred men—was edging cautiously out of the woods toward Costa's camp. But the rocket cover was doing them no good; the missiles were being sprayed haphazardly. As the soldiers picked their way through the field's stumps and boulders, they came into the teeth of Costa's mercenaries. The Thais, although down to less than a dozen men, reacted like the trained killers they were. Dug into defensive positions around the trucks, as the front ranks of the Chinese emerged into the open field from the forest, the Thais opened up with withering fire. The Chinese front line was ripped apart. When the second line of Chinese soldiers saw what was in store for them, they broke ranks and fled for the woods.

Seeing victory was theirs, the handful of surviving Thais shouted and chased after the Chinese, mowing many down from behind. Between spurts of machine gun fire, Jack could hear Ban's walkie talkie crackling.

And then the gun fire stopped as abruptly as it had started. Jack peered over the railing of the truck again. He and Chin were alone. Dead Chinese soldiers and a few Thai guerillas littered the field. Nothing moved. One last rocket crossed the sky and found its mark over behind the heroin lab. A white flash lit the night. Jack had thought the Chinese soldiers would be the answer, but he should have known. They were just green kids who had never been in battle. Now all he could do was pray that the KIA showed up. Soon.

Ban and the handful of surviving Thai guerillas straggled out of the mist. They clambered up into the trucks, and drove the remaining distance to Costa's camp. Two of the men pushed Jack and Chin off the edge of the truck and down to the ground. Lying in the dirt, Jack lifted his head and looked around. His charcoal trucks were lined up right in front of him. Over in a corner of the fenced-in pen, he saw the drivers cowering.

At Ban's instructions, the Thais untied their captives' ankles and herded Jack and Chin along the fence line toward the front of what remained of Costa's camp. Jack glanced over at the girls congregated at the other end of the pen. There were many more now, close to two hundred, standing behind the fence or crouched in the dirt. They were alive; none appeared injured from the shooting. And this time, they all stared back at him, terrified.

Jack peered through the compound. The camp's buildings smoldered. Flames licked the decimated cottages and drug labs. Somehow, the camp's generators were still running, and the lights remained on. The feedstock yard was intact, and so was the front-end loader, but there was no sign of any workers.

Next to the parking lot, the same old shrew mindlessly tended the cooking fire in front of the picnic area, ignoring the destruction around her. Charred strips of meat hung over the coals, on rebar rods glowing orange. Incongruous in the midst of the battleground, a brand-new Toyota Land Cruiser sat in the lot, covered with ash.

The front door of the office building banged open and Costa stepped outside. He saw Jack and the men walking toward him, and clapped his hands, rubbing them together. "Party time," he called back inside. In his fatigues, Costa turned and waddled toward Jack, pistol flapping against his thigh. A dirty, bloodstained bandage was wrapped around Costa's head, covering his nose and the lower half of his face like a bandana. Ignoring Chin, he drew himself up in front of Jack. "You didn't really think you could run stones without me, did you?" he sneered. "Where's the Imperial jade?"

Jack didn't answer.

"Where is it, goddamnit!" Costa said, smashing his pistol upside Jack's head.

Jack sunk to his knees, holding his face together with both hands. Lights flashed in his head, and his eardrum rattled. Warm blood leaked between his loosened teeth. Like when he got water in his ear surfing, he could hear a sucking sound inside his head.

"I'll show this motherfucker who the white tiger is around here," Costa said to Ban, dropping his pistol back in his holster. "Get them inside."

"We lose many men," Ban said to Costa, standing his ground, his automatic weapon strapped over his back. "KIA come very soon," he warned, looking over his shoulder toward the direction of the charcoal-cutting plain. Jack had never seen Ban concerned before.

"We'll leave when I get the good stuff," Costa said, spitting on the ground at Jack's feet before he walked over to the office building and disappeared inside.

Jack heard Ban curse under his breath. He herded Jack and Chin across the yard and in the front door of the office building.

Other than a desk and some bookshelves in one corner and a beat-up couch in the other, the spartan interior of the building consisted of a front room occupied by a large round wooden table and a dozen broken-down chairs, with a back bedroom accessible via a half-open door. The space was well-lit by lights hanging from the ceiling. A pile of bulging black duffle bags clogged the doorway between the rooms. Smoke hung in the air. It smelled like someone had been cooking something, but there was no kitchen. A bottle of *baiju* and paper plates holding scraps of greasy meat littered the wooden table.

Tao sat across the table. He was slumped forward, his head lying sideways. Out cold, a crusty trail of blood dripped out of marks on his forearms. As if on the witness stand, Victor sat upright next to him, semi-conscious.

Costa shoved Jack into a chair next to Victor, Chin slumping down beside him, as Ban tried to retreat out the front door. "Wait there," Costa ordered Ban, motioning for him to stand by the door. "I'm going to need you."

Victor stirred. Opening his eyes, he saw Jack and tried to warn him. "They know…the Imperial jade," he managed to say between bloodied lips.

"Fucking Polack," Costa said, grabbing the last pieces of meat off the paper plate and shoveling them into his mouth. Chewing nonchalantly, he slid around the table and used his pistol to slam Victor across the head, knocking him out of his chair and onto the floor.

The door to the back room opened, and Jimmi Zeng walked in. The golden boy's eyes were wide, his hair disheveled. He was wearing a fashionable body armor vest that wouldn't have stopped a pellet gun. Ignoring Jack, he scolded Costa. "The KIA is coming. We've got to get the hell out of here!"

"Shut up, pansy ass," Costa said to Jimmi.

"Will you quit this fucking nonsense?" Jimmi screamed at Costa again. "Mei, get the hell in here and count out this cash," he said, stepping over the pile of duffle bags stacked up in the doorway between the rooms.

The door to the back room opened wider, and Mei appeared. She refused to look at Jack. Dressed in jeans, a flannel shirt, and construction boots, with a headband wrapped around her forehead, her hair was up and hidden. She looked like a man. Bent over as she focused on the big duffle bags, she dragged one through the doorway.

The saliva ducts began to flow in Jack's mouth. He felt like he was going to puke. He could no longer make any sense of where he was or what he was doing. Staring numbly at Mei, he didn't want to believe what his eyes were telling him. Crushed, he sat still and mute, wanting to ask her to explain. But he couldn't mouth the words. Terrified she would confirm his worst fears, he pressed his lips together, fighting the inescapability of the scene playing out in front of him, waiting for any shred of hope.

Restless, looking like he wanted to scatter, Ban didn't move from where he stood by the door.

Costa couldn't have cared less about the KIA, behaving as if he was in no hurry. "That Imperial jade's mine," he said out aloud. He grabbed the bottle of *baiju*, took a swig, and stared at Jack. "Where the fuck is it?" he yelled at him, his red-rimmed eyes shining like a pig's.

Jack sat silently, watching Mei, wracking his brain, trying to fit the pieces together. He looked over at Tao's head resting sideways on his arm, stupidly realizing for the first time that the man's forearm was scarred with burn marks. At least he appeared to be breathing. Down on the floor, Victor was breathing too. Chin leaned back in his chair, oddly comfortable.

"Davis probably never got the stuff," Jimmi yelled one more time at Costa. "Just shoot him, and let's get out of here. We've got to finish loading the charcoal and get the girls in the trucks. Now!"

"This won't take long," Costa said, walking over to the table and slapping Jack across the face. "Stand up and empty your pockets, fuck face."

Knowing he was going to die soon, Jack kept looking at Mei as he stood up, hoping his last waking thought would be to learn she was there against her will. He pulled his pockets out of his pants to show Costa there was nothing in them.

"For Chrissakes," Costa said, walking over and checking out Jack's pockets for himself. "What the fuck did you do with the goddamn stones?" Without another word, he turned around and hustled out the front door. Jack heard him opening and slamming shut the Forland's doors, yelling. Jack couldn't take his eyes off Mei. Complying with Jimmi's instructions like an automaton while the lazy bastard just stood there, she was busy hauling the big duffel bags out of the back room toward the front door. She had not looked at Jack once. Surely she was there under duress. But no one was holding a gun to her head. As Jack's mind cleared, his hopes plummeted.

Costa banged the front door open as he stomped back inside. "Think you're so fucking smart?" Costa yelled across the room at Jack. "You swallowed them!" he shrieked, cackling in a high, childlike pitch. "What an amateur." He looked over at Jimmi. "You want to tell him what happens to stupid amateurs?"

"You're the stupid amateur," Jimmi said to Costa, pulling a Glock 17 revolver out from under his body armor and checking the magazine nervously. "Shoot him, or I will."

"Watch, we'll make him shit them out," Costa said to Jimmi, as if that would make it all OK. "Pull your pants down," Costa ordered

Jack, rubbing his hands together as he headed back out the front door. "Ban, get a pan."

Costa and Ban walked outside as Jack sat down in his chair. Mei disappeared into the back room. It was quiet. Jimmi behaved as if Jack wasn't there, re-checking the action of his gun as he walked toward the front door. Jack unbuckled his belt and started to slide his pants down his legs in order to get his hand on the snub-nosed pistol strapped around his ankle.

Costa strode back through the open door, holding a smoking rebar rod, its exposed tip a dull orange. "Get the goddamned pan under his ass," Costa called to Ban who was following him with a cooking pan.

Jimmi blocked their way, holding his pistol out in front of him, pointing it at Costa from ten feet away. "Put it down," he said.

Costa stopped in his tracks and glared at Jimmi. "Ban, shoot the stupid motherfucker," Costa said, holding the rebar rod in front of him toward Jimmi. Ban started to bend down to put the pan on the floor.

Then everyone froze as they heard the pop-pop-pop of single-action gunfire far off down the mountain.

Costa lunged toward Jimmi with the hot rebar, and Jimmi shot him square in the forehead. As Jimmi swung around and leveled his pistol toward him, Jack ripped the snub-nosed four-ten off his ankle and blew Jimmi out the door.

A red hole the size of a dime appeared in Costa's forehead, his eyes in disbelief. He dropped the rebar as he fell, his face bouncing off the floorboards. Bluish, cordite-laced smoke gathered up at the ceiling as Ban and Jack studied each other across the room. Another fusillade of shots rang out from off in the woods behind the office building, and Jack looked over his shoulder. When he turned back around, Ban was gone.

Victor groaned on the floor.

Jack cinched up his pants and knelt down over Victor. "You OK?"

Victor opened his eyes, and looked up at Jack, and then past Jack's shoulder. "Yeah. But you're not."

"Give me your gun, Jack," Mei said, standing behind him.

CHAPTER 18

Jack turned around to see Mei training a Glock 17 on him, extending it out in front of her with both hands. He stared at her, wishing her mean-looking face would simply disappear, confirming this was all a nightmare. "You don't need to do that." He pulled his gun out of his pocket and handed it to her. "It only has one shot," he said. "Remember?"

She took the gun and jammed it in her back pocket. "Thank you for killing him. That makes things much easier."

"Just answer one question," Jack said in the quiet of the room.

Mei didn't speak, but kept holding the gun on him. Underneath the headband, her face didn't look like Mei's anymore, but harder, like a man's. Jack was glad for that.

"That artist's palette necklace you wear," Jack said. "It was all part of an act, right?"

Mei exhaled. "I'm sorry, Jack. I read about you. I made up my mind I could count on you. And you came through." For a moment, the vein came out under her eye as her face softened; she almost smiled.

"What do you want us to do, Jack?" Victor said from behind him where he and Tao had both recovered, and were sitting in their seats.

Jack looked over his shoulder and saw the two men, their arms hidden. "Don't," he said.

Mei shifted her Glock toward the men. "Chin, take their guns," she ordered.

From his seat, Chin scrambled down onto the floor where Tao and Victor sat and came up a minute later with their snub-nosed pistols. "Sorry, boss," he said to Jack as he stood up in front of him and handed the pistols, still in their holsters, to Mei.

She tossed them as well as Jack's gun past the pile of duffel bags, into the other room. "Go and fish the car keys out of Jimmi's pants," Mei said to Chin, still holding the gun on Jack and the men at the table. "Hurry; we've got to go."

Jack knew there was no chance left; he could speak. "Why?" he croaked.

Mei looked at him, and smiled a sad smile. "You couldn't love someone like me," she said softly. "Not really. You might think you do now, here in China, but that would end soon enough."

"You're wrong."

"I don't think so," Mei said, her smile gone, face hard again. "Anyway, it's too late now, isn't it? Jimmi's dead—that's what I wanted the most. And I'm going back to Kunming and take over his business. I was practically running it myself before you came along. Investing his cash."

"What makes you think I won't come after you?" Jack asked.

Chin came back into the room, his hands covered with blood. "Here is," he said, showing Mei the keys. The sound of remote gunfire leaked through the open front door. "We must go," Chin said to her. "KIA come now."

"Grab two of those bags and start up the car. I'm right behind you," Mei said.

Chin lifted up two of the duffle bags and dragged them out.

Mei kept the gun trained on Jack and the men. "There's no reason to come after me," she said to Jack. "I don't want you. I used you to kill Jimmi. And I don't care about the money or your jade. He owed me what I'm taking; the rest is yours." Mei looked at him one last time as she stuffed the Glock into the waistband of her jeans, and then stepped over Costa's body and walked out the door.

Jack heard the Toyota start up, and creak down the rocky road past the feedstock yard, stealing back to China. He slumped in a chair at the table.

Tao went over to the next room and retrieved their guns. He knelt down and fastened one onto his ankle. He stepped over to Costa's body, pulled the dead man's pistol out of his holster, and handed it and another snub-nosed gun to Victor. Then he went out the front door, returned a minute later with Jimmi's Glock, handed it to Jack with his empty gun, and slapped him on the shoulder. "KIA come now," he said to the men. "We must be strong." He pulled the duffle bags of cash over to where they sat at the table.

Victor managed to fish a crumpled cigarette out of his pocket and light up. The three men sat around the table, not speaking, staring into space. Ten minutes later, a squad of KIA soldiers led by Major Maran banged open the office door. Men pointed rifles around the room as Major Maran studied the scene in front of him. He was missing his hat, and looked like he needed a haircut.

CHAPTER 19

An hour later, while the KIA men handed out bottles of water to the women in the cage, Tao organized the Forland drivers, who began to load the twenty-four remaining trucks with charcoal for the trip back to Dehong.

Jack and Victor sat alone in the office. Victor counted out the cash in Jimmi's duffle bags while Jack watched him.

Jack asked, "How much is in there?"

"It looks like each bag contains twenty-five million RMB," Victor said, zipping up the one he had just counted.

Jack drew a deep breath. "Looks like we're going to be able to go home," he said.

"On a Lear jet if you like," Victor said. "This is just Jimmi's cash. Don't forget about the Imperial jade you had for dinner last night."

"And the KIA jade in the trucks," Jack said. "I guess we've got to find a new customer, though."

"It'll sell," Victor said.

Jack was glad to have business issues to talk about. With effort, he continued, things around him moving in slow motion. "We don't even have to pay Costa for charcoal," he said. But he didn't give a damn about the money. All he wanted to do was picture Mei's beautiful face, the way she had looked sitting next to him on the plane, her smile when she cooked for him in the morning, the expression in her eyes when he made love to her. When her hideous countenance from an hour earlier invaded his consciousness, he rejected it.

SOUTH OF THE CLOUDS

"Let's see what Jimmi was thinking," Victor went on, as if knowing he needed to keep Jack in the here-and-now. "Six bags at twenty-five million each is a hundred-fifty million RMB. Start with the girls. If Jimmi was going to pay Costa thirty thousand a copy, two hundred girls is six million RMB, or a million bucks."

"I'll bet he needed to pay Costa ten times that to feed them a heroin dinner," Jack murmured.

"Right. Figure Costa would have been into Jimmi for over a hundred million RMB," Victor said. "Which would have left the king of karaoke with a balance of fifty million RMB, or around two thousand RMB a kilo to pay us for the KIA jade. Meaning he was going to shaft us," Victor said, dropping the last duffle bag and walking over to the front door where KIA soldiers were shoveling up Jimmi's remains. "I guess he'll think twice before doing that again."

"Do you think she would have shot me?" Jack asked Victor. He had to.

"Not a chance," Victor said. "You heard her: her target was the karaoke king."

Jack got up and joined Victor at the door, looking out toward the cage where most of the girls still cowered. A few brave ones had come outside the fence and were mingling with the KIA soldiers. "So what are we going to do with them?" Jack said to Victor.

Victor said, "We don't have to do anything. Major Maran's going to take them."

"That's not what I mean."

"I know," Victor said. "What do you want to do?"

"How many are there?" Jack asked.

Victor said, "Two hundred is a safe bet."

"And how much is this?" Jack asked, sticking his hand into one of Jimmi's duffle bags and pulling out a taped package of hundred RMB notes.

"The same as it's always been: one hundred thousand RMB," Victor said. "A nice round number."

"Let's make sure those girls don't end up like Mei," Jack said.

"Sure," Victor said, scanning his partner's wounded eyes. "Just tell me what you want."

"I'd like to give each of the girls one of these," Jack said, holding up a slab of bills.

"Like a party favor," Victor said.

Jack said, "Let's run the rest of this cash back to the bank first thing tomorrow morning, and get them to wire it out of the country as soon as possible. And then be on the next plane out of here ourselves. I don't even want to go back to the smelter."

"You don't ever have to go back to that place again," Victor said.

CHAPTER 20

The taxi from Kennedy Airport dropped Jack in front of his Manhattan townhouse at six on a chilly Christmas morning. Snow was just starting to fall. The streets were muffled and silent. Jack punched the security code into the panel and pushed open his front door. The hallway smelled clean, like floor polish. He said a silent thank you to Vivian, who had contacted the housekeeper to let her know Jack was coming home.

He stepped inside. He opened the tall wooden cabinet that served as a coat closet and hung up his bush jacket. Hooking it on a peg, he wondered if he'd ever put it on again. Setting down his bags in the hallway, he walked to the kitchen overlooking the garden at the rear of the house. Opening up a cabinet door above the sink, he grabbed a highball glass and loaded it with ice from the freezer. He moved over to the liquor cabinet, filled the glass half-full with Myers' rum, splashed some orange juice on top, and went back to his study at the front of the house.

He sat down in his favorite chair, took a long drink, and waited for the alcohol to hit his bloodstream. He looked around the room slowly, absorbing everything. He had thought about doing this every day he had been in Dehong, through the rain and the bugs and the fear, before Mei and during Mei. In the good days, he had thought about bringing her here, sharing New York City with her, showing her there was a world far removed from the horror show she had endured in Chinatown.

He wondered if that could have made a difference, if that could have saved her.

He got up and went over to his backpack in the hallway. He fished out the photograph he had taken of Mei standing next to the bougainvillea in Teng Chong, and the silver frame he had picked up at the Tiffany's gift store in the Hong Kong airport. He fitted Mei's photograph into the frame and held it up, scrutinizing his work. She looked beautiful. Maybe he had not been able to save her, but she had saved him.

He set the photograph of Mei on the Steinway, alongside his other loved ones.

ABOUT THE AUTHOR

In addition to *South of the Clouds*, John D. Kuhns is the author of *China Fortunes* and *Ballad of a Tin Man*. A businessman, he has taken six companies from inception to their IPOs. From 2007 to 2012, he owned and operated a silicon smelter, like the one in *South of the Clouds*, in the Yunnan province of China on the Burmese border. He is currently the CEO of a company mining gold on Bougainville, an island in the South Pacific. Kuhns graduated from Georgetown University and also earned an MFA from the University of Chicago and an MBA from Harvard Business School.